THE MAGIC OF BLOOD

DAGOBERTO GILB

The Magic of Blood

Grove Press
New York

I owe thanks to many editors who have honored my work in their book and magazine pages, but above all I need to thank Wendy Lesser: I sent her a story, SASE enclosed, in a plain manila envelope.

I am grateful to the following publications, in which these stories originally appeared: *The Threepenny Review:* "Where the Sun Don't Shine," "Parking Places," "Getting a Job in Dell City," "The Señora," "Ballad," "Look on the Bright Side," "Something Foolish"; *Puerto Del Sol:* "Down in the West Texas Town," "Recipe," "Photographs Near a Rolls Royce," "The Rat"; *Fiction Network Magazine:* "Vic Damone's Music," "Hollywood!"; *Kingfisher:* "The Magic of Blood," "Al, in Phoenix"; *American Short Fiction:* "The Death Mask of Pancho Villa," "Truck," "Churchgoers"; *Short Story Review:* "Winners on the Pass Line"; *The Blue Mesa Review* and *Iron:* "I Danced with the Prettiest Girl"; *Buffalo:* "Love in L.A."; *Tonantzin:* "Franklin Delano Roosevelt Was a Democrat"; *New Chicana/Chicano Writing:* "Romero's Shirt"; *High Plains Literary Review:* "The Prize," *The Sonora Review:* "Nancy Flores"; "Down in the West Texas Town," "The Desperado," "Where the Sun Don't Shine," "Love in L.A.," "Photographs Near a Rolls Royce," "Parking Places," "Winners on the Pass Line," and "Recipe" were printed in *Winners on the Pass Line* (Cinco Puntos Press); "Hollywood!" also appeared in *West, North of the Border: The Mexican-American Experience in Short Fiction,* and *Pieces of the Heart: New Chicano Fiction*; "Vic Damone's Music" in *North of the Border*; "Getting a Job in Dell City" in *New Growth: Contemporary Short Stories by Texas Writers*; "I Danced with the Prettiest Girl" in *New Growth 2*; "The Señora" and "Ballad" in *Best of the West* (3 and 4); "The Death Mask of Pancho Villa" in *Mirrors Beneath the Earth: Short Fiction by Chicano Writers*; "Look on the Bright Side" in *The Pushcart Prize XVII: Best of the Small Presses (1992–93)*; "Truck" aired on National Public Radio's "The Sound of Writing" and appeared in *The Sound of Writing #2*.

First published in the United States of America in 1993 by the University of New Mexico Press
Grove Press paperback edition published in 1994

Published simultaneously in Canada
Printed in the United States of America

Library of Congress Cataloging-in-Publication Data

Gilb, Dagoberto, 1950–
The magic of blood/Dagoberto Gilb.
ISBN 0-8021-3399-1
1. Mexican Americans—California—Los Angeles—Fiction.
2. Working class—California—Los Angeles—Fiction.
3. Mexican Americans—Texas—El Paso—Fiction.
4. Working class—Texas—El Paso—Fiction.
5. Los Angeles (Calif.)—Fiction. 6. El Paso (Tex.)—Fiction. I. Title.
[PS3557.I296M3 1994]   813.54—dc20   94-4315

Illustrations by Luis Jimenez
Design by Linda M. Tratechaud

Grove Press
841 Broadway
New York, NY 10003

01 02 03 04   10 9 8 7 6 5 4 3

To Rebeca, Antonio, and Ricardo,
for all the joy

CONTENTS

PART ONE

PART TWO

PART THREE

P A R T   O N E

LOOK ON THE BRIGHT SIDE

The way I see it, a man can have all the money in the world but if he can't keep his self-respect, he don't have shit. A man has to stand up for things even when it may not be very practical. A man can't have pride and give up his rights.

This is exactly what I told my wife when Mrs. Kevovian raised our rent illegally. I say illegally because, well aside from it being obviously unfriendly and greedy whenever a landlord or lady wants money above the exceptional amount she wanted when you moved in not so long ago, here in this enlightened city of Los Angeles it's against the law to raise it above a certain percentage and then only once every twelve months, which is often enough. Now the wife argued that since Mrs. Kevovian was a little ignorant, nasty, and hard to communicate with, we should have gone ahead and paid the increase—added up it was only sixty some-odd bones, a figure the landlady'd come up with getting the percentage right, but this time she tried to get it two months too early. My wife told me to pay it and not have the hassle. She knew me better than this. We'd already put up with the cucarachas and rodents, I fixed the plumbing myself, and our back porch was screaming to become dust and probably would just when one of our little why nots—we have three of them—snuck onto it. People don't turn into dust on the way down, they splat first. One time I tried to explain this to Mrs. Kevovian, without success. You think I was going to pay more rent when I shouldn't have to?

[3]

My wife offered the check for the right amount to the landlady when she came to our door for her money and wouldn't
take it. My wife tried to explain how there was a mistake, but
when I got home from work the check was still on the mantle
where it sat waiting. Should I have called her and talked it
over? Not me. This was her problem and she could call. In the
meantime, I could leave the money in the bank and feel that
much richer for that much longer, and if she was so stupid I
could leave it in the savings and let it earn interest. And the
truth was that she was stupid enough, and stubborn, and mean.
I'd talked to the other tenants, and I'd talked to tenants that'd
left before us, so I wasn't at all surprised about the Pay or Quit
notice we finally got. To me, it all seemed kind of fun. This lady
wasn't nice, as God Himself would witness, and maybe, since I
learned it would take about three months before we'd go to
court, maybe we'd get three free months. We hadn't stopped
talking about moving out since we unpacked.

You'd probably say that this is how things always go, and
you'd probably be right. Yeah, about this same time I got laid
off. I'd been laid off lots of times so it was no big deal, but
the circumstances—well, the company I was working for went
bankrupt and a couple of my paychecks bounced and it wasn't
the best season of the year in what were not the best years for
working people. Which could have really set me off, made me
pretty unhappy, but that's not the kind of man I am. I believe
in making whatever you have the right situation for you at the
right moment for you. And look, besides the extra money from
not paying rent, I was going to get a big tax return, and we
also get unemployment compensation in this great country. It
was a good time for a vacation, so I bunched the kids in the
car with the old lady and drove to Baja. I deserved it, we
all did.

Like my wife said, I should have figured how things were
when we crossed back to come home. I think we were in the
slowest line on the border. Cars next to us would pull up and

within minutes be at that red-light green-light signal. You know how it is when you pick the worst line to wait in. I was going nuts. A poor dude in front of us idled so long that his radiator overheated and he had to push the old heap forward by himself. My wife told me to settle down and wait because if we changed lanes then it would stop moving. I turned the ignition off then on again when we moved a spot. When we did get there I felt a lot better, cheerful even. There's no prettier place for a vacation than Baja and we really had a good time. I smiled forgivingly at the customs guy who looked as kind as Captain Stubbing on the TV show "Love Boat."

"I'm American," I said, prepared like the sign told us to be. My wife said the same thing. I said, "The kids are American too. Though I haven't checked out the backseat for a while."

Captain Stubbing didn't think that was very funny. "What do you have to declare?"

"Let's see. A six-pack of Bohemia beer. A blanket. Some shells we found. A couple holy pictures. Puppets for the kids. Well, two blankets."

"No other liquor? No fruits? Vegetables? No animal life?"

I shook my head to each of them.

"So what were you doing in Mexico?"

"Sleeping on the beach, swimming in the ocean. Eating the rich folks's lobster." It seemed like he didn't understand what I meant. "Vacation. We took a vacation."

"How long were you in Mexico?" He made himself comfortable on the stool outside his booth after he'd run a license plate check through the computer.

"Just a few days," I said, starting to lose my good humor.

"How many days?"

"You mean exactly?"

"Exactly."

"Five days. Six. Five nights and six days."

"Did you spend a lot of money in Mexico?"

I couldn't believe this, and someone else in a car behind us couldn't either because he blasted the horn. Captain Stubbing made a mental note of him. "We spent some good money there. Not that much though. Why?" My wife grabbed my knee.

"Where exactly did you stay?"

"On the beach. Near Estero Beach."

"Don't you work?"

I looked at my wife. She was telling me to go along with it without saying so. "Of course I work."

"Why aren't you at work now?"

"Cuz I got laid off, man!"

"Did you do something wrong?"

"I said I got *laid off,* not *fired!*"

"What do you do?"

"Laborer!"

"What kind of laborer?"

"Construction!"

"And there's no other work? Where do you live?"

"No! Los Angeles!"

"Shouldn't you be looking for a job? Isn't that more important than taking a vacation?"

I was so hot I think my hair was turning red. I just glared at this guy.

"Are you receiving unemployment benefits?"

"Yeah I am."

"You're receiving unemployment and you took a vacation?"

"That's it! I ain't listening to this shit no more!"

"You watch your language, sir." He filled out a slip of paper and slid it under my windshield wiper. "Pull over there."

My wife was a little worried about the two smokes I never did and still had stashed in my wallet. She was wanting to tell me to take it easy as they went through the car, but that was hard for her because our oldest baby was crying. All I wanted to do was put in a complaint about that jerk to somebody higher up. As a matter of fact I wanted him fired, but anything to make him some trouble. I felt like they would've listened better if they hadn't found those four bottles of rum I was trying to sneak over. At that point I lost some confidence, though not my sense of being right. When this other customs man suggested that I might be detained further if I pressed the situation, I paid the penalty charges for the confiscated liquor and shut up. It wasn't worth a strip search, or finding out what kind of crime it was crossing the border with some B-grade marijuana.

●

Time passed back home and there was still nothing coming out of the union hall. There were a lot of men worried but at least I felt like I had the unpaid rent money to wait it out. I was fortunate to have a landlady like Mrs. Kevovian helping us through these bad times. She'd gotten a real smart lawyer for me too. He'd attached papers on his Unlawful Detainer to prove *my* case, which seemed so ridiculous that I called the city housing department just to make sure I couldn't be wrong about it all. I wasn't. I rested a lot easier without a rent payment, even took some guys out for some cold ones when I got the document with the official court date stamped on it, still more than a month away.

I really hadn't started out with any plan. But now that I was unemployed there were all these complications. I didn't have all the money it took to get into another place, and our rent, as much as it had been, was in comparison to lots still cheap, and rodents and roaches weren't that bad a problem to me. Still, I took a few ugly pictures like I was told to and had the city inspect the hazardous back porch and went to court on the assigned day hoping for something to ease our bills.

Her lawyer was Yassir Arafat without the bedsheet. He wore this suit with a vest that was supposed to make him look cool, but I've seen enough Ziedler & Ziedler commercials to recognize discount fashion. Mrs. Kevovian sat on that hard varnished bench with that wrinkled forehead of hers. Her daughter translated whatever she didn't understand when the lawyer discussed the process. I could hear every word even though there were all these other people because the lawyer's voice carried in the long white hall and polished floor of justice. He talked as confidently as a dude with a sharp blade.

"You're the defendant?" he asked five minutes before court was to be in session.

"That's me, and that's my wife," I pointed. "We're both defendants."

"I'm Mr. Villalobos, attorney representing the plaintiff."

"All right! Law school, huh? You did the people proud, eh? So how come you're working for the wrong side? That ain't a nice lady you're helping to evict us, man."

"You're the one who refuses to pay the rent."

"I'm disappointed in you, compa. You should know I been trying to pay the rent. You think I should beg her to take it? She wants more money than she's supposed to get, and because I wanna pay her what's right, she's trying to throw us onto the streets."

Yassir Villalobos scowled over my defense papers while I gloated. I swore it was the first time he saw them or the ones he turned in. "Well, I'll do this. Reimburse Mrs. Kevovian for the back rent and I'll drop the charges."

"You'll drop the charges? Are you making a joke, man? You talk like I'm the one who done something wrong. I'm *here* now. Unless you wanna say drop what I owe her, something like that, then I won't let the judge see how you people tried to harrass me unlawfully."

Villalobos didn't like what I was saying, and he didn't like my attitude one bit.

"I'm the one who's right," I emphasized. "I know it, and you know it too." He was squirming mad. I figured he was worried about looking like a fool in the court. "Unless you offer me something better, I'd just as soon see what that judge has to say."

"There's no free rent," he said finally. "I'll just drop these charges and re-serve you." He said that as an ultimatum, real pissed.

I smiled. "You think I can't wait another three months?"

That did it. He stiff-armed the swinging door and made arrangements with the court secretary, and my old lady and me picked the kids up from the babysitter's a lot earlier than we'd planned. The truth was I was relieved. I did have the money, but now that I'd been out of work so long it was getting close. If I didn't get some work soon we wouldn't have enough to pay it all. I'd been counting on that big income tax check, and when the government decided to take all of it except nine dollars and some change, what remained of a debt from some other year and the penalties it included, I was almost worried. I wasn't happy with the US Govt and I tried to explain to it on the phone how hard I worked and how it was only that I didn't understand those letters they sent me and couldn't they show some kindness to the unemployed, to a family that obviously hadn't planned to run with that tax advantage down to Costa Rica and hire bodyguards to watch over an estate. The thing is, it's no use being right when the US Govt thinks it's not wrong.

Fortunately, we still had Mrs. Kevovian as our landlady. I don't know how we'd have lived without her. Unemployment money covers things when you don't have to pay rent. And I didn't want to for as long as possible. The business agent at the union hall said there was supposed to be a lot of work breaking soon, but in the meantime I told everyone in our home who talked and didn't crawl to lay low and not answer any doors to strangers with summonses. My wife didn't like peeking around corners when she walked the oldest to school, though the oldest liked it a mess. We waited and waited but nobody came. Instead it got nailed to the front door very impolitely.

So another few months had passed and what fool would complain about that? Not this one. Still, I wanted justice. I wanted The Law to hand down fair punishment to these evil people who were conspiring to take away my family's home.

Man, I wanted that judge to be so pissed that he'd pound that gavel and it'd ring in my ears like a Vegas jackpot. I didn't want to pay any money back. And not because I didn't have the money, or I didn't have a job, or that pretty soon they'd be cutting off my unemployment. I'm not denying their influence on my thinking, but mostly it was the principle of the thing. It seemed to me if I had so much to lose for being wrong, I should have something equal to win for being right.

"There's no free rent," Villalobos told me again five minutes before we were supposed to swing through those doors and please rise. "You don't have the money, do you?"

"Of course I have the money. But I don't see why I should settle this with you now and get nothing out of it. Seems like I had to go outa my way to come down here. It ain't easy finding a babysitter for our kids, who you wanna throw on the streets, and we didn't, and we had to pay that expensive parking across the street. This has been a mess of trouble for me to go, sure, I'll pay what I owe without the mistaken rent increase, no problem."

"The judge isn't going to offer you free rent."

"I'd rather hear what he has to say."

Villalobos was some brother, but I guess that's what happens with some education and a couple of cheap suits and ties. I swore right then that if I ever worked again I wasn't paying for my kids' college education.

The judge turned out to be a sister whose people hadn't gotten much justice either and that gave me hope. And I was real pleased we were the first case because the kids were fidgeting like crazy and my wife was miserable trying to keep them settled down. I wanted the judge to see what a big happy family we were so I brought them right up to our assigned "defendant" table.

"I think it would be much easier if your wife took your children out to the corridor," the judge told me.

"She's one of the named defendants, your honor."

"I'm sure you can represent your case adequately without the baby crying in your wife's arms."

"Yes ma'am, your honor."

The first witness for the plaintiff was this black guy who looked like they pulled a bottle away from the night before, who claimed to have come by my place to serve me all these times but I wouldn't answer the door. The sleaze was all lie up until when he said he attached it to my door, which was a generous exaggeration. Then Mrs. Kevovian took the witness stand. Villalobos asked her a couple of unimportant questions, and then I got to ask questions. I've watched enough lawyer shows and I was ready.

I heard the gavel but it didn't tinkle like a line of cherries.

"You can state your case in the witness stand at the proper moment," the judge said.

"But your honor, I just wanna show how this landlady . . ."

"You don't have to try your case through this witness."

"Yes ma'am, your honor."

So when that moment came all I could do was show her those polaroids of how bad things got and tell her about roaches and rats and fire hazards and answer oh yes, your honor, I've been putting that money away, something which concerned the judge more than anything else did.

I suppose that's the way of swift justice. Back at home, my wife, pessimistic as always, started packing the valuable stuff into the best boxes. She couldn't believe that anything good was going to come from the verdict in the mail. The business agent at the hall was still telling us about all the work about to break any day now, but I went ahead and started reading the help wanted ads in the newspaper.

A couple of weeks later the judgment came in an envelope. We won. The judge figured up all the debt and then cut it by twenty percent. Victory is sweet, probably, when there's a lot of coins clinking around the pants' pockets, but I couldn't let up. Now that I was proven right I figured we could do some serious negotiating over payment. A little now and a little later and a little bit now and again. That's what I'd offer when Mrs. Kevovian came for the money, which she was supposed to do the next night by 5 p.m., according to the legal document. "The money to be collected by the usual procedure," were the words, which meant Mrs. Kevovian was supposed to knock on the door and, knowing her, at five o'clock exactly.

Maybe I was a tiny bit worried. What if she wouldn't take anything less than all of it? Then I'd threaten to give her nothing and to disappear into the mounds of other uncollected debts. Mrs. Kevovian needed this money, I knew that. Better all of it over a long period than none of it over a longer one, right? That's what I'd tell her, and I'd be standing there with my self-confidence more muscled-up than ever.

Except she never came. There was no knock on the door. A touch nervous, I started calling lawyers. I had a stack of junk-mail letters from all these legal experts advising me that for a small fee they'd help me with my eviction procedure. None of them seemed to understand my problem over the phone, though maybe if I came by their office. One of them did seem to catch enough though. He said if the money wasn't collected by that time then the plaintiff had the right to reclaim the premises. Actually the lawyer didn't say that, the judgment paper did, and I'd read it to him over the phone. All the lawyer said was, "The marshall will physically evict you in ten days." He didn't charge a fee for the information.

We had a garage sale. You know, miscellaneous things, things easy to replace, that you could buy anywhere when the time was right again, like beds and lamps and furniture. We stashed the valuables in the trunk of the car—a perfect fit—and Grey-hound was having a special sale which made it an ideal moment for a visit to the abuelitos back home, who hadn't been able to see their grandkids and daughter in such a long time. You have to look on the bright side. I wouldn't have to pay any of that money back, and there was the chance to start a new career, just like they say, and I'd been finding lots of opportunities from reading the newspaper. Probably any day I'd be going back to work at one of those jobs about to break. Meanwhile, we left a mattress in the apartment for me to sleep on so I could have the place until a marshal beat on the door. Or soon I'd send back for the family from a house with a front and backyard I promised I'd find and rent. However it worked out. Or there was always the car with that big backseat.

●

One of those jobs I read about in the want ads was as a painter for the city. I applied, listed all this made-up experience I had, but I still had to pass some test. So I went down to the library to look over one of those books on the subject. I guess I didn't think much about the hours libraries keep, and I guess I was a few hours early, and so I took a seat next to this pile of newspapers on this cement bench not that far from the front doors. The bench smelled like piss, but since I was feeling pretty open-minded about things I didn't let it bother me. I wanted to enjoy all the scenery, which was nice for the big city, with all the trees and dewy grass, though the other early risers weren't so involved with the love of nature. One guy not so far away was rolling from one side of his body to the other, back and forth like that, from under a tree. He just went on and on. This other man, or maybe woman—wearing a sweater on top that was too baggy to make chest impressions on and another sweater below that, wrapped around like a skirt, and pants under that, cords, and unisex homemade sandals made out of old tennis shoes and leather, and finally, on the head, long braided hair which wasn't braided too good—this person was foraging off the cement path, digging through the trash for something. I thought aluminum too but there were about five empty beer cans nearby and the person kicked those away. It was something that this person knew by smell, because that's how he or she tested whether it was the right thing or not. I figured this was someone to keep my eye on.

Then without warning came a monster howl, and those pigeons bundled-up on the lawn scattered to the trees. I swore somebody took a shot at me. "Traitor! You can't get away with it!" Those were the words I got out of the tail end of the loud speech from this dude who came out of nowhere, who looked pretty normal, hip even if it weren't for the clothes. He had one of those great, long graying beards and hair, like some wise man, some Einstein. I was sure a photographer would be along to take his picture if they hadn't already. You know how Indians and winos make the most interesting photographs. His clothes were bad though, took away from his cool. Like he'd done caca and spilled his spaghetti and rolled around in the slime for a lot of years since mama'd washed a bagful of the dirties. The guy really had some voice, and just when it seemed like he'd settled back into a stroll like anyone else, just when those pigeons trickled back down onto the lawn into a coo-cooing lump, he cut loose again. It was pretty hard to understand, even with his volume so high, but I figured it out to be about patriotism, justice, and fidelity.

"That guy's gone," John said when he came up to me with a bag of groceries he dropped next to me. He'd told me his name right off. "John. John. The name's John, they call me John." He pulled out a loaf of white bread and started tearing up the slices into big and little chunks and throwing them onto the grass. The pigeons picked up on this quick. "Look at 'em, they act like they ain't eaten in weeks, they're eatin like vultures, like they're starvin, like vultures, good thing I bought three loafs of bread, they're so hungry, but they'll calm down, they'll calm down after they eat some." John was blond and could almost claim to have a perm if you'd asked me. He'd shaven some days ago so the stubble on his face wasn't so bad. He'd never have much of a beard anyway. "They can't get enough, look at 'em, look at 'em, good thing I bought three loafs, I usually buy two." He moved like he talked—nervously, in jerks, and without pausing—and, when someone passed by, his conversation didn't break up. "Hey good morning, got any spare change for some food? No? So how ya gonna get to Heaven?" A man in a business suit turned his head with a smile, but didn't change direction. "I'll bury you deeper in Hell then, I'll dig ya deeper!" John went back to feeding the birds, who couldn't get enough. "That's how ya gotta talk to 'em," he told me. "Ya gotta talk to 'em like that and like ya can back it up, like ya can back it up."

I sort of got to liking John. He reminded me of a hippie, and it was sort of nice to see hippies again. He had his problems, of course, and he told me about them too, about how a dude at the hotel he stayed at kept his SSI check, how he called the police but they wouldn't pay attention, that his hotel was just a hangout for winos and hypes and pimps and he was gonna move out, turn that guy in and go to court and testify or maybe he'd get a gun and blow the fucker away, surprise him. He had those kind of troubles but seemed pretty intelligent otherwise to me. Even if he was a little wired, he wasn't like the guy who was still rolling around under the tree or the one screaming at the top of his lungs.

While we both sat at the bench watching those pigeons clean up what became only visible to them in the grass, one of the things John said before he took off was this: "Animals are good people. They're not like people, people are no good, they don't care about nobody. People won't do nothing for ya. That's the age we live in, that's how it is. Hitler had that plan. I think it was Hitler, maybe it was somebody else, it coulda been somebody else." We were both staring at this pigeon with only one foot, the other foot being a balled-up red stump, hopping around, pecking at the lawn. "I didn't think much of him gettin rid of the cripples and the mentals and the old people. That was no good, that was no good. It musta been Hitler, or Preacher Jobe. It was him, or it musta been somebody else I heard. Who was I thinkin of? Hey you got any change? How ya gonna get to Heaven? I wish I could remember who it was I was thinkin of."

I sure didn't know, but I promised John that if I thought of it, or if something else came up, I'd look him up at the address he gave me and filed in my pocket. I had to show him a couple of times it was still there. I was getting a little tired from such a long morning already, and I wished that library would hurry up and open so I could study for the test. I didn't have the slightest idea what they could ask me on a test for painting either. But then jobs at the hall were bound to break and probably I wouldn't have to worry too much anyway.

I was really sleepy by now, and I was getting used to the bench, even when I did catch that whiff of piss. I leaned back and closed the tired eyes and it wasn't so bad. I thought I'd give it a try—you know, why not?—and I scooted over and nuzzled my head into that stack of newspapers and tucked my legs into my chest. I shut them good this time and yawned. I didn't see why I should fight it, and it was just until the library opened.

THE DEATH MASK OF PANCHO VILLA

It's late, very late. I've been in bed since eleven o'clock, for almost four hours, trying to get some sleep. I haven't been going to bed this early, but it's Sunday night and there's nothing on television. Not that I really like to watch television late at night the rest of the days. I do it too much because I don't know what else to do with myself. Probably I could listen to music on the radio. That's not true, I almost forgot. There's nothing on on the radio anymore, and around here, whether it's El Paso tejano or Juárez ranchera, pop from Mexico City, hard or soft American rock, it's all boring, and anyway there's commercial after commercial, just as irritating, maybe even more so, as the ones on late-night television. Okay, so maybe it's me.

Really it's not late, it's early, early morning, and one other reason I need to get some sleep is that I have to be somewhere in the morning. I've arranged, finally, to see about getting some work. I've been treating it pretty easy for a while, telling myself I was sick of doing physical labor and trying hard to blame my age for feeling that way. Unsuccessfully. So I've been sitting around, not doing as much as I probably should, getting soft. Doing too much television, I'll you the truth. I gotta admit, that isn't what I consider having a great time, but it can't be called suffering either. Our bills might be getting paid, my kids might be running around laughing and breaking things, my wife might finally keep a job for a while, but we're not getting rich.

Not that I ever really lived my life trying to get rich. Which is why I've been feeling guilty about my working situation, my lack of it. It's gotten me jumpy and nervous, worried about something really bad happening to us while I'm doing nothing about a paycheck. Which might help explain why I think the worst when I hear that pounding at the door. I don't even realize what it is, and my wife's so asleep I have to shake her awake.

What I do is pick up my son's aluminum baseball bat. I even think of putting on my boots. I guess that's some deal I have, not wanting to get into late night violence barefooted. Why do I think it might be something violent? Good question. I guess it shows how I'm thinking, even if it doesn't make much sense—because obviously violent criminals aren't going to be knocking on the door, ringing the bell to wake me up. I'm just asleep and not reasoning too clearly. Also there's been a lot of talk in the papers about thieves breaking in. Desperate young punks from the other side of the river disobeying all the rules of thief etiquette.

But when I finally get the door open it's just a friend and some other guy I don't know. One of my oldest, best friends in all the world, a guy I started hanging out with in high school, then after that worked a few construction jobs with. We shared a lot of girlfriends, a lot of bottles and cans, and traveled together often when we did . . . well, outlaw business years ago. All to say that I've had some of the best times I've ever had with the guy. We're still friends, but time has passed. We both ended up married—him first!—and we both have kids, and our wives talked to each other more than we did. Which is how I heard he was having some home troubles. First he got suspended from his job at the railroad. Then he got caught, or accused, of being bad with another woman and Dora, his wife, threw him out of the house. In fact she did the whole routine—threw his clothes out onto the driveway with an empty suitcase and locked all the doors and windows.

"You whore," I tell him after I turn on the yellow outdoor light. Gabe's wearing a tight, too-small, white T-shirt and still looks in good shape, particularly for a man in his late-thirties. It makes me feel bad that there he is, like always, a beer in his hand, a glaze in his eyes, somehow being healthier than me, drunk and whatever else. The only thing not like him is that the T-shirt and jeans are a little dirty and wrinkled, and his hair, which when he worked steady he didn't keep so long, looks like it just got off a pillow, the same as mine. Stuff his wife, it would seem, has been taking care of for a long time.

I open the door and go onto the front porch with my socks on. "Everybody in the house is asleep," I say, an explanation for why I'm not offering them the indoor accommodations. We shake hands, then wrap arms around one another for a long-time-no-see abrazo. "I been wondering about you. Hear about you having too much fun."

"Gotta have fun sometimes. You know that." Gabe's grin is almost exuberant.

"I heard about the clothes on the driveway too."

"Which ones?" he asks, still smiling.

"Whadaya mean?"

"There were two sets of them."

I don't understand, and I don't say anything.

"A day or two after the old lady handed me a suitcase, that other bitch came over and threw a pile she had on the driveway too," he tells me, and we laugh pretty good. "You know what I said when Dora called me about that? 'She didn't hit the grease spot, did she?' When she hung on me my fucking ear hurt."

We're both laughing while Gabe's friend keeps this steady smile throughout. "This is Ortíz," Gabe says, finally introducing us. "Román Ortíz." I shake his friend's hand. Despite the smile, the man's gauntness, for me, translates into something else I can't quite put a name on, and my first impression is that his loose western-style clothes don't seem to suit his character.

It gets too quiet for a moment. Not a dog, not even the shuffle of a breeze. It looks very dark beyond the yellow porch, and cold, though it isn't.

"You wanna beer?" Gabe asks me, plucking a can off from the vine of three he'd carried to the porch.

"No. It's kinda late for me. Or early."

Gabe looks at me disappointed and the other guy looks at Gabe, though still with that smile. Gabe breaks the tab from the can he'd offered me.

I feel bad, immediately, for saying no. Somehow I've done something to spoil the visit, I've brought things down a notch. "So how you been really?" I ask.

"All right," he tells me, uneffusive. He takes a couple swallows of beer.

"What about that job?" I ask. "You gonna get back there?" Working at the railroad, you have to understand, is one of the best paying jobs in the city.

Gabe makes a sour face and leans against the porch railing. "A bunch of suckass culeros. I'll find something better."

Very few people could. Very few people would want to leave that job. Gabe can do both. I know it as well as he does. I used to feel the same way about myself, though not anymore. I try to blame that on El Paso or the times or my age. But I'm only a year older than Gabe. It's another thing I admire about him and dislike about me.

Ortíz hasn't so much as moved except to sip on his beer. "You mind if I piss over there?" he asks, indicating beyond the porch.

"Of course not," I say. "I do it all the time." I don't do it all the time, but once in a while, just to keep in practice.

Gabe and I don't say anything until we hear Ortíz's stream hitting the hard dirt that is my front yard.

"So what's up?" I finally ask.

"This guy has something I thought you'd want to see," Gabe says. "Remember that time we were in Mexico and that old dude said he had pictures of him with Pancho Villa?"

I was into collecting Pancho Villa stuff years ago because he was my hero. More than that really. Anyway, I'd found letters he'd written, bought a holster and pistol that were supposed to be his, and in our front room I still have a framed document Villa'd signed for my great-uncle saying what an honor it'd been to fight together during the revolution. It has been a while since I'd thought about any of this though. I guess because I had children and got married. And worked a lot. And because I got older. I've got all kinds of excuses if I let myself think about it.

"So he has photographs?" I say, trying to sound interested. I'm not at all.

"A mask," says Gabe.

Ortíz is stepping back up onto the porch. "His death mask."

"I never heard of such a thing," I say.

"There were three of them made," Ortíz says. Same smile. "A Hollywood producer has one and a senator has the other." Ortíz opens another can of beer. No change in the smile, but the face around it seems prouder now.

My first impression isn't improving. I'm pretty sure Gabe's just met the guy in a bar, and in my humble opinion . . . well, I'd call it bar talk.

Gabe lights a joint. I'm wishing I were back in bed, the door locked. Which makes me feel bad again. What's happened to me? I don't think anything's wrong with marijuana, and I like smoking it the same as I always have. That's what I say anyway. The only thing is I don't smoke it very often anymore. I even have about two or three joints worth in a bag that was given to me almost a year ago. I guess I never want to smoke it by myself, and I'd be embarrassed now to use it with anyone else because it's so dried out. I should throw it away. I will throw it away.

I go ahead and smoke some because I don't know how to say no to this too, though the truth is that's what I feel like saying. I don't know why we're not talking. I think it has something to do with me, with me standing in my socks, not inviting them in, not saying let's go. Though maybe it's Gabe. He's too quiet, and it can't only be that he's unhappy because I don't feel like drinking beer. Maybe it's something between him and Ortíz. When we used to hang out together a lot, it was Gabe who usually met the guys like this in the first place. Gabe was the one who'd listen and believe, while I was the one who was skeptical. Gabe'd get all the information, I'd put it together, then we'd both come up with a conclusion, a decision—you know, we'd solve another little human-oddball mystery, and sometimes actually do something with the person. Either buy or sell. Was this guy trying to sell Gabe something? Or trade? Or was Gabe thinking of a sale to him? But why would he need me after all these years? And if he did, why doesn't he just say something to me straight out? Then maybe he thinks I'd just want to buy it. But why right now? It's about three a.m., or later, and I can't think.

"So are you selling this thing or what?" I ask Ortíz.

"Absolutely not."

He stares at me with that smile. I look for some kind of indication from Gabe, but there's none. We're finishing off the joint.

"Then what you are you doing with it?"

"He's got it at his place," Gabe says. "Let's go see it."

"You haven't seen it?" I ask him.

"Sure. I want you to see it. All you gotta do is get some shoes." He drops the roach and grinds it out with the sole of his boot. Then he pops another can of beer. He stops leaning on the wrought-iron railing around the porch and stands like he's ready to get going.

Gabe's push isn't out of exuberance now, but it's along the lines of it, some excess of something, and I can't figure it out. I start thinking about the problems he's having. No job, being away from his kids. Except that's not Gabe at all. I know him too well. He'll get back together with Dora whether she thinks she never wants to see him again right now or not, he'll get his job back or a better one, and I know he believes that too, and even if it didn't turn out that way a few years from now, I know he wouldn't think it wouldn't. So it's not that, it's not like he needs me, needs a friend or some TV emotion like that. And somehow it doesn't seem like he really wants me to hang out either. He wants me to go with him, but it doesn't seem personal, it doesn't seem to me like he's asking. It's more like he's telling me to go with them. Like it's for my own good or something.

"I can't go tonight," I say, thinking it's not tonight but this morning.

"How come?" Gabe asks. He's disappointed again.

"I gotta do things. In a few hours, as a matter of fact. Normal shit."

All the sudden a cop car cruises by. Not slow and not fast, just on a routine pass through the neighborhood. Except from behind us, from the dirt alley where we wouldn't have expected that blue-and-white to come from, and a dog starts barking at him because a dispatcher talks over the police radio and the window on the driver's side is down.

"Normal shit?" says Gabe. "Since when did you worry about doing normal shit?"

That stings because he's right. Or used to be. "Why don't I just see it tomorrow? You taking it out of town or something?" I'm feeling a little defensive now. "Somebody buying it?" I look at Gabe. He's not looking back at me.

"I'm giving it away," says Ortíz. "There are only three of them, and I'm sending mine to Moscow." His smile is the same but it's fading.

"Moscow?" I look at Gabe once more and feel stoned. He hits on his beer.

"In Russia," says Ortíz.

"I know where it is," I tell him. "Why there?"

"Because that's where John Reed is buried," Ortíz says. "John Reed wrote about the Mexican Revolution, then went to Russia and wrote about the Russian Revolution."

A smile starts to come on me because now the cop car is

cruising by again, only this time in front of us, and it seems so ridiculous especially because we're about to talk about communism or something at three or so in the morning and I don't have shoes on. Then another cop car goes by. We know it has to be another one because it's coming from another street, toward us, too soon after the last one. It turns right, opposite the direction the first one did. And now more dogs are barking in the neighborhood.

"I better turn off the light," I say. I open the screen door, then the other, and reach inside to turn off the yellow porch light. A cop car passes a second later. "You guys better not leave for a while."

"I don't need a DWI," says Ortíz.

Ortíz's car, I notice for the first time, is faded green, or blue, I can't be positive in this dark, with a peeling vinyl roof.

"So how'd you get this mask?" I ask.

"I just did," Ortíz says, finishing his beer.

"How do you know it's Villa?"

"People have seen it. Warren Beatty saw it and wanted it."

Warren Beatty, the actor. Now I am smiling the most. Dogs are barking all over the neighborhood and another cop car passes us. I swear it's a third one. I'm sure we can't be seen without the porch light on though.

"Why not just keep it right here, right here in El Paso?" I suggest. "Probably a lot of people would like to see it. It'd be a great contribution. It seems to me anyway."

Ortíz turns his head away from me and my naiveté. "People here wouldn't respect it enough, and it's fragile. Over there they care about things more than they do here. All of Europe is like that too. They have museums to take care of important cultural things. In Germany there are probably thirty opera houses to every one here." The speech erases Ortíz's smile, and he steps over and reaches down to get the last can of beer.

"So you've been to Europe, to Germany?" I ask.

"No," Ortíz says, humorless.

It's that I've stolen his smile. I'm looking for cop cars and watching lights go on in the house across the street where a dog is barking the loudest and steadiest. "Moscow, huh?"

Ortíz gathers himself after a big swallow of the beer. "The Mexican Revolution was the first in the century, and the bolsheviks used it as an example of common people rising up. John Reed was there for both revolutions and was buried at the Kremlin as a hero. They'll put the mask near him as a memorial."

I'm still smiling, but not because I'm unconvinced or skeptical. More that the cops have quit driving by and the dog across the street won't stop barking, which is probably why another dog still barks farther down the street. I'm smiling just thinking about how we're having this conversation about Russians and death masks in the dark and quiet right on my El Paso porch with the light out, all while I'm in my socks.

"I'd really like to see it some time," I say.

Neither of them say anything.

"I guess I should probably get a couple hours in," I say.

Gabe looks a little disappointed again. Or maybe apologetic. I don't want him to feel bad for coming by, for banging on my door. I haven't done anything for weeks but watch the stupid television.

"You guys better look around to see if the police are waiting for you to pull away," I say. I wish I knew how to say more.

Gabe just shrugs my worry off. He never did care about things like that, and, maybe because he didn't, never had to.

They both stop and piss before they get into Ortíz's car. It starts with a cheap gas and old motor sound, and finally rolls away without headlights for a few yards.

I lock the door and climb back in bed. I'm thinking that I probably can wait on seeing about this job, and I'm thinking how nice it feels being stoned and sleepy. My wife asks me who it was and I say it was Gabe and wait for her to ask me some more. She doesn't, but in my head I start asking questions for her and answering them. Or asking for myself: He wanted me to go out with him. To go see something this guy he knows had. No, I don't really know why I didn't go. No, I really don't know why he wanted me to. Maybe he thought because of Pancho Villa. Or maybe because he thought I'd have a good time. Which I haven't had in a long time. No, I don't know why I didn't go, I don't know why it didn't seem like I should. I used to not think about it, I used to just go. Gabe and I used to do things together. Things just like this.

I'm on my back in bed and my wife, after I've been lying there all this time, finally asks me what Gabe wanted. Nothing, I tell her, except he wanted me to go look at Pancho Villa's death mask. That makes me smile all over again. At what? she asks. Don't think about it, I say. But what time is it? she asks. What's the difference? I say.

NANCY FLORES

Nancy Flores moved in across the street from us when I was in elementary school. She had two older sisters. Within the first months after they unloaded their belongings, before anybody in the neighborhood knew much of anything about her family, the oldest sister got married. That was on a Saturday. I was playing football on the street with some other kids, I was quarterback, and we were about to score another TD. The end zone was the line of Nancy's driveway. We called time as her sister came out of the house in a white wedding gown—it must have been satin, since the late afternoon sun lit it up like she was in moonlight. Her dad, who we heard was a union laborer, followed behind in a richman's black tuxedo which, since he was stretching his arms and tugging at it, must have been too tight on him. He opened the door of their family car, a new two-tone, four-door Chevrolet decorated by blue streamers and red ribbons, and, both of them cautious, helped his daughter and the long dress into the backseat. Nancy and her other older sister and her mom stepped through the front door right afterwards in pink gowns. Nancy's was shorter than the others, at her knees, and her white petticoat showed, and she was gripping a bouquet of white flowers as though they were as fragile as blown glass. Her black shoes, with a brass buckled strap across pink socks, flashed blue in the sun, a wet sheen matched by her hair. I remember this so well because I'd never seen Nancy, and I'd never seen a girl with the new hairstyle like hers—long bangs across her forehead, then straight until it curled under at her shoulders.

Kids played at our house because nobody was around to tell us not to—my mom was at work and came home late or was out for the night, and my older brother, who was in high school, wasn't around much either and I didn't know why, and my father didn't live with us. I could be inside with my friends if I wanted, but outside was better. We played baseball with the front stairs of the house as the catcher, football with curbs as the sidelines, or we skated down the hill on pie tins, or jumped over soft hedges to see how high we could jump. There was always something. We had a big front yard, and we weren't like some in the neighborhood whose lawn was for looks. Like Nancy's. Nancy Flores never played outside, at least not in the front. I knew because I was out there every day until it was dark, even after the other kids had gone home, and I wondered about her while I'd throw a ball against the steps, or when I'd climb up the neighbor's tree or toss a stick for another neighbor's dog who was always loose. All I knew for sure about her was that she went to the Catholic school, St. Xavier, because mornings I'd see her get into their car with her dad and sister, wearing the Catholic uniform for girls.

One weekend night my mom was out on a date and my brother had some of his friends over. They were going pretty wild in the house, laughing and playing 45s on somebody's record player, hitting each other and stuff, mixing orange juice and some vodka one of the boys stole from his house, and I was hanging around as close as I could without my brother telling me to get lost. They were talking about girls, doing things with them I wasn't exactly sure about yet except that I knew it was interesting, and nasty, and I overheard one guy telling my brother about Nancy's sister. He went to the same church as she did—we didn't go to church ever anymore, not even for Christmas or Easter—and he was telling my brother how he and Nancy's sister were in confirmation class together. He told my brother how Nancy's family didn't like us because we didn't take care of our house, how my mom was a divorced Mexican woman who made the Mexican people look bad. In our neighborhood there were all kinds of kids and my brother didn't like it when anybody talked about us being, like some dirty word, *Mexican*—we practically never spoke Spanish—and he didn't like it when anybody talked about our mom, even if he himself was almost always mad at her like he was. So my brother got pissed off and said Nancy's mom and sister were ugly bitches and he told his friend to tell them he said so. Then he got their phone number from information and called their house. My brother's friends stood around, excited and scared, and so did I while he dialed and then waited as the phone rang. When somebody finally picked up the other end, he said, I fucked your daughter, and he hung up. A few of his friends laughed after a second, but they didn't really laugh like they thought it was funny, and I knew my brother didn't laugh because he thought he'd been so funny either. They sort of shuffled around, not knowing what to say or do next. My brother dialed again. This time he didn't have to wait so long for the phone to be answered. He said, I fucked your daughter and she sucked me too, and he hung it up fast like the first time.

●

In eighth grade, Nancy was assigned the desk directly behind me in two of my classes and almost sat next to me at one of the heavy, black tables in Science. She sat on a stool at the right end of one, I was given the stool at the left end of the other—only an aisle separated us. One person more or less at the low-end of the alphabet would have made us partners at the four-person table, diagramming amoebas and sponges, dissecting worms and frogs and crayfish together. I'd heard from the neighborhood gossip—one of my friends lived down the street from her, and his mom was always on the phone talking about everybody else—why she started public school: her dad had been caught with another woman and was thrown out, they didn't have a car now, they were having problems with money. Though her older sister still went to the St. Xavier because she had some friends with a car, the reason Nancy stopped was either that her mom couldn't afford it for both of them, or that Nancy got in trouble with the nuns and didn't like being there anymore.

For the first few months—it seemed like months anyway—Nancy didn't say much to me, though she didn't talk much to anybody, so it wasn't personal. She was shy and kept to herself, even at the morning snack and at the lunch period. I knew because I saw her sitting by herself at a lunchtable, with paper and pencil and an opened book. I wished I had the hair to go sit with her, could fake being concerned about homework. Instead I walked past her and went to the field to toss a football or to the courts to shoot hoops with the guys, or, if not that, I hung around the bleachers and laughed and goofed with them and with some of the school bad girls too, who we liked being around not only because they popped each other's bra straps but the ones on the unsuspecting goody-goodies who came by, all of them whelping like only girls did.

Then one morning I heard Nancy talk to me before class started. She'd just taken her seat behind me. I knew she was at her desk because I always knew exactly what she was doing, but, like always, I pretended I hadn't seen or heard her yet. I thought this was how it was supposed to be for a guy, like he had all kinds of important things on his mind.

Hi, Richie, she said.

Though she'd been saying this to me for weeks, I'd been too deaf. This morning I *heard:* the hesitancy in her voice wasn't ordinary sincerity but a lot of it, and her tone wasn't only friendly, it was intimate, private, *longing*. The words, quiet and simple as they were, were strong, deep tosses that landed close, and loud. She'd been leaning into her desk, aiming at my ears. I didn't see her of course, I couldn't with my back to her, but

I could tell. And so I said back, Hi, Nancy. Matter of fact, quick, cool, tough. Now I especially couldn't look at her, and I wouldn't. I only shifted my head a little in her direction, and I turned forward toward the green chalkboard.

And right then, at thirteen years old going on fourteen, I knew I'd never been in love before. I might have daydreamed romances, wished and worried about what might go right or wrong, what if and what if not, but the ringing in my ears now told me what was real, frightening, sickening, one and only being in love. Nothing in heaven or on earth could distract me from Nancy Flores, and Nancy Flores was the most beautiful girl I or anyone else had ever seen—and she *really* was, really she was, it was true, it was *true,* and nothing I did or thought or imagined could possibly not include her.

I don't remember how long she kept at saying hi to me in class before the bell. Or even if she began saying it in the other class she sat behind me. She was doing her best to encourage me to move along, but I didn't know what else to do back besides say Hi, Nancy. I got better at this, I was sure of that much. By now I could turn around and look right at her and smile. I wanted her to know I cared, but I didn't think I should let her see just how much yet. I was afraid that if she knew, she'd laugh at how sick I was with this love. My fever made my brother's Dee Clark and Jimmy Clanton songs—so many raindrops, falling from my eyes, eyes; just a dream, just a dream—too painfully serious for me to listen to. In classes I hugged the top of my wooden desk for secrecy and I drained fountain-pen cartridges etching her name on notebook paper, line after line, in every style of handwriting I was capable of, before I'd throw it away. All over my PeeChee folder I'd engraved her name in letters so small and secret no one could possibly read them. In big letters I wrote, I LOVE NANCY FLORES along one of its diagonal lines, going over it with those words so many times in capitals and smalls, in longhand and print, I turned it into a long, illegible bar of blotted ink so that no one could know. I

knew though. I saw it there on the cover, an announcement to
the world even if I were the only one who could read it. I did
nothing else but lovedream about Nancy. It wasn't like I ever
saw her in specific fantasies. She was more like the music that
played over the scenes. In the two classes she sat behind me, it
was as if I could see her warm, beautiful breath. Sometimes I'd
get to feeling so good I'd worry about having to stand up. I'd
have to sneak my hand down and adjust my erection so the
elastic in my underwear would hide it up against my groin and
stomach, and I'd hope and pray my Pendleton or long-tailed
shirt would do the rest so I wouldn't die of embarrassment.

Then one day she was absent. And another day, and another.
I was miserable. Ever since the time my brother called her
house, Nancy's mother or sister wouldn't so much as glance in
our direction if, by accident, a normal, neighborly encounter
happened. I had learned through the gossip that her mom
was gone at least some afternoons, babysitting for the married
daughter. I didn't know much more, but I decided to take the
chance—I really couldn't do anything else, I wasn't able to stop
myself—and I headed over to Nancy's house. I thought it out,
worked up an excuse in case. I'd ask her if she'd want me to
bring the assignments she'd missed, or the ones that would
come if she had to miss more. I needed to know if she was going
to be absent any more days. I had to see her, make sure she
hadn't forgotten all about me.

My hands in my baggy pants, I walked straight across the
street, down the middle of the sidewalk, down the middle of her
concrete walkway, then manneredly and formally and officially
up the two steps to the porch. I rang the doorbell, returning that
free hand to its pocket. I wasn't sure how bad it could get if her
mom was there. Is Nancy home? is the line I'd been practicing
to say on the way over. If her mom opened the door, I had to say
this fast and not freeze up. I rang the doorbell again and
knocked on the screen door for emphasis.

A curtain bent before the front door opened. It was Nancy.

Hi, she said. She said it simply, bashfully, perfect.

Like I'd figured out, I told her how I wondered if she wanted me to get any school junk for her, how I didn't think she'd want to get behind. It came out like I'd memorized it, like I did. Nancy was hidden behind the screen door, a step away from being close to it.

No, she said. I'll be back in school tomorrow.

I must have smiled too big, sighed too heavily, because when she smiled at me she moved closer to the screen door and looked right at me with her beautiful brown eyes.

Which way do you go? I asked. Because I walk every day and I never see you.

She pointed.

I realized I went a long, odd direction because I stopped by a friend's house. Every morning I did that.

My mom wouldn't let me walk with you, she said.

I guess not, I said, not letting her explain what I already knew. I stood there trying to think of something else, anything.

I'll see you later, I said.

See you tomorrow, she said.

I only walked back across the street, but when I got home, I knew how much farther I'd traveled.

●

We began by talking outside the classes we had together. I'd wait for her, making sure to get there early so I'd run into her by accident. Then we started getting together during lunch period, after she ate with a couple of girls she'd made friends with, me with the friends I'd been eating lunch with for years. We sat on bleachers away from everybody, and once in a while we'd brush against each other's hand or arm or shoulder—always by accident—each little contact as sensual as a kiss.

One week in P.E., the boys' class and the girls' class were put together to learn how to slow dance. We lined up facing what were supposed to be our partners, until everybody scattered around once we'd been told what was arranged for us to do. The girls giggled, the boys squalled, the coaches yelled at us to act mature and take the person directly in front of us. Nancy and I found ourselves across from one another. I put my hand on her waist, she rested a palm on my back, and the fingers of our other hand weaved into each other's. I don't remember anything after that except that I didn't care about anybody or anything else.

Nancy loved me, I loved her. Everybody knew it. We quit pretending we weren't sure. The coaches and teachers joked and raised their eyebrows and winked at us, or sometimes just gave off a smile as inward as it was outward, like adults do. The other kids, boys and girls, packed together around us, yet kept a curious and whispering distance. My old friends left me alone—didn't ask me a single question, not that I would've heard one if it came by—because they were in awe, speechless about this mystery world I'd joined and they hadn't. And especially since it wasn't only my own opinion that Nancy was the best-looking girl in eighth grade. Besides her beautiful hair and eyes and lips, her beautiful everything, Nancy had a figure like a woman, with breasts, and in eighth grade most of the other girls didn't have very much, and this was something that all the boys noticed, not only myself. And since all these guys knew this was the very girl that liked me, all of them envied my incredible fortune.

Nancy and I began walking home together. If her mother wasn't babysitting, I'd say goodbye before we turned the block onto our street. If she was, if she weren't home, well, for a few days we sat on the front steps of my house. But since Nancy worried about that so much, worried a neighbor would see us and tell her sister or mom, we went inside to the couch in my living room, near the front window, so we'd hear if anybody was coming. At first we only kissed on the lips and felt embarrassed. Then we practiced with our tongues and developed that for a long while. My hand took time to wander over her back, my fingers over and back down her bra strap, and I would feel her breasts against my chest. Nancy and I would kiss, and kiss, and finally I'd try to slide my hand over to the front. She'd stop me, and, within a minute or two, she'd get up and have to leave before her mom or sister got back. The next day and next chance I'd be there again though, and soon enough I realized that she really did like this battle some, and so I'd try more often, with both more patience and more insistence. I began by reaching under the back of her blouse, running my hand on her skin, a finger slipping under the strap. I'd run my finger the length of the elastic, to the side where the band widened. Wherever I left off the last time, I could be sure to reach the next. And the day arrived when I didn't let her stop me, or she didn't, when my entire palm embraced her bulge, rested over the crusty fabric that still hid what I hadn't yet touched. I wasn't allowed that flesh easily, and on this Nancy fought for a long time. She liked my touching her too, though—I was sure of that even if I didn't understand her point of view, and one day I unhooked her bra, and she didn't stop me. Nothing I've ever desired has been so satisfying as when I caressed her breasts, the tender, babylike skin which shaped them, no pleasure so tireless as squeezing those taut nipples. Nothing before and nothing since, nothing, has measured up to that simple joy I'd been blessed with right then.

When she had to leave that day we stammered and stumbled as much as we did the first time we spoke or walked home together or kissed. Neither of us could look each other in the eye. For all our mature discoveries, we knew how young we felt, how afraid we still were. Nancy got up off the couch. She said bye, I said see you tomorrow.

●

Joseph Schlee was a gawky, tall German boy with a difficult accent who wore thick glasses and a goofy smile that never left him. His jeans were washed and ironed, his black, wing-tipped shoes never scuffed the schoolyard unpolished, and his white dress shirt—bleached and ironed too, maybe even starched—was tucked in so that it didn't come loose from the pants. He was a boy who nobody openly disliked, but who nobody hung around with either. This, it seemed, he accepted as friendliness itself, or friendly enough.

It was the morning after I'd touched Nancy's breasts, and I was still drunken with their pleasures.

Schlee was standing on the highest wooden step going up to the bungalow where our class met. He was in my gym class, first period, and he was already there, as neat as ever. Other kids were around the stairs too, below him, waiting for the teacher, who was hurrying toward us but still a football field away, to open the locked door. When Schlee saw me walking up, his dumb eyes looked down at Nancy, who had her three-ring binder and texts pressed against her chest, and he smiled stupid like he did. Since everybody knew about us, he did too.

Your husband is coming, he told her.

Nancy didn't shift a toe, even once I got there, but she blushed. I stood outside the crowd of kids, at the perimeter, but I felt like I was right next to her. Kids were looking at us. I was proud.

Schlee gaped above both of us now. Do you know what Richie told me? he asked Nancy.

Nancy didn't and didn't answer.

Schlee guffawed, his screwy eyes fixated onto the lumps on her chest. Richie told me, he said, that what the Lord has forgotten, you filled with cotton. Schlee laughed even stupider than usual.

Just about everyone took a second or two to register his meaning. Even Nancy grinned at the strangeness of the words. But once a snicker clouded the group, and a laugh darkened that, the bright, shiny color in Nancy's face went into the shade. I didn't respond at all because I didn't understand, and, besides, I wasn't listening. I couldn't hear anybody any more than I could see anybody except Nancy. But my reaction was to chuckle out of politeness, to go along—I was so content with the world, I could get along with anyone and any comment. That was before I'd noticed how unfunny Nancy took the remark. The teacher pushed up the stairs, slipped the key in the door and let us in. Nancy'd become even more upset behind me at her desk. I still couldn't figure out what she and everyone else had heard.

Nancy rushed out after the bell rang. Once I caught up with her, she shoved me away, pushing my shoulder so that I lost my balance a little. That got me mad because all my friends were watching and, like all these other firsts, they laughed at me like nobody'd ever done before. So out of self-respect, and because of my confusion, I let her run off and I acted like I didn't care where she went. Go on then! I yelled. I didn't know what else to do. Next period I played casual, unconcerned, even when I had to ask—I hated this—one of the guys what exactly this Schlee had said, but even after he repeated the words, after a few of them laughed again, my lovesick brain couldn't make sense of them. I honestly still did not get it, even after they told me it was about padding her bra. Why would this make Nancy so upset with *me,* what did any of it have to do with *us?* If she wanted me to go after this Schlee for insulting her, I would. But did she have to get so mad at me? Still confused, I chose to play being mad back at her. Anyway, she couldn't come over to my house that afternoon because her mom would be home. And so that day I hung around with the guys at snack period and lunch to punish her for showing me up, for being disrespectful to me in front of all of them.

On the way home, while I was alone, with none of the guys around, by myself and without Nancy, I got it. Slow as I obviously was, the realization struck like bad food: she thought I talked about her, she thought I bragged to the guys about feeling her up. Worse, maybe she thought I lied and told them I did it with her. She was probably sure I told them about the day before, the day she'd been fighting off so long, what she'd finally surrendered to.

I was numb, then sick. Then the pain made me panic and that got me reckless. I had to talk to her and right then. If my brain suggested I wait patiently until the next day, for its safety, my legs pressured me out the door. They ripped over our crabgrass and dug into her mother's soft, lush grass, and they leaped over the steps right onto the porch. I held down the doorbell button and I pounded on the screen door. Nancy couldn't open the door faster than I could speak.

I didn't tell them nothing! I swore to her. And I didn't know what that dumbshit Schlee was talking about!

I don't believe you, she told me. She meant it, but her voice was weak and hopeful.

You have to believe me! I pleaded.

That was when her mother came out of the darkness behind her. Up close, I saw how matronly and stern she was—nothing, in comparison, like my mom, who seemed young and girlish.

What, she snipped, is he talking about? When my mother lost it, which she often did at us, her whole body showed it. Nancy's mother only allowed anger to show in her eyes and through the wide spaces between each of her words.

I didn't say what, and Nancy didn't either.

Nancy's mom scowled at us both. I cannot believe what I think I'm seeing, she told Nancy in Spanish, the same dying air between her words. With a stabbing eye movement, she had Nancy clear away from the frame of the door, and she physically stepped between us.

You, she said to me with contempt. Then without taking her eyes off me, without blinking, she yelled at Nancy to get to her room. Never, she resumed, *never* come here again. She shut and locked their front door.

Before my mother had crossed the threshold into our house, the phone was ringing. She went straight to it. She only offered polite syllables for a while, but she spoke up one time: I don't care what you think of me, she said, but I won't permit anyone to talk about my sons like that. She listened a little bit more, then she hung up the phone rudely.

I was in my bedroom. It had become mine because my brother slept in the garage, which he'd made into his bedroom—he decided he was too old to share with me—and I expected to be screamed at like she'd screamed at my brother over the years. My mother often came home from work dragging, but when she came in my bedroom she looked worse than usual.

Nancy told her mother everything about you two, she said. She says you can't see her again.

Even in front of my mom I felt I should hold back tears, but some squeezed by.

I'm sorry, she told me without any of the anger I was sure was going to wail on me. I'm very tired, she said, and I have to go change my clothes, and she turned toward her bedroom.

But I was not going to give up Nancy Flores. And I was going to get her back. The next morning after homeroom, I ran to first period, to P.E., as fast as I could. Schlee was already suited up and on the field, near the coach. So I had to wait until I caught up with him between classes. I palmed him in the chest to drive out that foul air in his lungs and called him names. Stupid fucker, geek, goon, pussy, fucking maricón asshole. I shoved him again and told him to take off his fucking glasses. When he hesitated, I punched him as hard as I could in the stomach.

Kids piled in on us, screaming about a fight. I punched Schlee in the gut again, calling him more names, taunting him to take off those glasses so I could hit his fucking face. That stupid smile of his quit him. He swung at me wild and clumsy, and though I dodged it, some of his blow caught my jaw. Schlee was big, bigger than me, and I felt it, but only enough to make me get more serious. I popped him in the face even with those glasses on, hit him square on the nose. He backed away from my barrage of punches. He had his fists up by now, but, if he knew how, he didn't use them. I kept coming at him with lefts and rights onto his mouth and nose and jaw, against his glasses, and he kept backing up, trying only to defend—he swung once more, but it missed because I was quicker than him. I called him names again, the crowd screaming and rolling forward with me, backward with him.

Schlee twisted in a way I didn't recognize, and his right leg, with that wing-tipped shoe at the end of it, wheeled up and plugged me dead between the legs. I moaned in pain, buckled, threw my hands onto my balls. Weakened and bent over as I was, Schlee easily hooked a right into my nose and eye so hard my head rose up and my body fell limp. I hit the ground and Schlee kicked me in the stomach and would have beaten me more if a teacher whose whistle we'd heard hadn't finally reached us.

We were both suspended from school for the rest of that week, and my mom, feeling sorry for me, let me miss a few more days because of my black eyes. When I did go back I was so humiliated I was glad that Nancy's seat assignment had been changed in Science and that she'd been transferred out of our other two classes. But I couldn't believe she wouldn't speak to me sooner or later.

She wouldn't though, absolutely would not, and so I tried to get even by acting like it didn't matter so much to me either. I even considered telling guys I did make it with her. But I didn't. I wouldn't say anything because really I missed her and I wanted to explain to her how I never had and never would say anything about her and me. I wanted us together like before, and I refused to believe we wouldn't be.

It was almost the end of the schoolyear when I saw her walking, happy, across the playground with Trey, the most popular boy in ninth grade. Trey was tall and lean and wore pointed shoes with taps and shirts with big collars. Trey's black hair was combed back on the sides and curled up into a pomp at the top, and it shined like neon on those Saturday nights when these older guys went out. It was said he already had a car. He dated younger girls, older girls, and all of them swooned—his school status was as heroic as a TV star's. Trey's fame existed in both name and body like it'd always been there, like he'd been born with a birthright, and even as his reputation soared sky-ward like a god's, he still owned more earth than any of us common people, and we gave ground helplessly.

And Nancy was holding his hand. No girl would blame her. No guy didn't understand, not even me. Still, as they passed together, I swore she let loose of his hand some, I swore she held back just a little for me, for *us*. I swore I saw a sadness in her, a longing to come back to me. Trey didn't feel any loosening of her grip and wouldn't have. He didn't see me, and if she'd told him anything, he surely didn't hear it. There was no battle-ground for me and him. He didn't care. I was no one who mattered if he'd heard, I was no one who mattered if he would've seen me right then. In his world, the one Nancy had ascended to, I was still suffering from childhood, and if she wanted to go back there with me, he'd let her. He was a man, and he was a big man. I still loved Nancy, so I hated this Trey, but only a little bit more than I envied and admired him.

That summer my mother married again, and we moved to another part of the city. Though I thought about her, saw something of her in every girl I thought I might like, I never heard or asked about Nancy again.

●

Four years later my mother had divorced and we'd moved to a different apartment and she remarried and we moved again to another man's house in a newer housing development. He was wealthier than her previous husband, and he bought my mother a new Mustang. I had to go to a new school. I was driving my stock but cherried-out '61 Impala with chrome rims, which I'd paid for by working, over a two-year period, in factories—a pipe factory, a paper factory, a machine shop—where nobody once considered the possibility that I lied about being eighteen. I'd worked for about three months on a swing shift, then quit for two or three months. It seemed better this way than working in a grocery store or a hamburger joint like the other kids my age who didn't lie.

My high school grades had always been passing—C's, a couple of D's, once in a while a B. But at this new school that meant I was slow, and so I was put in classes for the slow people and the fuckoffs. It didn't make any difference to me. I wouldn't quit school because I didn't want to go in the army yet. My brother had just gotten out, come back from the jungles, and, much like he did when I was younger, was never around home except to sleep—he'd stagger in drunk and stoned, though now he was obvious about it, mocking what anybody thought or said. My mother's new husband didn't like my brother or his attitude, but she felt sorry for him, even guilty I heard her say once, so she refused to kick him out. I decided not to be around very much. I wanted things to be different for me. On weekends I kept on dating a girl from my last neighborhood, and I went on saving money so I could go off on my own. I'd already found a graveyard shift job—I dumped the trash and cleaned ashtrays in the offices of a big oil company—and I was, in my opinion, making good money. I'd sleep in class, after school, and on Sunday from afternoon until it was time to go to work.

The kids at this new school weren't like those at any other I'd been to. They all seemed to wear the new shopping mall's clothes straight off the shelves and racks. The first days I looked around for who might be trouble later, but there was no one who I didn't think I could handle if it came down to it. I also didn't see any girls I might like—they were all cheerleader types, and I'd never been out with girls like that. Besides, I was still of the opinion that the best-looking, sexiest ones went to my last high school and cruised the boulevards near it. I considered myself an expert on these matters, and I was so sure of my facts I didn't even feel the need to prove them.

Which is why I think I was singled out in this one class, Health Science it was called. The teacher spoke friendly—we should feel free to talk about anything, he told the students, though I sure didn't believe him—and asked what kids from this school considered daring questions about sex. He'd ask his questions and make the students raise their hands, and they'd giggle and blush. I never put up my hand for anything, never had anywhere else either, and at first this teacher would ask me why, right in front of everybody. I said nothing, no explanation or excuse, which seemed to get me more attention from the other students, made me feel even more in the wrong place, made the teacher more conscious of and hostile toward me. I didn't like this much, but I wasn't threatened. What could he do to me? I wasn't doing anything wrong. The year before I hadn't minded coming to school because there were girls, but at this school I didn't like anything. Then again I was not going to follow in my brother's footsteps—I planned to stay for the diploma, like it or not. Mostly I missed my old neighborhood, my friends there, cruising the streets at night, those girls there who were the best.

I didn't pay much attention to the one named Della who sat next to me. She was too skinny, and she ratted her hair up like she thought she was a pachuca except hers was dirty blond. She wore short, black dresses, brushed wide swathes of skyblue eyeshadow between her blackened eyebrows and the thick eye- liner above her lashes. She chewed and popped gum, and the leg she had crossed over the other swung nervously, scuffing loud the nylons she wore. We sat at tables in this room, not individual desks, and lots of times she'd work it so fast she'd kick me. I finally got it into my head that she was doing this on purpose.

Della was into amphetamines and psychedelics. I didn't

know what those words were yet. Speed, she whispered to me, and acid. I knew those words. I did whites and black beauties to party sometimes, but that other chemical stuff I thought made people not just crazy but also impotent. I told her I could score weed, some downers. She didn't need those, she said, but she'd keep it in mind. Her chair scooted closer to me, and my hand started teasing and playing under the table for something to do. I touched her, and she didn't stop me. Finally this class took on meaning and value for me, and when the teacher showed movies, Della and I got to be the real show—everybody was aware of what was going on. The teacher, who finally had to separate us, didn't like either of us.

I didn't want to go out with her though. On the weekends I saw my girlfriend, and even after we broke up, I still wanted to hang out there in the old neighborhood, not around here. Della wasn't good enough for me. Though one time before I went to work I'd gone over to her house after school and I did it with her. It was there, that was why. I came away ashamed of myself. I wasn't just a dog who made it with any bitch in heat. I'd walked away from lots of girls. I still saw myself as that guy in junior high with Nancy Flores. I liked the best.

But Della began to carry on about us going out. She'd call my mom's and my stepfather's house, leaving messages for me in the morning when everybody was just getting up, or at night when they were asleep and I was at work. One day she insisted I take her home again and made a frantic scene about it. During lunch the only dude I hung out with was this black guy who was new to the school too and didn't have any friends there either, so it wasn't as though I should have felt pressured. But I did. And I promised to take her home that day so we could talk it over. I figured I'd lie about having a new girlfriend, tell her how I liked her but but but, and no hard feelings.

She lived in a cheap tract development that was beginning to show signs—the brick trim which edged the bottom perimeter of the house was falling off, and, along with a few partially and definitely no good parts, car and motorcycle oil was like a deep-coated wax on the driveway. Her living room was a mess of beer cans and full ashtrays, dinner plates with dried-up steak bones on them. The first time I was there she snuck me into her bedroom, to her bed, even though nobody was home then either. This time I told her I didn't want to do that, I was afraid we'd get caught, and maybe we should just talk. Talk wasn't on her mind, and she started getting nasty with me on the couch. I didn't fight her off as much as I'd intended.

Then she saw an old, primered-gray Plymouth pull up against the curb in front of the house. Rusted chrome mags indicated the car was once upon a time thought better of, but now it didn't get washed.

It's my boyfriend! Della squealed as she jumped, stuffing herself back into her clothes. I peeked over the edge of the couch to make out how big the dude was and was ready for my analysis as he was stepping out of the car. Quick, Della had cut him off at the sidewalk before his heel could make any divot on the grass toward the front door. While she did the talking, I focused my eyes, squinting with disbelief through the smudged up pane of the living room picture window. It did look like just like the famous Trey, only he was thinner than before, less substantial, shorter.

I got up, headed toward the front door, opened it, and strutted right up next to both of them. I was proud of myself not only for wanting to do this, but for doing it. I got near enough to be absolutely sure it was him.

It seemed like he hadn't even bought new clothes since junior high. He *was* shorter than me. His black hair was still combed the same, but somehow, like everything else about him now, it'd gone limp and lifeless, droopy, ordinary. Or even less. Of course, he didn't know me, and he couldn't—would have had no reason to—remember me from before. And now, here, this time, it seemed like he wouldn't remember me again, didn't want to think I mattered. He glimpsed me from the corner of his eyes, glared at the house and my car. He was pissed off, but he wasn't going to do, or say, nothing to me.

I gotta go to work now, I told Della and Trey, and I took off for my car.

Della hung back for a few seconds, then caught up after I'd closed my car door. She clung onto the window sill as I was starting the engine.

Hey, she said intimately, I don't like that jerk no more. I just don't know how to get rid of him. I like *you*.

I was dazed, wobbled by this blow of chance—by such a force that it didn't seem undesigned at all. I was stoned, I was drunk. I was awake, I was dreaming.

My biology satisfied, even it had lost interest in Della. But then again I was grateful to her beyond words or explanations because she was his girlfriend, because he was hers. I felt good. Tall. I felt strong, in mind and muscle, like the man I'd always thought I'd be, both the one that Nancy Flores missed out on when she chose that punk, and the one she dumped me for.

Be with him, I said to Della. Like I been telling you, I don't like you that much. He's the right guy for you.

●

I moved out after high school and rented an apartment with an old friend. He was into partying, and in the beginning I went along with him too, but I was also enrolled at the junior college. I liked school more than I was willing to admit to anybody. I was embarrassed by this, as surprised as anyone else would've been. Every subject had become like meeting a new girl, and there wasn't a subject I didn't want to learn. None of my other friends went to school—a couple tried, but most of them ended up in the service, or married, cashing weekly paychecks. I planned to transfer to a four-year school. I was proud of myself, and I showed my pride with a college decal on the back window of my '61 Impala—which I still kept cherry—and where I neatly lined up the semester parking passes on my bumper, the evidence that I wasn't just faking it like those who only had a decal.

I worked six days a week as a stockboy at a department store. It paid less than what I made as a janitor at the oil company, but it was better because my work hours were fit around my college schedule. I worked two weekdays, two nights, and Saturday and Sunday—and Sunday was double-time. I paid my bills, bought my books.

My boss, Rudy, was an older guy with lots of gray in his beard. He had nine kids. Even though he was there from morning to night, he was cheerful about it. High-strung, he was quick to do whatever a department manager wanted him to. Too quick according to some. He loved the job, he loved being a boss. But I liked working for Rudy anyway, and he trusted me because I did.

One morning we were tying our blue smocks on near the freight elevator, about to push the aluminum bins loaded with clothes or boxes out to the sections where they belonged—the store wouldn't open for three hours, and each department had clerks and a manager to stock their shelves and racks—when Rudy came over to me to say how I should work with this new kid. Sure, I said, it's no problem with me.

The new stockboy was Trey. He looked worse than the last time. Ripe pimples colored his cheeks and neck, and otherwise he was pale and gaunt. His dirty clothes were faded and over-washed. His hair showed only the greasy residue of its heroic gloss, dangling there on his scalp, tired of it all, remorseful about its former glory.

I don't know where they find 'em, Rudy confided to me, shaking his head.

Trey didn't remember me. Not a cell in his brain had re-corded a sighting of me. I still couldn't look at him straight. My impulses groaned with pent-up words and sentences. What I could tell this guy! Yet there was another strong urge too, and I reached back for that, overcame the onslaught of emotion: wasn't this a magical present, because wasn't he—the most hated and envied hero of my childhood mythology—here for me again? As alive as he was inside me, I'd never been born to him. I made him an exercise of virtue and weakness. If I had to work with him, I didn't have to say anything. I'd take and not give.

He didn't say much either. He worked preoccupied.

I really needed this job, he said finally.

I didn't say anything about that. I told him where to push the carts, which carts to push. We steered and then unloaded one heavy one together.

It's a pretty good job, isn't it? he asked me.

I said I thought it was. For me anyway.

I couldn't find any other jobs, he said. I put in applications everywhere.

We didn't talk much for a long time, though nobody did in the morning. Everybody was expected to be working their hardest before the store opened for customers.

Rudy pulled him away from me for another job he needed done.

Whada you think of him? Rudy asked me when he came back. It was clear what he thought.

I said I didn't know, I'd only just started working with him.

I don't like him, Rudy admitted out loud. I have to be around him all day, everyday. He's not a student like you and the rest of the crew. Something about that kid rubs me wrong. You think he's all right?

I said I couldn't say. That he was the boss.

You tell me what you think later, Rudy told me.

At break, Trey found me in the loading area and sat next to me.

You married? he asked.

No. You?

Yeah. One kid, and my old lady's pregnant again.

I shook my head. I was thinking.

You got pictures? I asked. Of your kid?

Sure. He pulled out his wallet, opened it to the baby. A little girl, he said.

I took hold of his wallet to get a closer look. Cute, I said. Then I flipped the see-throughs to find others.

That's the old lady, he told me.

It wasn't Della or Nancy. I gave the wallet back.

After break the store opened. We were still partners.

I hate working, he said. I hate fuckin' jobs like this.

I thought you wanted it.

Hell no, I don't want it. I don't want any fuckin' job like this.

We didn't say much to each other for a while.

I should go to school, huh? Like you.

Don't ask me, I said.

Or go in the Marines, he said.

I don't know about that either.

He moped around for a while.

Hey, I had a Mexican girlfriend once, he told me. He looked at me apologetically. Chicano, he said. Or whatever. You know.

I hated this kind of conversation, but I *was* curious.

Nancy, he told me.

He didn't go on right away. Then he said, My grandmother's Mexican. You know that?

I avoided sarcasm and shook my head.

Nancy. He squinted to recall. Nancy Flores, that was it.

And there it was, waiting for me. All I had to do was go along, push innocently, and I would know all that I could want. I could plumb my jealousy and envy, pit love against hate. I could learn just the facts. I might find out more, get a whole new story. Where she went, where she was right now. If I didn't like what I heard, if it were bad news and it made me too bitter and resentful, I still owned him, I could hit him with those times I shared with Della.

I let it go along as it was, with no interference. This was taking an almost inhuman strength and will and I was straining.

Flowers, right?

Excuse me? I asked.

Her name was flowers. Flores means flowers, don't it?

That's true, I told him.

Shaking, blood rushing, I'd snapped it up there, and when I dropped the barbells, the stockroom dust exploded—danced, like a pollen of slivered glass—from the cement field of stockroom into the cardboard haze, and as I gasped to regain my breath, it was as though my lungs had sucked in heaven. I was at peace: what *he* remembered was so *stupid*. I'd been the one in love with Nancy Flores, and I was the one who would never forget her.

Less than an hour later, Rudy came for Trey again. Hey, he said like a boss, I got a job for you.

At lunch, I was sitting near the loading dock with a part-timer when Rudy walked over.

He's gone, he told us. Some little kid upchucked out there and he wouldn't clean it up. I told him he had to, it was part of his job. He wouldn't do it, so he's gone.

I'd never have cleaned it up either. I never had, never would. Rudy knew that. There were a few stockboys who wouldn't, Rudy knew which of us. Usually he did it himself.

I didn't like him no ways, Rudy said. Whada you think? he asked me. You think I was too quick?

I couldn't say, I told him. You're the boss. I didn't get a chance to know him.

Yeah. Well, I did, I knew enough. He wasn't gonna work out.

I DANCED WITH THE PRETTIEST GIRL

(a Tex-Mex song)

The best place for music is Austin, and that's where we were going. Both Lee Roy and I thought we were decent on the guitar, though Lee Roy surely did play it better than me, and, big man that he was, he had a voice somewhere between Hoyt Axton and Tom Waits, which was why I liked him to sing my songs. I wrote better music than he did, but Lee Roy was major star material and I knew my place. My success in the music business improved by my knowing him the same way it did when we did construction together—I'd work anyway, but with him around it was like having a guaranteed income.

I met him framing a Motel 6 in Tucson, where there was so much work and dry sunshine. My first sight of him was rolling 2x6 joists, grabbing up four or so and holding them rock-a-bye style and practically running with them and then running back for more. He took to the tops of walls like other humans do to sidewalks. I was stooped-over all that day banging treated sixteens and dripping sweat and listening to this foreman scream at us that we weren't going fast enough while that huge animal slopped around all lonesome slamming joist and block-ing and decking and singing like to tell us that this ain't shit to him. He approved of what the foreman allowed musically, particularly Conway Twitty and George Jones. Once he started yelling "What ever happened to Hank Snow?!" and single-swatted nails to prove how serious he considered the radio station's failing to be. The first time we talked he'd come down to help us raise this long, double-studded party wall. He says, "They oughta hire a few more a you Mexicans to help do this, or else help me so I don't care." Sometimes I say things without thinking about who would win. I said, "They oughta hire one more big ugly white boy and breed singing cows."

We became friends and pretty soon learned to play music together. I've played lots of music, learned acoustic bass from a neighbor and sang in his mariachi band when I was still a boy. Love ballads were my strong suit. But I got ripped-off because I was the cute attraction at this Mexican restaurant and didn't even get an equal share. My revenge was to forget it all by twelve and listen to rock'n'roll which I preferred anyway. All this was about the same time my mother finally gave up waiting for my old man and remarried and we moved to a better neighborhood. These days I've got my favorites narrowed down: Ritchie Valens, Buddy Holly, early Elvis and Jerry Lee, Bobby Blue Bland, Jerry Jeff Walker. Lee Roy was into music young too. His old man played some bands and might have had a career if he hadn't been an alcoholic and done time for counterfeiting. Lee Roy still tells about going around different towns spending oily twenties on albums with his daddy waiting in a car. He likes any musician with redneck credentials.

The reason we stopped in El Paso was that I was driving and I got off the interstate and pulled into this bar's parking lot and kept hold of the keys. Lee Roy insisted that we should only get one beer and take a six-pack or two if I thought it was absolutely necessary, which of course for him it was. But he wanted to keep going until dark so we could make it to Austin the next day.

"This is where I was born, where my mother and father met," I explained, wanting to look around some.

Lee Roy wasn't much into my sentiment. "One beer," he said. "And besides, I thought you told me your old man *dumped* your momma without knowing you were gonna be *born*." He thought he had me between the legs.

"He was gonna come back. He was like a cowboy and had to follow the work."

Lee Roy got a kick out of that.

The Bullring was a modern bar with a big-screen TV and a happy hour. Even though Texas was playing Oklahoma there weren't many patrons, and they didn't seem too enthusiastic. Lee Roy and I changed this. It was like we kicked open the swinging doors. We took the stools at the counter, the bartender asked us what we gentlemen preferred, and Lee Roy tore into the free food.

"What's that music you got here tonight?" I asked the bartender.

"Progressive country, a little Charlie Daniels and Heart."

Lee Roy and I both laughed and ordered a couple more.

"Whada you guys do?"

"Lee Roy sings. Otherwise we play the hammer and nails."

We drank two for one and stayed on after the game ended and an evening crowd started in. We made acquaintances with the band members and in no time at all felt like regulars. We started getting free drinks, which stimulated Lee Roy to do his typical asshole routine, though nobody seemed to mind. He took center stage while I stayed put at the bar thinking about El Paso and trying to make up some verses to a tune I'd been playing around with. I put it down as the band warmed up, which was at the same time I fell in love with the prettiest girl I'd ever seen. She came in with this other female who might only be considered average looking in comparison.

"Look," I tried getting through to Lee Roy, "that other one's just right for you, and I'm in love. You gotta get ahold of yourself so we can work this as a team."

It was hopeless. He was too busy being drunk and I had to brave it alone.

"Um excuse me, but I had to introduce myself. May I sit down? Believe it or not I'm not good at this, but, well you're the best looking thing I've ever seen. I mean it. You are the prettiest woman my sorry eyes have ever looked at. You already know that, don't you? You probably got guys under your feet when you walk, you probably had to get an unlisted phone number. Can I buy you both a drink? I'm just passing through town. Me and that big drunk white guy over there. We're on our way to Austin. We're musicians. Guitar. What else is new, huh? I was born here in El Paso. My parents are from El Paso. Well, you know, more or less. Really my mother. I'm not that sure about my father to be honest. But anyway that's why we stopped. Look, would you like to dance?"

Have you ever been on a dance floor with the prettiest girl? Let me tell you, your boots move differently, the world is a changed place. You sway to the earth and your animal heart beats young blood and your tainted eyes sparkle. You feel like a real man.

Her name was Alma and she was seventeen years old. She could obviously pass for legal age but she made sure by coming with her sister, Luisa, who really was harmed much more than she deserved by her sister's control of nature. I was convinced that it would all work out, that Alma loved me as much as I her, convinced that Lee Roy, despite himself, was making a good impression on Luisa, who had her own apartment.

"Lee Roy," I pleaded back at the bar, "her sister is very pretty. Don't you got eyes, man?"

"You take beautiful and I help you out with the other. You think I'm a dumb Mexican?"

Lee Roy ordered himself another beer. He and I had known each other for a while by then, and the truth was that much of our friendship was based on a truce: no racist talk at me. I'm sensitive and irritable about it for obvious and not so obvious reasons, and I've made it clear to him that I don't find it cute. Very seldom does he refer to "Mexicans" around me. Like any good old boy, he loves racial slurs and epithets and finds it very hard to refer to non-white people without calling them something. One time we were in a car and these black guys took a little too long in a crosswalk for Lee Roy—he'd been drinking of course—and he screamed something about niggers. I told him that time that if something came up as a result, he should know whose side I was on, that I wouldn't back nobody up for bullshit like that. I remember it made an impression on him and I was glad. Still, around a group of musicians, after a few shots and chugs, he'd sometimes refer to me as his little Mexican songwriter and partner. He meant it good-naturedly, and I tried to accept it in the same way he did when I talked about him as a white boy.

"Are you that drunk? You're lucky to stand a *chance* with the big sister. Look, *look* at her for a second. If Alma wasn't in the place you'd kill for her. And it's only a miracle that Alma seems to have taken a liking to me. I'm afraid she'll stop drinking and drop me cold."

"Maybe next time, little buddy. I ain't seen all the cards yet to fold my hand."

I should say this. I'm not so little. Lee Roy's about six-four and he's bigger, but lots of times that isn't big enough. I was pissed, but then I wasn't about to let him spoil my evening.

●

Everybody knows that fights don't start over a single incident, not even between strangers. The fight's already there, just waiting, just looking for something to fire it up. You always know when a guy in a bar is there to get into it. Well that guy was staring at Lee Roy, and Lee Roy, who probably wouldn't have cared any less anyway, was too drunk to pay him any attention. This guy was a tall, lean Chicano with a long reach, a man hard and strong in the spirit of Alexis Arguello. What he was saying was that he didn't like it that Lee Roy was drinking Coors. He would've found something else to not like if he had to, there was no question of that. The guy had some hair and he wasn't just in it to take *any* somebody out, he wanted to be challenged. He was also drinking beer, but in his case it was to chase his shots of either whiskey or tequila, I couldn't tell which for sure.

Meanwhile, things were falling in place for me. Alma and I danced and talked and she not only didn't seem to be getting bored, she was interested. Only Luisa wanted to leave. I wasn't sure how to handle this. There were certain questions of manners and taste to be considered, certain complications of Alma's youth. An easy "Let's you and me lose your sister" line wasn't gonna work. The game had to be played by old style conventions, so I had to convince Lee Roy to double date, to entertain big sister.

"Would you come *on*," I begged him. "As a favor to me if nothing else. I'm like having a dream come true here. I can't believe I've met her and that now she wants to be with me. And I swear to God, Luisa likes you, disgusting as you are."

Lee Roy finished a can and asked the waitress to bring him another. He'd won a couple games of eight ball for five dollars a rack. "Nah," he said, examining an angle. "Specially not right now."

I nodded my head and tightened my jaw. I shouldn't have been so surprised but I was.

The waitress came with the beer just as I was about to go back to my table.

"Dígale a su amigo que no compramos Coors aquí," that homeboy told me, "that here the people don't drink racist beer."

I decided to wait where I was a minute. "You can tell him, compa. He'll understand."

Lee Roy looked up. "I don't give a fuck what Mexicans drink or don't drink. They can swallow piss for all I care."

Guys moved away from the center of the room and got closer to the walls, made room. The Chicano's friends moved to his side.

Lee Roy had a pool cue in his hand and had casually brought the heavy end up. "I might need a little help here, partner," he said to me. "Looks like this boy don't think he can go it alone."

I'll be honest. Generally I hate this kind of shit. I dread it and feel very much like trying to work the problem out some other way, say by leaving. It's just not relaxing at all. But my heart pumped for this one. I took a long second. "I'll be there if any other guy jumps in," I told the ones behind the homeboy. "Otherwise," I wanted Lee Roy to understand, "que viva la raza, asshole."

Lee Roy tossed the pool cue onto the table. The Chicano came in first, popping Lee Roy twice with narrow-toe boots and a left-right combination. Lee Roy let him get through with a couple more and grabbed the Chicano by his shirt, unsnapping most of the buttons on it as he flung him and landed two solid blows into a mouth and against a nose. The two of them rolled around a bit and it was anyone's guess who was getting the worst of it. The Chicano was able to get up but missed, locking his boot under Lee Roy's neck, and went down again. They stood up together.

Of course, the excitement around this was intense and enthusiastic, except for the bar owner and his bouncer, who was a football player at the university. You knew that because it said so on his T-shirt. They obviously didn't appreciate the mess and were hollering about police. I really don't think he wanted to, but I suppose the bouncer, a heavy-set black dude, felt an obligation to grab someone, so he reached in for the homeboy, only because he was closer. That was probably a mistake. That Chicano made wind of his fists and the bouncer was against a wall, dazed, before he realized he should have been more polite. When he focused he was mad. Things got out of control at that point. Somebody hit me in the face and I hit him back and Lee Roy was fighting off three guys. Some white guy was helping him out, trying to pull a body off Lee Roy's back. I heard sirens.

I went to Alma and her big sister. They told me to follow them. Since I had the keys, I had the car, and right or wrong it didn't seem fair to leave Lee Roy behind. As tempted as I was, I went back for him. He was a mess, groaning as much as his pride would allow, but I think he was glad I was still friend enough to let him slump over in the back seat.

The fight enhanced things for me considerably. It gave me an excuse to go up to Luisa's apartment, it gave us a mutual story to share and drink coffee over, it made my interest in Alma seem more than just a one night hustle, which it was, but which it wasn't. I killed 'em dead when I got out my guitar and sang a few songs with that swelling, discolored spot on my cheekbone.

Much too forgivingly, Luisa tended to Lee Roy until he finally passed out on the couch. Then she excused herself and went to bed, though not before she gave her little sister a big sister warning about staying up. Alma and I went outside onto the balcony. El Paso's a quiet city under that load of stars and half-moon and wide black sky. Besides ourselves, we could only hear an odd rig on the avenue nearby and a rooster with a bad sense of dawn.

"That's where my dad works," she said, pointing to this unnatural blot of man-made lights on the horizon. "At the smelter."

"Right now he's there?"

"Almost every night."

"So he makes lotsa bucks anyway."

"There's too many of us, and they don't pay that good."

I took a second or two and I kissed her on the neck. "So how come we're talking about your dad?"

"I was thinking about him. He doesn't think I should stay with my sister even one night. He's afraid I'll get myself in trouble."

"Oh?" I wavered. "Have you been getting yourself in trouble?"

She took a second or two. "Tonight's the first time I brought a guy up here."

I had to think of something to say. "I'm telling you, it's true love."

"You always kid around, don't you?"

"I'm serious."

Finally we started making out. We kept at it. She acted seventeen, almost eighteen, about it.

"I gotta make love to you," I told her.

She didn't say anything.

"*Please.* You're so beautiful I can't stand it."

"How come you never write songs in Spanish?"

I moaned loud. She knew what I meant, but waited for my answer. "I dunno. I stopped when I was young. I hang around guys that sing in English."

"You should write some in Spanish."

I nodded. "Tonight's made me think about it." I kissed her again and we made out again. She was getting tired and she broke.

"We'll go in. Where were you gonna sleep?"

"Usually when I stay, on the couch, but Luisa said I should sleep with her."

We went inside and slid the glass door closed. I took one of the blankets off Lee Roy and then rolled him off the couch. I took the cushions. I laid the blanket on top of them, and Alma came back with two more.

"In the kitchen?"

"I'm hungry."

"I never slept with a guy before," she told me slyly.

"And don't you ever sleep with another."

●

Let me tell you, she was the prettiest girl. I was the happiest man to ever fall asleep. Is there any joy greater than sleeping with a woman you've fallen in love with? When she is still becoming one, when that wild sensation of innocence can still prey upon and consume a man's spirit? I had thoughts! My mind soared with possibility and hope, with certainties and destinies. I knew why the Lord put me on this earth, and I loved Him too.

"You won't come back, will you? Otherwise you'd stay."

"Alma, I'm telling you, I'll be back. We just gotta make this gig in Austin. It's a big break for us. Come with me if you want."

"You know I can't."

"It's only a couple nights there. Then I'll come back."

We both went back to sleep, and Lee Roy finally kicked me to wake up late in the morning. "Let's hit the road, Jack." Luisa came out of her bedroom when she heard us talking and offered to make breakfast. She woke up Alma and the two of them whispered and Alma kept the blanket around her and grabbed up her things and headed for the bathroom. I looked at Luisa guiltily. She told me it was love at first sight and I felt better. I offered to go to the store but she insisted that no, we only had to give her our first album when it came out.

"You know," Lee Roy told me, "you were right about big sister. She's a very pretty one. I missed out."

My thinking wasn't too clear about Lee Roy. His face was pretty messed-up though, and I did not feel sorry about that. "I'll have to drive the whole way. You better be able to sing tomorrow night."

"Don't be so tough on me, partner. You know I don't mean no harm."

It was an awkward goodbye. All of us were sleepy and exhausted, Lee Roy and I were hungover, I couldn't say for sure about the sisters, and Alma and I were trying to find the words.

"I'll call you when I get there," I said. "It'll only be a few days."

As I drove off, I kept wondering how I was gonna go back, about how I could do it, about what I might be passing up in Austin. Then I got to thinking how all this was a good omen for us, how the muse was with me and wanted me to write my songs, how good it was to be wandering. I pulled over to the side of the highway and stopped in a dry, dusty cloud of desert soil. I took a piss on some hearty flora and told Lee Roy that he had to drive for a while because I wanted to write this tune about El Paso.

"About how I'm gonna go back for her," I told him.

He laughed.

"I'm not lying, man. I think I love her."

He howled out the window.

"You don't believe me?"

Lee Roy kept on laughing. I hopped in the back seat and stretched-out my legs and strummed the guitar with a pencil in my ear and a piece of paper on my lap. The song was about how I danced with the prettiest girl, and I wouldn't ever let Lee Roy sing it.

THE MAGIC OF BLOOD

It wasn't late unless you were a baby or maybe just past that, asleep in the backseat of the car, or old. Very old was how old my great-grandmother was, and she was in the frontseat, tired. I was driving her home from my uncle's suburban house in Garden Grove, where we'd celebrated her birthday, though nobody was sure what number it was or even if it was the exact date. I hadn't wanted to take her because my car hadn't been washed in months—which around here seems more important than it did at home—and was loaded down with beer cans and bottles and greasy workrags and all that paper and stuff that never gets thrown out once you've stopped thinking about it. My car didn't seem the best for someone who meant so much to my family, but since my sister and I live in Hollywood too it didn't seem right not to take her either. It was also a clear night on the freeway, meaning it was dark black around us, thick as dirty oil, and headlights beamed sharply into it. There was a soothing hum to the road, and the people, with their elbows out an open window in all the big and small cars that glided past us, were so in focus that they looked costumed and made-up to suit the setting behind them, like this was all part of some chic American movie.

Once every so often my nephew, the baby, would cry and my sister would say little things to him. My great-grandmother wouldn't turn away from the fuzzy windshield, which was pitted by the desert storms back home and water-spotted and plain dirty from here, and she would say, "Pobrecito, pobrecito, que bebito tan lindo tan chistoso" in this sing-song voice. Which was nice, except our words would end at that for a couple of miles and in the silence I'd notice how firmly she'd be gripping her hand to the top lip of the dashboard. Before we got going I'd asked my sister to sit in the frontseat because required conversation made me miserable, but all she said was, "With the baby?"—sort of like I was suggesting we put the boy on the hood of the car. So, silence being worse than small talk, I took lead of the discussion.

"No, I haven't heard from him in many years," great-grandmother answered me about a certain relative I had met once. "The family is too spread apart. They are here, they are there. And this one won't talk to that one, there's this thing or that thing. Really, it is not good, it is very rare."

"I didn't even know what most of my uncles and aunts looked like," I threw in to support her theory and to keep it alive.

"Nobody cares what happens to anybody," she said. "Nobody thinks it is important. The family is all broken up."

I glanced in the rearview mirror for that one. Did my sister hear? I couldn't help treating our great-grandmother's remarks as larger than maybe she meant them, and I was thinking it would be good for my sister to catch that one, for our mother's sake at the very least. Sometimes, in spite of myself, I really did want my sister to be punished for the creep she'd married and the life she led.

It's not simple to explain why my sister married that cabrón. We're not a dumb or poor family. My old man always brought home a paycheck and he taught me more than one trade to make a living. My sister had lots of chances too. She's good-looking and she's smart and she always seemed to know exactly what to do. But she used to say that she didn't like being at home, that she didn't want to end up settled-down in some boring house the rest of her life, raising kids until her body became as pretty as a dishcloth. My mom would get very resentful about this attitude of hers and talk about what a bad example she was setting for her younger sisters. There are five children in the family and I'm the only man. I don't suppose that sounds so important, but I always accepted it as a responsibility and so did my mom. My old man didn't ever seem to think about this kind of thing, which is, in the spoken opinion of my mother, more evidence. Maybe it seems like I'm wandering off the subject but I'm not. My great-grandmother is my father's grandmother. And my sister came to L.A. because my great-grandmother did.

Great-grandmother is from Mexico, some small town on the way to Mexico City. She wasn't stupid either, and she wanted all the life that most people want but can't have. Nobody's explained this to me very well, maybe because nobody knows the story very well, it being so long ago and coming down to us the way it has, but my great-grandmother married this very wealthy man who had something to do with the government. She was just fourteen. She became pregnant right away, and after a year the man died. Some relatives say he was killed, some say it was some freak disease, some say he was just old—he was real old, they say—and died like everyone else dies, just like some say he deserved to for having such a young girl for a wife. So my great-grandmother, who was about sixteen at this point, was rich or at least powerful in some sense and in a position she wanted to be in. She left her baby with her mother back in their small town and she came to the United States. You can figure for yourself how many years ago that must have been and what it was like. I don't know where she went first, if she traveled around the country or only in the Southwest or what. That's another one of the subjects no one seems to want to speak clearly about. And I don't think anyone feels comfortable asking great-grandmother directly, which I take to be also part of my father's tradition. I do know it was said that my great-grandmother ended up in California and eventually got into the beginnings of the film industry. Nobody knows whether she got rich by it, or famous, or anything, though we do know she married some movie director—he was also old and he also died, but no one talks about any intrigue concerning his death. What mattered, to all of us, was this one glamorous, and verifiable, detail: she had a Hollywood address. It was like believing there was magic in our blood.

My sister was the first one in my family who acted on that. She ran away from home when she was sixteen and came to L.A. My father wanted to kill her at first, but overnight he was resigned to it and he told my mother he would leave the girl alone and that she should too. It was her life, what she had chosen, he told her. My mom argued and cried, then she obeyed. That was how my old man was about things, how my mom got along with him. She said it was impossible to disagree with him when he got these ideas in his head. It was like my great-grandmother, and probably it was like my sister, and probably he was right. But I saw it like my mother did before she gave up the fight. I wanted to know why he didn't drop everything and go after her. Wasn't that what he was supposed to do? Everybody has said that I take after my mom. Which is probably why my old man had to hit me when I told him how I'd go after her if he wasn't father enough to. I shoved him, he shoved me. Then I hit him in the shoulder as hard as I could. And he shoved me with both his arms. I got my balance back and I swung and missed and he hit me in the stomach so deep I couldn't breathe. I would have bet he didn't stand a chance against me, and for a little while after, after the first few weeks and months, my pride mumbled about how if I'd really gone at him, if I'd hit him in the face with all I could. It wasn't true though. He would've beaten the shit out of me. And so I did what he said because he was right about a lot too. I accepted it in the same way I did when he taught me how to take a car apart before I under-stood—I'd have to learn myself if his way was the best or just what he knew.

My sister won't say what she did those first months here in L.A., not even now. I do know that she didn't stay at my aunt and uncle's house in Garden Grove. That's what everybody here at home believed, but I asked them and they told me she didn't even drop by once. What I do know is what we all know, that she started hanging out with this older guy, a jailbird and a gangster my mom called him. We knew about him because when she finally started writing home she sent pictures. One with Mundo in baggy pants and an undershirt and tattoos on each arm and a mustache and slicked-back hair. Another where he'd dressed in a white suit and a black shirt and a white tie, a black handkerchief in the jacket pocket, that mustache, some long straggly hairs on his chin, that polished hair textured by wide teethmarks of a comb. In both photos my sister looks good, if I can say so even though I'm her brother, and sexy, like there wouldn't be a man in the world who wouldn't want any time he could get with her. I also know she was having a good time. He got her into nightclubs, even though she was underage, which, according to her, Mundo sang in, ones right on Sunset Boulevard. Nobody believed her about that. It was hard to for some reason. But one thing about my sister was that she didn't lie— though she might not tell, she never lied. I also suppose you could say Mundo did all right by her in a lot of ways, since she was dressed in the best clothes and she didn't work. Oh yeah, she got to Hollywood in the first place by stealing an envelope full of money from our parents' bedroom dresser. It was quite a bit, and when she finally mentioned it in a letter she said she was sorry and she'd pay it all back as soon as she could. Which she did, or Mundo did. My old man was very impressed by this. My mom said he took it as proof of how he was right about her and we'd been wrong.

I didn't come out here for my sister like everyone said. She did suggest it, that's true, but I decided to come for my own reasons. My sister had this place in Hollywood and she wanted help with the rent. She'd broken up with Mundo months before—we don't know why and she hasn't explained it to me either, though I guess it's obvious enough. She told him to leave her and the baby alone, at least until she was ready to let him back in her life. She gets letters from him that are all apologetic, she says, with comments about how he loves her and how he's changing. She tells me she doesn't write him or call him, but I'm not so sure. She got this great job at a music studio. She admits she got it because of Mundo's connections, but she claims it doesn't matter how she got it because everybody gets a good job for some reason. It's forty hours sometimes, sometimes twenty, and a neighbor, a Mexican lady, takes care of the baby when she's not home. Anyway, she didn't need me like everyone said, and even if she did I still would have come for my own purposes. You might say I wanted to find out what it was like, if I'm more than my mother's son. I have a job at a Firestone station. It's temporary.

●

Great-grandmother's party was a big one. Relatives came from everywhere, from every state in the Southwest, from Mexico. They roasted a goat in the backyard and my uncle hired maria-chis from Santa Ana to play for two hours. Everybody talked about Disneyland and Knott's Berry Farm and Sea World. Everybody was staying at separate hotels and motels, including my parents and younger sisters. Not even the relatives from Mexico stayed with my aunt and uncle. All this is part of a tradition which, my mother explains disapprovingly, is also why they say my great-grandmother refuses to live with anyone but herself, whatever her state of health, or so *they*—my mother would say—want to believe.

There were many questions I could think of for my great-grandmother now that she was in my car. I hadn't asked not because of shyness, or because today was the first day I'd seen and met her. I hadn't because I didn't think I should, and it seemed forbidden to ask someone else in the family if it was forbidden to ask her. So, aside from that list of questions, I didn't know what to talk about. In every silence I went back to wishing my sister would talk or the baby would cry again. Or I'd start to worry about this old car I was driving. What if it broke down? How would she feel if we were stopped on the shoulder of the freeway? And I'd been drinking. I wasn't drunk, but what I was did add to the blackness of the night, to that quality of old and new, of young and old. I felt like we were underground, not on top of the earth, that I was driving but not in control of the destination we were rolling toward. I'd had rides like this on roads away from the city back home. I'd driven this very car, headlights turned off, the windows down, wind blowing, and I'd felt a similar sensation, but there it was the stars and the moonlight on the cactus and weeds and on the dirt and rocks. That felt old to me, like I was seeing the past, seeing it like every man who ever passed through at any time saw it. But freeway driving was the future, with its light hanging over us in squares and rectangles, circles and ovals, their reflections on the waxed colors, on steel and aluminum, on the billboards of young women rubbing themselves with tanning oil, or young men with rippling stomach muscles modeling pants. Both experiences excited me, but this one was with my great-grandmother staring at it alongside me, her clear, wet eyes wild and squinting past the dirty window of my dirty car.

All I could talk about was relatives I didn't know or didn't even think about.

"I've received letters from them all sometime," she said in a voice that seemed easier than how scared she looked. "Every one of them writes me at some time about going here or there. Or sometimes it is about a new house, or a marriage, and then they send me baby pictures too. I have many, many pictures. I don't throw them away. I keep them in a drawer."

"It must be impossible to keep all the names straight. There must be hundreds of pictures."

"Yes," she said indifferently.

"Keeping the names straight. You probably don't know who these people are!"

"I try to learn," she said indifferently.

"So grandmother," I said. "You don't mind being alone where you live? It doesn't bother you?" I knew right away that this was something my old man would say was none of my business, but it flew out of me, like my mother's voice.

"Well, there are my little cats. They are such sweet babies. They keep me company. I have very few visitors now."

All of the sudden the baby cried and great-grandmother chanted "Pobrecito, pobrecito, que bebito tan lindo tan chistoso." I wondered about the visitors while my sister calmed him down. I was imagining movie people or who knows what with occupations I didn't know about or understand coming to her house for old-time's sake. I didn't know if everybody in the family had the same photograph, but my family owned one which was taken at a portrait studio in Hollywood, on Vine Street. I knew where because it was stamped on the back of the stiff, yellowing 8x10. She looked young, sexy, like a starlet. The resemblance was still there, only she was a whole lot older.

"I don't know what I would do without my little cats," she said, resuming the conversation without me. "They bring me so much happiness. I once had tenants live in the other bedroom, but they would steal from me or not pay the rent. It was very aggravating. I could use the money, but it's much too hard. People expect much too much."

"Are you doing okay?" I asked, getting deeper into it. "You don't need money or anything, do you?" God knows what I could have done, but I felt it and my mouth moved.

She didn't flinch. "It isn't as easy as it once was because I can't work now. But my expenses aren't so great."

She said this so reasonably that I knew she'd never thought she deserved better or more.

"But don't you wish the family was near you? Don't you

wish someone would visit you every day?" My mom would be proud of me for coming out with this. There was no holding back.

"Oh yes. I would like that very much. But the family is always too spread apart. It is very rare, but it is how it is."

"You wouldn't want to live with someone? With my aunt and uncle in Garden Grove? With my mom and dad?"

"No, no. I am very used to my home. I couldn't live in anyone else's."

So much for my mother's way of thinking.

Once we smashed through the lights downtown—their shards almost like a daylight—we stopped talking. My great-grandmother and I were on our own personal freeways and she'd even let loose of the dashboard. The baby had fallen into a deep sleep and my sister had dropped off too. We looped onto the Hollywood Freeway and the drive was no longer so un-familiar. Green exit signs slipped past us until I followed the one closest to her house. Great-grandmother gave me directions, though I did somewhat know the way since I'd had my sister drive me by as soon as I'd gotten into town. My sister told me then how she did the same thing when she got here, and later she had even stopped in more than once with Mundo. "No big deal" were her words.

It was a normal house. Not much different than the ones at home really, though there was something about the street and the lawns, the palm trees all around. The neighborhood wasn't very nice. In front of a house across the street a car without tires or rims was blocked up and sprayed with gang graffiti. People cruised by or walked past who didn't look common, at least in any place but Hollywood, where sleaze mixes in easy. There was loud rock music, maybe from a bar on the boulevard, maybe from one of the nearby houses. It probably was a pretty home once though, and my great-grandmother's house would still look good with some fresh paint on it. Whatever, to me it was something to be here. It was the address I'd memorized. And now I wasn't just locating it on a map or seeing it with my sister, I was involved, I'd stepped into part of its history.

Great-grandmother did need help getting into the house, especially, she told me, after she'd been sitting for some time. I'm not used to this sort of thing either. I don't know how much help is help and how much is too much. I opened the door for her and held out my hand and she grabbed on, lifted each leg out the car door and onto the street curb, then pulled herself up. She also needed help walking. I offered my arm and she clung to it to keep steady. The walking was better once she was in her house, she explained. I kept up with her, matching her deliberate pace. It was a hard walk for me too—her touch was so fragile and delicate and so perishable, with nothing soft or innocent about it, nothing like a child's. The stairs to her front door were the hardest for both of us, and at the top we were both exhausted in our own way.

She had to lean against the stuccoed wall between the door and window to dig through her old purse for the housekeys. She kept saying, "They're here, they're in the bag," though not with confidence. Two of her cats split the curtains and rubbed themselves against the screen, clawing the mesh, meowing steadily, both frantic and happy. The light behind them inside was so bright they seemed more like silhouettes. Up close, I could see they were motley gray tabbies. While my great-grandmother hunted her keys, she was chanting in her sing-song, "Pobrecitos, pobrecitos, que gatitos tan lindos tan chistosos." I went back to the car for her sack of presents and leftover food.

When I returned she'd found the keys and was wrestling with the locks. There were two, one below the doorknob and part of that hardware, and a deadbolt above. She hadn't remembered to leave on the porch light so it was dark. What little light there was came from the window where another cat had joined in the waul, and it wasn't much help. My great-grandmother kept going back and forth between keys and locks, tugging and pushing, saying how she wished she had left the light on, how she'd have to go around the back, how these weren't the right keys. I offered to try but she told me no. I heard crickets somehow through all this, or maybe one loud cricket, then a burglar alarm from a distant building.

"I'll have to go around the back. I'll have to go around the back." She was shaken and upset. "Something is wrong with these keys."

"Let me have them," I finally insisted. "I can see they're the right keys. They're turning." I was nervous because she was nervous, but I told myself that there were only so many possible left and right turns and one of the combinations had to be the correct one. She was still talking about going around the back, or breaking windows, or knocking the door in. She talked to cats or chanted when she didn't talk to me. I swore she was trembling and I worried about her falling over and dying right there from the trauma of this. "I'll get it, I can open this," I assured her and myself. The top key to the left, then take the keys out, the other key to the right, push, to the left, push. The top key to the right . . .

It was a sticky door and when I got it the first time I didn't realize it because it didn't open. So I went through the process again. I pushed hard, mad, the next time, and it gave.

"The kitties, the kitties!" My great-grandmother was transformed with the door open. Her change was as distinct as the moist stench of catbox which soaked the house. She walked in talking to the cats and to me, "Come in, there's some cookies in the tin, I know how hungry you are, pobrecitos, pobrecitos." The kitties leaned against and weaved around her weak legs. "Are you thirsty?" I almost said yes since it wasn't clear if she was only talking to her cats.

I completely forgot about the odor while I was looking at the pictures on the walls, Hollywood photos, black-and-whites, of her and some other actors and actresses I didn't recognize. She was in costume in most of them, Spanish costume, but also in one which I didn't know the nationality. I felt this swirl of relief because, much as I wanted it to be true, I always doubted, worried it was a story I'd been fool enough to believe. But now I was here, in this otherwise normal, otherwise sadly furnished, smelly house.

"I better go," I said. "The baby."

"Oh yes! El pobrecito!" She was so happy to be home, and she thanked me many times as I went to the door.

AL, IN PHOENIX

My car needed a new wheel bearing. I knew it because I'd been hearing it in there for over a year, but also because of that, for it so long always sounding the same, no better no worse, I wasn't so worried. I didn't want it to freeze up and ruin the axle too, so I knew I should do something, at least have something done since I hate to work on my own car now, on anybody's car, though sometimes I'll do this or that on somebody else's, you know how that goes. Most of the time it's easy enough really and I almost always know what's wrong, what to fix, because I did it so much when I was a kid. I was concerned enough anyway to see what might be done, what this mechanic in Blythe would say about it. I knew the guy, I knew the place, because I almost always stop for gas on my way through, one time to change a tire, another to take a look at some loose tappets I heard. Blythe's the last real stop before Phoenix, and it's a long, sandy desert between, and not a great place to break down. I'd have thought the guy'd remember me and my car, since one like this can't come through that often I'm sure, and that time he snugged-up my tappets I had him go ahead and tune it up too, and I went out and bought us some beers. He didn't act like it though, or if he did he wasn't giving me any deals. I'd asked about a new tire first and he wanted twice as much as I'd ever paid anywhere, looked at me like I was from a different planet when I asked suggestively if he couldn't do just a touch better

[75]

than that, or if not, give me some idea of a place in town that might. I needed the tire too, it was in bad shape, closing in on the first layer of ply. So then I asked about the wheel bearing, how much he thought it'd cost me if I let him have at it. He had no idea, he'd have to tear it down first and see. That didn't sound too reasonable to me, as you can imagine, since once it was apart I'd have already lost time and money if his price was gonna be high. So that was it for Blythe. Like I told him, I was feeling lucky, so I decided I'd get it to Phoenix, maybe get the tire there at a discount place I knew, I had a good spare anyway, and I'd have the other work done there where prices wouldn't be so last-chance high.

My luck held too. The wheel bearing wore out within the Phoenix city limits. I drove it slow, on the shoulder of the freeway to be exact, until I got it to an off-ramp, and then I coasted, the wheel smoking and stinking until I'm over to the side of the road in front of a business establishment, which lets me use its phone to call Triple-A, which I consider one of the really great American services, which everyone always welcomes you to use the phone to call. In no time at all I have a tow-truck pulling up and hooking me on.

"So where d'ya wanna take it?" the tow-truck driver asks. He's a young guy, with long straight blond hair that's neat, cut well, and clean.

"You know a good mechanic? You know, not too much, not so cheap you worry the guy's stupid?"

"Not really. My station's good though. We got this mechanic named Al there. He's maybe the best I've ever seen."

I think this guy's an innocent, a true-believer type, hasn't been around long enough to know. Has a first kid, a young wife, thinks he's got a good job. "I don't trust Triple-A stations, if you know what I mean. They know they've got ya."

"I don't know any other place," he says. "I do know that my station'll get you in and out, and that Al'll do it right. I don't get any money for saying that, or taking you there either."

An innocent. It probably never occurred to him that if he didn't take the breakdowns to his station he wouldn't have the job. On the other hand, what'd be the difference? How much could a wheel bearing be if the guy charged too much? More than in Blythe? Probably not. And if the guy is fast I could get back on the highway and save spending the night in Phoenix. So far everything'd been going smooth and on schedule. "Take me to your leader," I tell him. "I wanna get it done."

"You'll get it done," he says, "and Al'll do it right. He'll find whatever's wrong and tell you what's about to go wrong too."

"Sounds heroic enough to me."

The tow-truck driver laughs. He drives straight and confidently, his dispatch radio blaring, then pulls into a station at the crossroads of two freeways. He's gone almost the moment he gets there, barely exchanging a word with the station mechanic whose oval name patch has "Al" stitched in it.

Al is either prematurely gray or a very healthy old guy in his sixties. He's working on a Cadillac, jumping a battery. He revs the engine, listens, and shuts it down. He adjusts some dials on the battery charger and lowers the hood about half-way. I'd swear he's humming a song to himself, one of those mellow classics everybody even my age knows for better or worse, but not a sound is parting Al's lips.

"So," I say to him to start up a conversation.

"Sir," he says, almost closing his eyes at me, "why don't you have a seat in the waiting room and I'll be with you."

"No problem," I say. I walk away nervously, because I'm always nervous, thinking I should be more patient, the guy must have tons of work to do and thousands of people to deal with. I wait, pacing around the station and not in the waiting room listening to the ting-ting of cars stopping for gas. A short, muscular guy takes care of them. Finally Al comes out from the back of the garage, as excited as ever, and goes over to my car, and starts up the engine.

"It's a wheel bearing," I tell him.

He doesn't respond. He rolls the car forward, into one of the stalls, then positions the steel arms of the hydraulic lift under the chassis. He stands up, goes over to the controls, moves the lever and brings the car up.

"Great invention," I say. "I remember when I was a kid this neighbor had a pit with stairs in it. He always had to carry around a light. It was always dark down there anyway, and greasy." Al is spinning the wheels of my car. "And he'd have to block the car up to work on the wheels, stoop over." I get close to my tire, the one that Al's near and about to take off to get at the wheel bearing.

"Sir," he says, "please wait in the waiting room. The sign says only employees are allowed in this work area." He stops what he's doing to say that to me directly, irritated.

"No problem," I say. "I understand." I do. It is hard to work all day with distractions, people under your feet. I'd be the same way if I had to work on these cars all day, everyday. So I go into the waiting room, this grease-coated room where they have two worn-out couches and a table between them. In the corner nearest the door leading into the work area is an up-to-date cash register, the plastic on it still polished, and above that a sign: ABSOLUTELY NO CHECKS! This all used to be the gas station office, now it's the waiting room, quote unquote. On the table there's a pile of newspapers and a stack of car magazines. The newspaper is today's, so I read it until Al comes in.

"It's only the wheel bearing, so you were lucky. I checked the one on the other side and you've had that one done recently. I'll have to have it pressed on. This is the cost." He has it itemized on a form. The price is good, average at best, not above anyway.

"Do it," I say. I sign the form. "How long you think it'll take?"

"Can't say."

"I mean estimate. More or less how long, that's what I mean."

"Can't say."

I don't like that much. That being his attitude. Like he

doesn't give a shit about me, me sitting here, waiting. I almost say something to him. Then I say this anyway. "I only wanna know so I can make some plans if I have to. Like get a motel room if I have to spend the night." It wasn't late, it was afternoon in fact, but I can see the possibility, it wouldn't be his fault or attitude that would make a part hard to get, and I understood that he was having the bearing pressed on somewhere else.

"I can't say, sir," he enunciates. "Everything takes time."

A real philosopher. I don't argue. The car is still up there on the lift, tires and axles off. I'd made good time today, and I figure I can afford to relax. I know a good motel, cheap, with a cable television. So I go on reading the paper, then I look at those magazines, shut my eyes a little, walk around this Phoenix gas station.

I talk to the short, husky-armed guy, name tag Nick, who works the full-serve and takes the money for the self-serve. "Your partner isn't the friendliest in the world."

"Al? Al and me get along pretty good. I understand him cuz we're both from Detroit."

That made sense. I don't try talking to him much after that. He's too busy anyway. I do listen to Al talk to this other couple from Georgia, Georgia plates anyway, who came in with an almost new car. Al has the hood open, staring and fiddling with all the tubes and wires it has. The couple stands by uncomfortably, wordless. Did I say listen? I mean I watch. There are no memorable words traded. Just about an ignition key and gas, what the car sounded like when the trouble started. Al disappears and the couple whisper. Maybe ten, fifteen minutes go by. He comes back, tells them what's wrong, a timing chain, how these cars are famous for this, and for all the work it's gonna cost them this big figure. He doesn't say it, but it's obvious that he's telling them he disapproves of their car, that it's the proverbial hunk of, but it's also clear he's not gouging them on account of his dislike of the car, it's not a willful price, and he gives them the figures on paper like he did me. He waits a moment or two, I can't hear what they say to him, but he walks away and they whisper some more and go to a phone booth. Al doesn't look under that hood again. They get into a taxi and drive away as quietly as they came.

I'm patient, I'm prepared for the long wait, but then I see a small foreign pickup squeal in and a delivery boy carrying my old axle with a new wheel bearing. In no time at all. Al gets right to it. In his way that is. Like I said, humming one of those old songs. I know better now though. But he does get right to it. I watch him without so much as putting my toe in the forbidden work zone, leaning into the door opening of the wait room. He greases the axles, slips them in, tightens a couple of bolts, then comes the drums, the tires. He checks the rear-end grease. He adjusts the brakes while it's up in the air. Methodically, unrushed. He lowers my car, disappears, returns with the bill. All this as disinterested as the rest.

I'd bought myself a soda, and I put in a couple extra quarters for him. "I'd have bought you a beer but the machine man must of forgot to put them in. Didn't know what kind you liked, so I guessed." I set the cold soda next to where he puts the paperwork.

"It's not necessary, sir. No thank you."

Okay. I pay cash. Not a dime more than what he'd said. I say thanks, leave the soda, and drive off. I couldn't believe how early it still was, how little it cost, I mean I really expected to pay much more, being on the road and all, and so I decide to take it easy and spend the night. First I buy a new tire. Then I check into that motel I mentioned. I take myself to a restaurant where there's a bar, drink a couple beers, and call it a night. I was happy between those crackly motel sheets, a cable movie on. I nodded out.

I was up early and felt great. I stopped for a big breakfast. Everything was going so well. I like to hit the road just as the dawn breaks, and I did. I gotta say I like driving through

Phoenix in the morning, I like the light, that pinkish-blue, mixed with black. Pretty. I also like leaving Phoenix. So I was rounding this on-ramp and I hear what I thought was like pieces of gravel under my floorboard. Then again. Then a bad sound, not like gravel, but like engine, like pieces of rod all of the sudden coming apart. I pull over. The oil-light had gone on. The sun was on the rise. The engine won't turn over. I walk over to the restaurant where I'd just eaten and use the phone to call Triple-A. I wait maybe half-an-hour, maybe forty-five minutes for a tow-truck. It wasn't the same driver or the same truck, but it's the same people.

"Take me to Al's station," I tell the driver, another young guy with long hair, only his more scraggly, like he isn't married, doesn't have a first kid.

"We got another station right over here, closer, if you want."

"No, I think this guy Al's a good mechanic, and I want a good mechanic." I am not feeling too happy.

"We got Hank over at the other station. He's a good mechanic too."

"As good as Al?"

"Maybe. About the same. Al's real good though."

"Take me to Al. I guess I trust him."

"Yeah, Al don't want anybody in his way, but he's good. One of the best. Maybe *the* best."

I feel like I haven't gotten enough sleep. "I'll bet you get tired of having to come for us breakdowns. All depressed and worried. I don't even wanna know what's wrong with this car. I don't even wanna hear it. It's bad news, I'm sure already."

"Nah, we make lotsa folks happy. Starting up a car that won't, fixing a flat. Al'll probably get you going too."

Naive, don't you think? The point isn't whether or not he can get me going, but whether he'll do it for a price I can pay. I've lost cars this way, two to be exact, two because I couldn't pay for the repairs. In both those cases it wasn't whether a mechanic was able, anybody can bolt-in a new engine, hook the wires back up. The question is, is it worth it? The question is, how many options do I have so far away from home, from friends, from tools?

When we get to the station, the truth is I'm embarrassed to be back, and I don't even want to talk to Al about what's wrong. Early as it is, he's already there, not humming any melodies I know, leaning under the hood of some other car. A simple tune-up, it looks like. This time I'm even nervous for me. Not just from the breakfast coffee. When he finally talks to the tow-truck driver about my troubles, I don't know, it just seems to me he's irritated, you know, the way someone says *What this time?* Like that, you know? And he doesn't go over to my car. He doesn't look over at me. He goes back to what he was doing, with the same sort of attitude toward it, no more, no less. I can barely take it.

Did I say I don't like Phoenix? I don't like Phoenix. There's something about the place. You wonder what draws people here at all. It's the weather, the climate. I do know this, I know that that's why all these easterners come out, why the city gets all the business it gets. I can see why someone'd want to live in Arizona, it's pretty, the country is, all desolate, rugged, but not Phoenix. Phoenix always seems about as interesting as that TV show that was set here, about the diner, if you know what I mean. I do like Goldwater, by that I mean only the man, but I'll bet he doesn't live in Phoenix. Like here at this gas station. What's unique? It's like every gas station anywhere. And beyond, in the neighborhood? Faceless buildings, an American flag, not even that big of one really, palm trees. Palm trees? Phoenix is not Hawaii, not even L.A. And then all these guys who work here. Uniforms with their names on them. And everyone of them has a beard. Not even interesting ones. They're all cut and cared for. Not like strong statements. Just uninteresting beards and bellies and blue uniforms.

So when Al's done playing with that tune-up, he goes over to a car he has up on the rack. A brake job, it looks like. Okay, so there's some cars ahead of me and I gotta wait my turn. I can understand that. Though he could take a look at what's with mine and give me an estimate so I can make some plans if I have to, make some decisions. That's what I think, that would seem like the courteous thing to do if you were to ask me. Then another tow-truck pulls in with another car. Al goes over to it, he talks to the owner, he pops the hood, he goes around, starts the engine, turns it over anyway, then has the driver do that while he looks under the hood. Then he talks some more. It's nothing at all like how I was treated, and, I don't know, maybe this other guy does look better than me, a suit and everything, a newer car on the expensive side, but so what? My money's the same as his, my money was good enough yesterday, my clothes were no fancier then either.

When he gets done with talking to that man, getting a phone number, and the man leaves in the tow-truck, Al goes back to the brake job. Now I'm upset, which I can be from time to time. I'm worried about my car you see, worried about my money, my life, and I'm worried that it's Friday, and the next day's the weekend, and maybe even if it can be it might not be done until the weekend's over, I mean I can understand how that could happen. I mean it's probably going to be a big job if I have them do it, and there's gonna be parts to find, all these things I can understand, so it's reasonable of me to be thinking the things I am, worrying about making plans.

So I go over to Al. "So whadaya think? When do you think you'll get at mine?"

"I can't say, sir." He doesn't even look at me.

"All I mean is when do you think you'll be able to tell me what you think is wrong?"

"Sir, I can't say. Everything takes time."

"Look," I say, biting my angry tongue, "all I wanna know is if you're gonna look at my car when you're done with this one, in an hour, in two. I have to make plans."

"Sir. Please. I cannot say. I'll get to it." He stares at me.

I can't believe it either, but what can I do? Have it towed somewhere else? Where? At what expense? I can do nothing now and I know it. I can do nothing but hate Phoenix, hate waiting.

I try the room for this, for waiting. I listen to the boys with the bellies. The only one without a beard, name tag Nick, the stocky guy with the arms, who's from Detroit too, like Al, tells how the guard at his prison wouldn't let him out this morning until he went back and shaved closer. He'd thought he'd shaved close enough, but the guard doesn't like him for racial reasons. Then he asks if he could have an extra hour at lunch, to get his horns clipped. A normal request, and the other guy with the blue shirt, name tag Rick, doesn't lose a moment from the newspaper to say why not. I spy what looks like a boss. A grayer beard, a bigger belly. He talks to Al once or twice, interrupts him, doesn't go to the pumps or collect money. I get his attention.

"I realize your man over there is busy, by himself, all that, but can you do me a favor? He's very hard to talk to. I need to know when my car's going to be looked at so I can make plans. I don't know if I'm going to have to reserve a motel room, get more money, nothing. All I'm asking for is the estimate, not the actual work. I wanna know when I'm probably gonna get that."

"Sure," this man, name tag Bill, says easily. "I'll find out for you." He comes right back, not thirty seconds. "Within the hour."

I don't know why Al couldn't tell me the same thing. I'm not happy about that, that being his attitude, and I'm still not happy about how long it all has been taking. But I try hard to have patience. I try to make contingency plans. I go to a phone booth and look up a bank where I can get some money. I find an address.

"Where's 2400 Van Buren?" I ask Rick, who's still reading the newspaper and now eating a pop-tart or whatever they're called that he bought off the roach coach that just came by. It's getting close to lunch.

"It depends," he tells me wisely.

I'm feeling like I'm working I'm so tired by now. "It depends?"

"Yeah. It depends."

I wait, but I figure out that I have to ask. "It depends on what?"

"Whether it's east or west. Whether it's 2400 East Van Buren or 2400 West Van Buren." To him, it's a dumb question, an obvious distinction.

"I'll go look it up again. Can you give me directions for both?"

He does that well, and quickly. I'm afraid to ask for a repeat, so I think to call the bank, ask for directions over the phone, but then I see that Al is pushing my car into the garage. I won't help or even think to. The guy with the arms does though.

I watch now. He gets it started, which makes me very pleased, excited even, because that means I didn't blow up the engine after all. That means it's the transmission, or something else. Al listens. I position myself at the doorway of the waiting room once again, and I listen too. Finally he takes the car up in the air. He takes out the drive shaft, gets the transmission out, works on the bell housing, takes that off, leaving the pressure plate. He disappears. Fifteen minutes later he steps into the waiting room with his paper and figures.

"The clutch was put in backwards. You need a new one. There were rocks in the bell housing too. Some bolts sheared off, probably because whoever did the clutch—it wasn't too old, but it's ruined—put in the saddle, which holds up the transmission, wrong and it's been twisted because of the angle."

He gives me the estimate. I can't believe how little it is, at least how reasonable. I mean it'd cost me this at home, at places I know to go, and his labor charge, well, it's only for two hours, and he's already spent one messing around with it. I sign the document willingly. "How about a beer? I'm so happy! I'll walk over to some store and buy a six-pack. Whadaya like?"

"That won't be necessary."

It's more than that. He doesn't want me to, I can sense that. Maybe he doesn't like me, like my type, my skin, my clothes, my eyes, my nose, my out-of-state plates, my talk. But who cares? I don't care! Fix my car and I'm on the road, I'm gone.

All I gotta do is wait again. It's lunch time, there's no reason I shouldn't go have a beer or two just because Al from Detroit doesn't want any, and maybe by the time I get back he'll be closing in on it. So I go across the street to this bar and slide over a stool. It's not much of a place, a hangout for real unattractive people who wouldn't think that about themselves, a crowd big on Levi jackets and earrings, on both sexes. Beer's beer though, and I have two of them. I ignore the activity I could stare at in the mirror, all the making-out in the back.

That's my lunch. Hours pass, my car's still up in the air, and I'm wondering.

"So, uh, when do you think you'll be through with mine?" I ask Al.

"I can't say, sir."

I can't understand what it could be. Other than this guy's attitude, I like him. I can't understand what it is he doesn't like about me. Or maybe my car. Maybe because the work on it is too shabby? Okay, so me and a friend didn't do it so right. That was years ago, we'd been drinking beers, and, after all, it's an older car, almost rare—who'd expect this thing to keep on going like it has? Or maybe it's the whole picture: me, my car, my looks. Maybe he thinks I don't live right. Maybe he thinks I should have a newer car, car payments, house payments, an office job, a white shirt and tie, at least some uniform with a name tag like him. Maybe he envies me, thinks I'm living loose, drinking beer, driving around with out-of-state plates in all these other states, playing with girls. Maybe he's not married and wants to be.

Maybe he is married and miserable. Maybe he's got a daughter, or two, or more, and he thinks it's guys like me. Maybe he's just a jerk who never learned not to be one.

"Look it, it's only that I need to know so I can make some plans. You can understand that, can't you?"

He almost scowls at me this time. "Sir, everything takes time. How can I say?"

So now I'm mad. It doesn't seem right to me. It seems discourteous, nasty, thoughtless, unbusinesslike. Which makes me think of Triple-A.

So I dial their number. The woman on the other end understands what I'm telling her, she agrees.

"I think he's a good mechanic, but I don't think there's any excuse for him treating customers the way he does, and I think if you send someone out here, like as an experiment, you'd see what I mean. I had my car towed here because it's a membership station, and I've come to expect, well, courtesy, and professionalism."

"I agree with you, sir."

"I am glad of that. Do me a favor though. Don't make the complaint today, however it works. I have my car here now, I can't take it anywhere else, and I don't want the work on my car to be stalled on account of this. I just think you people should reprimand this station, so that other people, in similar situations, won't have this, this aggravation."

"Thank you for telling me about this, sir."

"No problem. Thank you."

It's late now, mid-afternoon, but Al's back on my car, a new clutch has been delivered, he's putting it in. I can still do some driving, I can get out of here. Then he throws down a part, cussing, and disappears the usual amount, then returns, holding the metal fork that takes the throw-out bearing.

"Whoever replaced your clutch should have replaced this too. It was a sloppy job. I have to buy another now. It'll cost this much more."

He shows me the numbers on the paper. No more labor, just that part. I nod my head. I want to ask him about finding it because I know it won't be easy, the car being unique and all. I do. "You can get it?"

"I can't say, sir."

I don't bother to ask about the time. I know the answer. I wait. Two more hours in that room. In Phoenix. Which I hate. I'm afraid even to turn on the radio since I hadn't heard it either of these days I've been waiting waiting. Then Al's working on my car again. Slipping parts back in, bolting. It's 4:30 p.m. when he's got the drive shaft back in and he can lower it down. He starts it up. There's this horrible sound. Like grinding rocks. The same sound that brought me in here by tow-truck. Al listens to this several times. It's ugly and causes him to cuss behind the wheel. Me, I'm thinking of money again, where I'll stay, the value of fixing versus the savings of walking away, my life. I'm tired. My legs hurt so much I feel like I've been holding that car up in the air all day.

Al doesn't talk to me. He brings the car back up and starts disassembling again, down to the pressure plate. I don't even bother to ask him, I know I'm in Phoenix for another day at the very least now, and I'm very worried about how much time it's taking him, the new expenses. I'm worried he's gonna say forget it, I'm done for the day and for the weekend and with this car, good luck, goodbye, and I'll still owe them money, which I don't have a tree full of.

Everybody else has gone home except Al and his Detroit friend with the arms and the prison sentence, name tag Nick.

"I can't believe it," I tell him. "I thought he had it. Now he's at the beginning again."

"It happens," Nick says.

"The guy's been on my car since this morning. I bet he can't stand working on it anymore."

"It goes that way sometimes."

"I'm afraid it's something else, and he's gotta figure out what it could be all over again."

"I know Al. He'll find it."

Nick doesn't appear to be the least worried about the hour, about his friend Al's will to work, and he shrugs off my concern like it's so much small change.

What can I do? I stick around. But I watch from a distance, because I feel bad about Al, who's still in there working, on the wrong thing I'm convinced, not that he wasn't right, but that there's more and he can't face it. The light in Phoenix is changing. It's as pretty as in the morning, pink and blue, the palm trees black silhouettes against that sky, the flag put away in the comfortable night air. The brightest light around is in the garage where Al is still working on the underside of my car, and the light gets brighter and brighter as the darkness gets darker and darker. Al keeps at it, methodically, unrushed, an even pace. Nick is closing one of the gas pump islands. I decide to go ahead and rent a room, I'm not gonna try to drive tonight, even if he does get it tonight, which he won't, but I'm not going to tell him to stop, I'm not going to say anything to him, go near that forbidden work area. I go over to this one motel. It's cheap enough, cheaper than that to be honest, but the best room, the room that doesn't have one broken window—it's the only one like it, this is what the owner or motel manager or clerk or whoever she is tells me—well, it's hard to describe, but the smell alone, and the stains on the rug, the bad ones I'm talking about, not all the others, and then the ones on the mattress and box springs and I'm talking about them because that's what I was shown, all these things reminded me of worse places than where those people in the bar hang their jackets, so I go across the street. The room is more money, more than the place I stayed last night, but it's got cable too, and I figure I'll get used to the smell—some kind of rug cleaner, or insect bomb—and otherwise it's not too bad. I take it, pay the money, turn on the tube, walk back to the station a half-hour later, and though from a distance I can see, without walking the two blocks, I can see Al still in there, still working, the car in the air, I walk over.

"I'm afraid to talk to him," I tell Nick. "I can't believe he's still at it."

"He won't give up. That's how he is."

"Here's the number of the motel where I'm staying. Give him it if he needs me."

"Sure thing."

I go back. I buy some donuts and milk from one of those establishments across the street. I watch half of an hour television program. I have to go back. I go the two blocks. I really can see him in there without going all the way to the station, I can see just by standing on the street in front of the motel. But I go, into the waiting room, not too close to the door that leads into the garage area. I don't think he sees me, and I don't go there so he does, but I go there. Every half-hour I do this, out of a need. After four of them I see he's putting things back together. I get further away to watch. He lowers the car. More sounds, not as serious, but the same kind, and he grinds the gears as he shifts. He takes the car up again, takes out the drive shaft, the transmission, and I can't watch, I walk back to the motel, tortured by the scene, miserable, guilt-ridden, exhausted. Several more half-hours. Each time Nick is doing something else that he does at the station, checking gas levels, cleaning an area, washing something, and he's as indifferent to Al's working as Al himself appears to be.

It's ten o'clock, a little bit after. A local news show has started. I go over to the station. Al's bolting down the drive shaft. Then he lowers the car. Goes around to the door. Turns the ignition. It starts. No ugly sounds. No grinding gears. He revs the engine, shifts the gears several more times, then stops. He pops the hood. He checks things. He checks the battery, puts in water, greases the clamps, then closes the hood. He disappears for his usual time, then comes to me with his paper.

It's the price he quoted, not a nickel more. I notice he's washed his hands, but I'm sure he hasn't touched another part of his body, and there's not a gray hair on his head or in his beard that is out of place, smudged, or damp. His friend from Detroit, with the arms, from the prison, Nick, is sweeping the waiting room where I'm counting cash. They don't say a word to each other.

"I can't believe you wouldn't give up on it," I tell him. "You gotta be starving."

"I won't let it beat me," he says directly.

"I guess not." I thank him and back out of the garage. I pull onto the street, but drive past the motel room I've rented to get the feel of the car. It's never felt better, never shifted smoother in all the time I've driven it.

ROMERO'S SHIRT

Juan Romero, a man not unlike many in this country, has had jobs in factories, shops, and stores. He has painted houses, dug ditches, planted trees, hammered, sawed, bolted, snaked pipes, picked cotton and chile and pecans, each and all for wages. Along the way he has married and raised his children and several years ago he finally arranged it so that his money might pay for the house he and his family live in. He is still more than twenty years away from being the owner. It is a modest house even by El Paso standards. The building, in an adobe style, is made of stone which is painted white, though the paint is gradually chipping off or being absorbed by the rock. It has two bedrooms, a den which is used as another, a small dining area, a living room, a kitchen, one bathroom, and a garage which, someday, he plans to turn into another place to live. Although in a development facing a paved street and in a neighborhood, it has the appearance of being on almost half an acre. At the front is a garden of cactus—nopal, ocotillo, and agave—and there are weeds that grow tall with yellow flowers which seed into thorn-hard burrs. The rest is dirt and rocks of various sizes, some of which have been lined up to form a narrow path out of the graded dirt, a walkway to the front porch—where, under a tile and one-by tongue and groove overhang, are a wooden chair and a love seat, covered by an old bedspread, its legless frame on the red cement slab. Once the porch looked onto oak trees. Two of them are dried-out stumps; the remaining one has a limb or two which still can produce leaves, but with so many amputations, its future is irreversible. Romero seldom runs water through a garden hose, though in the back yard some patchy grass can almost seem suburban, at least to him, when he does. Near the corner of his land, in the front, next to the sidewalk, is a juniper shrub, his only bright green plant, and Romero does not want it to yellow and die, so he makes special efforts on its behalf, washing off dust, keeping its leaves neatly pruned and shaped.

These days Romero calls himself a handyman. He does odd jobs, which is exactly how he advertises—"no job too small"—in the throwaway paper. He hangs wallpaper and doors, he paints, lays carpet, does just about anything someone will call and ask him to do. It doesn't earn him much, and sometimes it's barely enough, but he's his own boss, and he's had so many bad jobs over those other years, ones no more dependable, he's learned that this suits him. At one time Romero did want more, and he'd believed that he could have it simply through work, but no matter what he did his children still had to be born at the county hospital. Even years later it was there that his oldest son went for serious medical treatment because Romero couldn't afford the private hospitals. He tried not to worry about how he earned his money. In Mexico, where his parents were born and he spent much of his youth, so many things weren't available, and any work which allowed for food, clothes, and housing was to be honored—by the standards there, Romero lived well. Except this wasn't Mexico, and even though there were those who did worse even here, there were many who did better and had more, and a young Romero too often felt ashamed by what he saw as his failure. But time passed, and he got older. As he saw it, he didn't live in poverty, and *here,* he finally came to realize, was where he was, where he and his family were going to stay. Life in El Paso was much like the land—hard, but one could make do with what was offered. Just as his parents had, Romero always thought it was a beautiful place for a home.

Yet people he knew left—to Houston, Dallas, Los Angeles, San Diego, Denver, Chicago—and came back for holidays with stories of high wages and acquisition. And more and more people crossed the river, in rags, taking work, his work, at any price. Romero constantly had to discipline himself by remembering the past, how his parents lived; he had to teach himself to appreciate what he did have. His car, for example, he'd kept up since his early twenties. He'd had it painted three times in that period and he worked on it so devotedly that even now it was in as good a condition as almost any car could be. For his children he tried to offer more—an assortment of clothes for his daughter, lots of toys for his sons. He denied his wife nothing, but she was a woman who asked for little. For himself, it was much less. He owned some work clothes and T-shirts necessary for his jobs as well as a set of good enough, he thought, shirts he'd had since before the car. He kept up a nice pair of custom boots, and in a closet hung a pair of slacks for a wedding or baptism or important mass. He owned two jackets, a leather one from Mexico and a warm nylon one for cold work days. And he owned a wool plaid Pendleton shirt, his favorite piece of clothing, which he'd bought right after the car and before his marriage because it really was good-looking besides being functional. He wore it anywhere and everywhere with confidence that its quality would always be both in style and appropriate.

●

The border was less than two miles below Romero's home, and he could see, down the dirt street which ran alongside his property, the desert and mountains of Mexico. The street was one of the few in the city which hadn't yet been paved. Romero liked it that way, despite the run-off problems when heavy rains passed by, as they had the day before this day. A night wind had blown hard behind the rains, and the air was so clean he could easily see buildings in Juárez. It was sunny, but a breeze told him to put on his favorite shirt before he pulled the car up alongside the house and dragged over the garden hose to wash it, which was something he still enjoyed doing as much as anything else. He was organized, had a special bucket, a special sponge, and he used warm water from the kitchen sink. When he started soaping the car he worried about getting his shirt sleeves wet, and once he was moving around he decided a T-shirt would keep him warm enough. So he took off the wool shirt and draped it, conspicuously, over the juniper near him, at the corner of his property. He thought that if he couldn't help but see it, he couldn't forget it, and forgetting something outside was losing it. He lived near a school, and teenagers passed by all the time, and also there was regular foot-traffic—many people walked the sidewalk in front of his house, many who had no work.

After the car was washed, Romero went inside and brought out the car wax. Waxing his car was another thing he still liked to do, especially on a weekday like this one when he was by himself, when no one in his family was home. He could work faster, but he took his time, spreading with a damp cloth, waiting, then wiping off the crust with a dry cloth. The exterior done, he went inside the car and waxed the dash, picked up some trash on the floorboard, cleaned out the glove compartment. Then he went for some pliers he kept in a toolbox in the garage, returned and began to wire up the rear license plate which had lost a nut and bolt and was hanging awkwardly. As he did this, he thought of other things he might do when he finished, like prune the juniper. Except his old shears had broken, and he hadn't found another used pair, because he wouldn't buy them new.

An old man walked up to him carrying a garden rake, a hoe, and some shears. He asked Romero if there was some yard work needing to be done. After spring, tall weeds grew in many yards, but it seemed a dumb question this time of year, particularly since there was obviously so little ever to be done in Romero's yard. But Romero listened to the old man. There were still a few weeds over there, and he could rake the dirt so it'd be even and level, he could clip that shrub, and probably there was something in the back if he were to look. Romero was usually brusque with requests such as these, but he found the old man unique and likeable and he listened and finally asked how much he would want for all those tasks. The old man thought as quickly as he spoke and threw out a number. Ten. Romero repeated the number, questioningly, and the old man backed up, saying well, eight, seven. Romero asked if that was for everything. Yes sir, the old man said, excited that he'd seemed to catch a customer. Romero asked if he would cut the juniper for three dollars. The old man kept his eyes on the evergreen, disappointed for a second, then thought better of it. Okay, okay, he said, but, I've been walking all day, you'll give me lunch? The old man rubbed his striped cotton shirt at his stomach.

Romero like the old man and agreed to it. He told him how he should follow the shape which was already there, to cut it evenly, to take a few inches off all of it just like a haircut. Then Romero went inside, scrambled enough eggs and chile and cheese for both of them and rolled it all in some tortillas. He brought out a beer.

The old man was clearly grateful, but since his gratitude was keeping the work from getting done—he might talk an hour about his little ranch in Mexico, about his little turkeys and his pig—Romero excused himself and went inside. The old man thanked Romero for the food, and, as soon as he was finished with the beer, went after the work sincerely. With dull shears— he sharpened them, so to speak, against a rock wall—the old man snipped garishly, hopping and jumping around the bush, around and around. It gave Romero such great pleasure to watch that this was all he did from his front window.

The work didn't take long, so, as the old man was raking up the clippings, Romero brought out a five-dollar bill. He felt that the old man's dancing around that bush, in those baggy old checkered pants, was more inspiring than religion, and a couple of extra dollars was a cheap price to see old eyes whiten like a boy's.

The old man was so pleased that he invited Romero to that little ranch of his in Mexico where he was sure they could share some aguardiente, or maybe Romero could buy a turkey from him—they were skinny but they could be fattened—but in any case they could enjoy a bottle of tequila together, with some sweet lemons. The happy old man swore he would come back no matter what, for he could do many things for Romero at his beautiful home. He swore he would return, maybe in a week or two, for surely there was work that needed to be done in the back yard.

Romero wasn't used to feeling so virtuous. He so often was disappointed, so often dwelled on the difficulties of life, that he had become hard, guarding against compassion and generosity. So much so that he'd even become spare with his words, even with his family. His wife whispered to the children that this was because he was tired, and, since it wasn't untrue, he accepted it as the explanation too. It spared him that worry, and from having to discuss why he liked working weekends and taking a day off during the week, like this one. But now an old man had made Romero wish his family were there with him so he could give as much, *more,* to them too, so he could watch their spin around dances—he'd missed so many—and Romero swore he would take them all into Juárez that night for dinner. He might even convince them to take a day, maybe two, for a drive to his uncle's house in Chihuahua instead, because he'd promised that so many years ago—so long ago they probably thought about somewhere else by now, like San Diego, or Los Angeles. Then he'd take them there! They'd go for a week, spend whatever it took. No expense could be so great, and if happiness was as easy as some tacos and a five-dollar bill, then how stupid it had been of him not to have offered it all this time.

Romero felt so good, felt such relief, he napped on the couch.

When he woke up he immediately remembered his shirt, that it was already gone before the old man had even arrived—he remembered they'd walked around the juniper before it was cut. Nevertheless, the possibility that the old man took it wouldn't leave Romero's mind. Since he'd never believed in letting down, giving into someone like that old man, the whole experience became suspect. Maybe it was part of some ruse which ended with the old man taking his shirt, some food, money. This was how Romero thought. Though he held a hope that he'd left it somewhere else, that it was a lapse of memory on his part—he went outside, inside, looked everywhere twice, then one more time after that—his cynicism had flowered, colorful and bitter.

●

Understand that it was his favorite shirt, that he'd never thought of replacing it and that its loss was all Romero could keep his mind on, though he knew very well it wasn't a son, or a daughter, or a wife, or a mother or father, not a disaster of any kind. It was a simple shirt, in the true value of things not very much to lose. But understand also that Romero was a good man who tried to do what was right and who would harm no one willfully. Understand that Romero was a man who had taught himself to not care, to not want, to not desire for so long that he'd lost many words, avoided many people, kept to himself, alone, almost always, even when his wife gave him his meals. Understand that it was his favorite shirt and though no more than that, for him it was no less. Then understand how he felt like a fool paying that old man who, he considered, might even have taken it, like a fool for feeling so friendly and generous, happy, when the shirt was already gone, like a fool for having all those and these thoughts for the love of a wool shirt, like a fool for not being able to stop thinking them all, but especially the one reminding him that this was what he had always believed in, that loss was what he was most prepared for.

And so then you might understand why he began to stare out the window of his home, waiting for someone to walk by absently with it on, for the thief to pass by, careless. He kept a watch out the window as each of his children came in, then his wife. He told them only what had happened and, as always, they left him alone. He stared out that window onto the dirt street, past the ocotillos and nopales and agaves, the junipers and oaks and mulberries in front of other homes of brick or stone, painted or not, past them to the buildings in Juárez, and he watched the horizon darken and the sky light up with the moon and stars, and the land spread with shimmering lights, so bright in the dark blot of night. He heard dogs barking until another might bark farther away, and then another, back and forth like that, the small rectangles and squares of their fences plotted out distinctly in his mind's eye as his lids closed. Then he heard a gust of wind bend around his house, and then came the train, the metal rhythm getting closer until it was as close as it could be, the steel pounding the earth like a beating heart, until it diminished and then faded away and then left the air to silence, to its quiet and dark, so still it was like death, or rest, sleep, until he could hear a grackle, and then another gust of wind, and then finally a car.

He looked in on his daughter still so young, so beautiful, becoming a woman who would leave that bed for another, his sons still boys when they were asleep, who dreamed like men when they were awake, and his wife, still young in his eyes in the morning shadows of their bed.

Romero went outside. The juniper had been cut just as he'd wanted it. He got cold and came back in and went to the bed and blankets his wife kept so clean, so neatly arranged as she slept under them without him, and he lay down beside her.

CHURCHGOERS

O.K. That was the superintendent's name, and it should have counted as the first warning. Don't men who use initials for a name always play some tougher-than-thou role? There were a couple of other signals too—the waving American flag decals he put on either side of his glossy white hardhat, which seemed to have been born on his head. Or when, the first time I got close enough to him, shoulder to shoulder on the narrow landing between sections of the metal scaffold stairs (I was on my way down, he was coming up), he didn't seem to hear me say good morning, or care if I did.

The hole, four stories down, was alongside Beaudry Street and gouged a city block, and was tied-back from 3rd Street on the west to 2nd on the east. Not only wide, the structure would be the tallest poured-in-place concrete highrise west of the Mississippi, and so lots of tradesmen would be needed. In the beginning though, besides O.K., the only other Hoff-Dunbar (the general contractor) men were a journeyman named Sean, who worked with Ramirez, the assistant super, and Curt, the layout foreman. Curt got me on. We'd known each other from a few years earlier. At the time, he'd been off so long—hurting—that he worried about keeping up. I was young and he was smart and we became partners, and when the job ended we shook hands, said we'd see each other again sometime. Which was this job.

Curt had been hired by an even bigger offsite boss, and O.K. didn't seem to have much to say to him, whereas Ramirez and Sean often took an earful of instructions which sounded more like reprimands. Curt read and acted on the blueprints without a question and he and I went about our business on our own. We laid out the column footings with lime, and two backhoes cut them out. The holes were fat, some ten-by-ten feet, six feet deep, while rough-sawn timbers, fourteen feet long and a foot square, were used both as planks to walk across and to nail the two-by-four templates the rodbusters would tie their steel rebar to. The building being a city block, it required a lot of columns, and we kept busy. Kicking up the dirt was always my favorite time at a job, and I liked the waul of earthmovers at the other end of the jobsite pounding the land into place here and scooping it out there, heaving up into an empty, idling rig a rich, moist soil which had gone hidden under the dirty city all this time. Only two of the eventual three tower cranes were up, and they swung at our end in comparative silence, just like any other sky animal, pallets and stacks gliding down from the street and landing as easy as gulls onto sand.

A crane picked the timbers and either me or Curt used hand signals to guide the operator. We liked to set them close to our final layout, and once they were down I'd prybar them a few inches this way or that. We'd been going along at it this way for a couple of weeks when one afternoon O.K., who was passing by (or whatever, since you could never be sure there wasn't some unspoken motive), stopped near Curt. The timber was still in mid-air, about eyelevel, when O.K. grabbed onto Curt's end and started pushing it, hollering at me to do the same. I'd gotten a hand on my end to walk it over toward my side of the footing hole, and I couldn't see any purpose in O.K. screaming or working up such a sweat since the crane had it under control— what he was doing didn't make any sense. But O.K. kept on shoving the timber, fighting. That was the only reason my end was difficult to keep steady. Once it landed, my end was an inch or two from where I'd finally stake it down, while Curt's side, now O.K.'s, was about a foot off. I walked the timber to its mid-point and unhooked the cables, then made the slow whirling signal to the crane operator to take it away.

Curt and O.K. were talking energetically, staring at me. In all the jobsite noise I couldn't hear a word, just saw their mouths moving. I went back to my end, measured from a layout marker, and bucked the timber a half-inch into place. I swung a doublejack, driving a stake on either side like I always did, and sank a few nails to hold them together. I was waiting until O.K.'s back was far enough in the distance to go around to the other side of the footing.

"So what was all that about?" I asked.

Curt's face was weathered brown, but it still revealed as much his youth as age. He never looked right wearing a hard-hat and he must not have felt right either because he took it off whenever he stood still too long. He ran his fingers through his gray hair, smiling as he shook his head. "He said he wanted me to fire you."

I wasn't really surprised. I knew I was supposed to do what O.K. wanted me to, sensible or not, and once he began yelling I was supposed to jump, fearful and obedient. I knew about these kinds of bosses, but I never respond too well to them, and these days I'd felt more comfortable than ever because I was working alongside Curt, who did things how I believed they ought to be done—smart, I'd say. In a way that made working a pleasure, not miserable. We got along, we got things done right the first time. "So that's it, huh? I'm cashing in today?"

Curt was combing his hair with his right hand. "I told him we were plenty ahead of schedule, and everything was going good with no complaints I'd been told of, and if he didn't like our work he'd have to tie a can to the both of us, because if you go, I go."

I *was* surprised by this. I didn't know Curt to make speeches. I felt as honored as I did bad for putting him in such a spot.

"Thanks," I said, humbled. "Nobody's ever backed me up like that before."

Now Curt fiddled with the plastic liner of his hardhat. "Well, don't be thanking me yet. We both may be handed our checks this afternoon."

"No way he can fire you," I told him. It had to be impractical to let Curt go—I'd been working for almost ten years, and he was the best I'd been around—but I wasn't as sure as I pretended to be. "And they're getting you cheap, too. You know more than him by a long ways."

"Tell you what," said Curt. "If you're wrong, you buy the beer tonight."

I wasn't wrong. That was the last time O.K. interfered with anything we did. I was so confident that I'd sneer and laugh when Sean would bitch about how disgusting O.K.'d get telling Ramirez and him to do something. Curt could scarcely smile.

For me it became the best job I'd ever had, and as more men came on—carpenters, laborers, rodbusters, plumbers, electricians, concrete finishers—it got even better. Ramirez took off his bags, and he made Sean one of the foremen. Curt and I kept two steps ahead on our work, which let Curt spend more time drinking coffee in a shack above the hole. Meanwhile, I did all the one-man jobs. I built storage boxes and ladders and sawhorses, a shed for the plumbers and ironworkers, I even built three-legged stools. And if there wasn't something like this, or a pour to watch or a template to make, I worked wherever I wanted, and nobody questioned it—because I worked for Curt. I loved coming to the job, and stayed late any night I was asked, no hesitation.

After the grade slab (the bottom floor) was poured, the next weeks the columns and walls began, then not too long after that the decks, and so practically all the men who'd been pacing around and waiting above every morning were hired on. There were hammers drumming and saws yowling, steel rebar being torched and aluminum joist being dropped; concrete fogged up the mornings, men slopping their rubber boots in that swampy mud, dragging heavy, throbbing hoses, jitterbugging and screeding. We were building a building, and it was going up, and it was like a celebration.

●

Then came the changes. First several foremen were let go, one by one, and replaced by nervous, ambitious strangers. These new foremen fixed their sights on their new men. They got rid of guys nobody liked, some nobody knew, and some everyone was sure didn't deserve it. As a downpour of men came and went, instead of a single green company hardhat, a rainbow of hats sweated it out for the bosses who wore those white ones—and especially for the man with the two flags on his. Even Sean was fired, I learned days after the deed, because he'd had one too many words with O.K.

I had no personal right to complain. I worked for Curt, and, as I said, when I got done with all he had for me, I worked where I wanted. Where I wanted to go was simple: anywhere O.K. didn't.

A compliment from O.K. was when he said nothing. Usually, though, he'd find something, and he'd narrow in on men whose work could be cussed about and put down. Sometimes he'd throw things, sometimes he'd rip apart what they were doing and tell them to start over, and then he'd pound over to a foreman and yell in his face. In the beginning, there were men who'd quit rather than take his bullshit, but as time passed the ones who stayed accepted the abuse, expecting the layoff check at the end of the day. Since I was lucky enough not to be required to stick around for one of O.K.'s tirades or tantrums, I'd joke about how I could smell him coming, and I took off if I claimed to whiff the scent. He and I, I swore, could not so much as make eye contact if I wanted to continue my employment for Hoff-Dunbar.

Thankfully, the possibilities for an accident like that weren't many because of the odd jobs Curt put me on. Like installing shelving and plywood cabinets in the electrician's shack, what I was doing the morning I saw Mrs. O.K. and their son on a visit to the jobsite. We were almost at street level, only a deck below, and men were stripping the column forms. The shack I was in had screen windows, which could be seen out of easier than anyone could see in. Mrs. O.K. was a modest, thin woman who was much younger than her husband but who dressed and groomed herself, intentionally or not, to appear older and un-attractive. She wore what I'd guess was a homemade cotton dress which was at her knees and to her neck, with gathered sleeves that covered most of her upper arms. The boy wore nothing in style either—ordinary running shoes, a T-shirt a little too small and faded, and off-brand, economy jeans. His hair looked like it'd been cut in the backyard. A few feet away from where I was, I saw proud, impressed smiles on their faces as they watched the big men below them hustling around.

They'd been there talking happily, their hands all over the safety rails, when I spied O.K. coming around the corner of the walkway. I decided to keep quiet—I was pretty sure he didn't know I was inside the shack, and I didn't want to draw any of his attention to my existence.

"What're you doing here?" he snapped. "Whadaya want?" He wasn't private with his voice. I was sure that men below could hear him if they wanted to.

The boy moved closer to his mother's skirt, and she backed up a little bit from the jobsite too. "We wanted to visit," Mrs. O.K. said, disappointed, realizing she'd made a mistake. "We came to see your building."

O.K. was a stocky, thick man of medium height. His arms raised a crop of long, colorless hairs, and because of that it was hard to tell if those stumps were muscular or plump. He had a puffy face with meaty cheeks and a bulbous, sunburned nose, its complexion about as shaded as noon glare. Upset, he squeezed the muscles in both his face and arms into their bones. It was all he could do to stand still, to maintain a respectful distance from his wife. He hadn't yet acknowledged his son. "What are you doing down here anyway?" he said after a considerable silence.

"What I told you," Mrs. O.K. said. Only O.K. and I could hear her, the men below couldn't.

"That's *not* what I'm talking about!" Anybody could hear that, and one of the men below even looked up, worried O.K. might be yelling at him.

Mrs. O.K. didn't move much, and neither did the little boy. "I had to pay that fee. You remember." She didn't reveal any emotion, but I felt her physically shrinking.

"If you had put it in the mail on time," he told her, "you could have saved a trip."

Mrs. O.K. nodded. More leaden silence between them. "Do you know what time you'll be home?"

"You know I don't. Why ask?" Finally he glanced down to the boy, who still clung to the other side of his mother's leg. "You like my job, Bubby?"

The little boy nodded his head slowly and fought back a smile that said he was happy his daddy recognized him.

"You better go," O.K. told his wife.

Mrs. O.K. and the boy turned and followed his quick pace toward the gate out. A distance away, but not too far, O.K. stopped, then held a palm up, a salute which, as impersonal as it might have appeared to a passerby, nevertheless was about the nicest gesture I'd seen from him.

●

The column crew had become the best crew because the latest foreman, Brown, was a steady, easy man who didn't need to stroke his power, didn't believe in using pressure tactics to get work done, and got away with it. Because they were not only close in age but also in sentiment, Curt and Brown became lunch buddies, the result of which was that I'd gotten rotated onto Brown's crew when the little jobs ran out and it was decided that Curt didn't need to have a man working with him anymore. It wasn't long after I began setting and plumbing columns regularly that I shook hands goodbye with Curt. Everybody knew it was O.K.'s spite, even if Curt claimed otherwise—he quit because he didn't want to be a deck foreman. O.K., Curt told me, didn't show any animosity or vengefulness, and was as polite as he could be about it. Right, I told him. Sure.

So I took it personally for him. It never was polite to let a man go (that was what it was; this other job was a demotion) before the job was finished. And Curt did know that this decision was made the first week the man who'd hired him had taken a vacation. Not that I didn't believe Curt could find another job. He knew what he was doing, and there always had to be work for someone like that. It was just that sometimes there wasn't. And I was sure that Curt, like anybody else, would rather not have to go find some other job and company even if almost any would've been better than this Hoff-Dunbar one.

We all knew our days were numbered. At the end of each we breathed like we'd snuck something out of there. Company man or a guy like me, O.K. had made us conscious of how precious the work we had was, how unimportant we were to the scheme of the job we were getting done. It wasn't like any of us didn't know this already. But every day we had to tell ourselves, and often each other, to ignore it and count that money while it kept coming.

I didn't like the idea of ignoring what I didn't like. Then again, I didn't want to be fool enough to leave when I still wanted the work.

"Quitting," my new partner Jackson advised me, "is for rich white boys. When the boss brings you a layoff check, you say, 'Thank you so very much, sir.' Then you be on your way, not before."

Jackson was born in Houston, Texas—that was how he said

it, naming both city and state—but lived in Compton, only a few blocks from where I grew up. He loaded up on both lithium *and* thorazine which the VA prescribed to him. He needed drugs to calm down, he said, because he had a violent temper and lost too many jobs. Always, he told me, squinting hard into my brown eyes, it was because he had an anger about the blue-eyed devils, especially as he was coming up in Houston, Texas. His daddy couldn't control him, jailers couldn't control him, and, he confessed, whispering to me confidentially, them young men in that black militant group he belonged to for years couldn't either.

"And you got to remember," Jackson told me, " 'What goes around, comes around.' "

That was like some religious tenet held by construction workers. I heard it all the time. To me, it was a wishful rationalization for not attacking someone for doing something ugly, for doing nothing about it. "You tell me how you're such a mean, smart, *bad* old man," I said, "so I'm thinking you must be tossing back a few above and beyond those prescriptions of yours."

Jackson's laugh could rouse dogs. "You got to believe, boy! You got to!" He had to catch his breath. "None of these other boys like working with old Mr. Jackson," he said. "How come Jackson don't seem to bother you none?"

"Old black men, blue-eyed devils," I responded, "it all pays the same."

Jackson laughed to the exclusion of all other things. Stopped whatever he was doing, opened that big mouth, bared his stained teeth, and howled skyward. Lots of guys, myself included, thought Jackson's laugh was about as funny as funny could be.

"You better shut down that hoot, old man," a young guy on the wall crew shouted, "or O.K.'s gonna make that black butt of yours walk."

"Wouldn't be the first time," Jackson hollered back. "Won't be the last."

In the same way I often enjoyed being around Jackson, so did this young guy, whose name on the job was Smooth. For a few days, while we were doing some columns near a wall he was putting together, Smooth took break with me and Jackson, but not really to listen, even though that's what first brought him there, instead only to talk. Smooth told street stories. He told them fast, speedy, and he stood the entire time, twitching around like it was happening to him right then: A car full of niggers comes by wanting to make some bad shit with Smooth, and Smooth fucks 'em up back, tells them how he'll give 'em gangster knots they fuck with him in his neighborhood—he liked to repeat himself and emphasize that one word—he'll give 'em some *gangster* knots they try to fuck with him, he'll own them motherfuckers.

"Maybe for a little while," Jackson told him, "but not for always. Ain't no man big enough for three, and ain't no man bigger than a well-aimed bullet."

Smooth was a small man in his mid-twenties, five-eight or less, a featherweight, with prominent veins crushed between the black skin and textured muscles of his upper arms. "I will fuck 'em up," he warned Jackson with misplaced defiance. "I can pop caps too, that's how they want it."

That Smooth had popped some caps into another man not even a year earlier was the singular piece of biography that everyone on the job knew. The story was that at another Hoff-Dunbar job, right after quitting time, he got into it with some stranger who pulled a gun to rob him while he was getting in his car. Smooth, it was said, had a gun in his car too. And Smooth, who was hit twice in the shoulder, won the shootout. Now there were also some who said the dead man wasn't a stranger, who said it wasn't self-defense. Smooth, with his personality, was not an inconspicuous man, but, above all, this large fact—and there were others—and the uncertainty about the details of the killing, added at least a foot to his stature.

Smooth had gotten on this job because the company was obligated to rehire him when he was ready to return to work, and he'd been put on the wall crew. Ever since Sean had left as foreman, the wall crew had become the worst, every couple of weeks losing a man or two who were replaced by another one or two, including foremen. Whether or not he was aware of it, this didn't seem to concern Smooth. He did his job energetically and happily, climbing up and down walers like a kid. He talked a lot, and he talked loud, and he got the work out.

The latest foreman looked Japanese even though his name was Langford. He was a big man, well over six-feet, and didn't say much. Langford didn't yell, he didn't get mad. He let the men do the work after he laid it out, then he either stood off at a distance and watched without interfering, or wasn't around. Even when he let men go, you didn't see him giving them their check, they just seemed to disappear.

Jackson and I weren't far away when we heard Smooth.

"What're you looking at?" he asked.

Smooth wasn't trying to be loud, didn't really seem to be raising his voice. But it stood out. I stopped what I was doing. Smooth was on top of an unpoured wall, tacking a pour strip inside. Standing about twenty feet away, a shoulder on the shady side of a cement column, was Langford.

Smooth stopped what he was doing. "Don't be looking at me," he told Langford. "I don't want you looking at me. You go look at anybody else, but don't you come snoop around and look at me." Smooth spoke calmly, though I could hear him clearly from where I was, and he seemed composed, except that when he was done, when he went back to nailing, I could see he was not.

Langford didn't even blink.

Then Smooth stood up at the top of the wall form. "So you go get the fuck away from me!" Smooth screamed this loud enough that, as big as this job was, everyone would hear him, either immediately or through an echo of gossip. "You go get the fuck away from me, you hear, man?!"

Langford heard right then, and he turned and walked off patiently, like he'd intended to anyway.

Smooth didn't get a layoff check the afternoon after the incident, and though it didn't seem possible for him to pull another full day, he was still with the wall crew toward the end of the next one when I heard Jackson howling near our foreman, Brown.

"That boy *is* crazy!" Jackson told me after their conversation.

Jackson set free a second hoot while I waited for his explanation. "Yes sir, he is one *wild* black-eyed devil. You know, we get taught how all God's creatures have their purpose, but sometimes it takes time for us churchgoers to see what that purpose might be so's to come to appreciate."

Jackson was obviously contented by what he'd heard, and finally I had to be direct and ask what he might be talking about so I could appreciate too.

"Brown says they wanted to lay Smooth off, and O.K. had him a check made out, but Langford said he wasn't fool enough to give it. Said it wasn't worth him dying over, said he was sure that boy was damn crazy enough to kill him."

I didn't know why I didn't believe Jackson. I thought he must have misunderstood Brown or something. But the next morning Langford didn't show, and Jackson was grinning.

"Laid off, like I told you."

He hadn't told me that part. Or that Brown was asked to run the wall crew until they got another foreman.

"And he won't give him the check either," Jackson went on.

"Brown won't?"

"Says O.K.'ll have to let him go too."

I might not have believed that either if I hadn't been around the next day. The entire jobsite was buzzing with snickers that were louder than skilsaws. The human energy was bigger than the machines'; all these men talking and whispering, working with a curious enthusiasm, their eyes open for Smooth—because Smooth had taken off his workbags. He'd decided he didn't have to drive nails anymore, only walk around the job, from one end to the other, up to the deck crew and down to the stripping crew, from wall crew to ours, strutting and talking shit, shooting off his mouth, though not about work or his situation, which he seemed to feel under control about, only about whatever else came to his mind, whatever he felt like. When Smooth first dropped in on us I was hooked up with a radio, acting as the rigger for the crane operator. Like he did it all the time and every day, Smooth pulled the radio out of the leather case on my belt. Smooth knew exactly how it worked, and pushed the talk button like he was a foreman.

"O.K., O.K., come in, please, over." No response after ten seconds. "O.K., please come in please, over." Nothing after another wait. "This is the smooth man, Mr. O.K., you know who, and he's wanting to come in, over." Only static, but this time Smooth cut short his civility. "Now O.K., you understand I'm wanting to talk with you, and I know you been listening to me. And I'm understanding you got something for me. Well I'm out here waiting for you to bring it. Cuz you know I got something for you too, O.K. Cuz you bring something *to me,* and I'll bring something *to you.* You understand that, don't you, O.K.? This is Smooth, over for now."

And off he took. As the day wore on he simplified his message, reduced it to basic. He strode up to the riggers and plucked their walkie-talkies at his whim, eventually making his voice mockingly sensual and intimate. "This is Smooth, O.K., and I'm still waiting for you. Cuz you got something for me, and I got something for you." No more over-and-out, no more please or come in, just straight–ahead over the radio and dead into O.K.'s inner ear.

The whole day was a Smooth holiday. We put in our time but didn't care if we got anything done; we were getting paid to watch the show. By early afternoon all the white hats disappeared for a conference with the now unseen O.K.—the suddenly *nowhere to be seen* O.K.—and everybody faked it until quitting time.

By morning the next day we learned that Ramirez, the assistant superintendent, had refused to take Smooth his check too. Men, both awed and disturbed, started talking issues. Top on the list was whether it was right that O.K. be killed for laying a man off. On the bottom was the one about whether or not Smooth should get paid for the time he put in without working.

Smooth arrived late in non-work clothes—a long, gleaming black shirt with tails hanging loosely over his hips, no hardhat, his hair a shiny Jheri Kurl for looking good. His eyes were glassy, and he slowly bobbed his head when he stood still. This morning he didn't use the radio. Much less cheerful than the day before, he lit a joint, and after he finished smoking it, he walked toward the parking structure ramp and went down, it was said, to the very bottom of the building, where he sat by himself and smoked more weed.

Brown told Jackson and me how Smooth had come into the office in the morning, right into O.K.'s den, and sat at one of the desks. O.K. wasn't there, but Brown and Ramirez were. Smooth landed his feet on the desktop and asked the secretary how to dial out for long distance. The secretary looked to Ramirez, who told her to go ahead and tell him. Smooth dialed out. He called his grandmother in Louisiana and talked to her for about a half-hour. Then he called his sister who lived in Palm Springs, his feet up the whole time. Not once did he talk about what was going on, Brown said. Only said he was using the office phone at his job.

"Amen!" Jackson howled out, and I laughed as hard as I could, not a second thought about it.

●

That afternoon, an hour before we called it a day, two police officers with ties on—one of them in a blue suit, the other in a tweed sports coat and brown pants—arrived at the jobsite. We were a few stories above ground level, and they had to climb ladders to reach the poured level most of us worked on. Then they climbed one more, to the level that was still being decked with plywood for concrete. I didn't know why they'd gone up there until I saw them with Smooth, grouped against a background of finished highrises and bluish, smoggy sky. It wouldn't have occurred to me to call these men large, but beside Smooth they appeared so—Smooth, especially from a distance, seemed so tiny. The three of them talked on the middle of the deck while the few men around in hardhats worked, or pretended to, along the sides of it. They conversed calmly, the detective in the sports coat keeping his hands in his pockets, looking around, probably because it was the first time he'd ever been on a building going up. A few minutes passed, and they went together toward the ladder and climbed down.

After work a group of men, including me, wanted to stick around and recount every aspect of the events, not to mention get the facts. We chipped in for a couple of cases of beer, and sat on a section of grass near the building. The beer freed ideas and darkened laughs. Smooth had said this, Smooth had done that. Once the detectives had handed Smooth the check O.K. was too terrified to give him, they also had to threaten him with arrest for harassment if he even came near this jobsite again. But nobody thought that would discourage Smooth. The police wouldn't live here, and Smooth knew how to drive by. If not tomorrow, then days after. Smooth wouldn't forget. Not Smooth. And hadn't he promised to bring something to O.K.? He would, he'd just take his time. He didn't need to rush. One way or another, Smooth had for sure killed one man they knew of, but he always hinted he'd killed others. It wasn't a problem for him.

Not once had O.K. shared any time with the men he was in charge of, so we tensed up and quieted down when we saw him coming toward us. Conditioned as I was, I was betting it was to tell us we couldn't drink beer near the job. Instead, he accepted a cold one. He sat down on the grass, taking off the white hardhat with those waving flags on either side. The skin on the top of his balding head was bright pink. Seeing him then almost made me feel sorry for him, but I still didn't like him, so to me that head looked infected and swollen. If I hadn't known the real reason, I might have suggested this to explain his pained, fearful, even embarrassed slump.

The congregation of men, just a little drunk, now sat awkwardly on the grass. The building—a handful of laborers still wandering around, putting away tools, rolling up cords and hoses—was raising a cool, jagged shadow that inched into them. The men weren't speechless, but sentences faltered, words spilled like nails when a man tried to grab too many. Finally one of the guys made a thought whole: "You never know how crazy a person is until you try to lay him off," he told O.K. His intention had been to cheer O.K. up, but the sentence got away from him, opening its arms like a quote from scripture, a proverb jarring us inward. None of us worked construction because we were rich, but neither did any let his body get this aching and exhausted and dirty only for love of money. It was a need, and what we learned, physically and mentally, was that not just anybody could do it, not week after week, month after month, year in and out. Our job was our pride, who we were around our families and neighbors, what we spent in doctors' and lawyers' and dentists' offices, what we carried camping and fishing and to ball games, what we sat back with, tired, at the bar or in an easy chair facing the tube. It was the sex the women liked about us, the muscles our children admired. Employed, it was what we were never ashamed of.

And so, in that accidental moment of spiritual reflection, we all remembered how bad it was to get that check we didn't want, the one handed to each of us more than once but especially that once when we knew we didn't deserve it, when it wasn't right, and how we wished the absolute worst on the man who made it so, how we prayed for an Old Testament God's wrath and justice. And when our eyes opened, and as they saw O.K.'s worried head turned down, they also saw another man, a friend—for me, Curt—who a week or a month or two ago loaded his heavy tools into the trunk of his car and drove away.

Smooth, sent by God as a lesson for O.K. about the danger of messing with a man's working life, was a messenger for us too. We were all to understand the parable. With a grinning reverence for such a happy ending, we would remember O.K., pale and scared, friendless among these men, *his* men, and Smooth, somewhere out there crazy, and connect them forever in our memory. Hallelujah. Amen.

SOMETHING FOOLISH

It was a Sunday night and late enough for Cristián to be yawning and wishing the weekend would be at least a day longer when the phone rang. It was his father. His *real* father was how he always learned to say it, though he'd never called the other men his mom married dad or father. Growing up, Cristián saw him maybe three days a year—each other's birthday, Christmas Eve—though sometimes more, and sometimes less. Once he was driver's license age it was mostly less. That was because he didn't think his father liked him very much. Cristián didn't blame him for this. It was one of those things. How could he like him if he'd never lived with him? He thought Cristián was like his mom. Irresponsible, always moving too much, avoiding bill collectors. His father was a bookkeeper, so he sided with them. It wasn't wrong to think this way. Like her, Cristián did not have a very good credit history.

"What's going on?" he said, immediately feeling dumb for answering as though he were talking to some guy, not his father. He was just caught off-guard. His father had *never* called him before, not once.

"I need a favor," he said directly.

"Sure," said Cristián, sitting up straight. Around him was his family. His wife was balled-up on the couch—they wanted a new one—with her eyes closed and her tongue out, while their son was using the light of their new 20-inch TV to color. He'd fanned-out all his new marking pens, mixed them in with his collection of matchbox cars, broken crayons, the plastic guys from Star Wars, which, no matter what he was doing, went everywhere with him, no exceptions. The images, dreamlike, linked up with his father's voice on the phone. "Sure," Cristián repeated. "Of course."

"Could you pick me up at the bus station in Hollywood? I don't have a ride home." His voice was shaky. Weak even. Not, in other words, like usual, which was stern and confident, even in his seventieth year. "I'm sorry to bother you."

"It's no bother," Cristián said. The bus station in Hollywood? As far as he knew, his father hadn't been out of Los Angeles since the war, which was before Cristián was born. He'd never even taken a vacation. Not one. Cristián used this astonishing fact about his real father's last forty-plus years as a defining characteristic of him. "Sure I'll take you home."

"I know it's late, and you have to get to work in the morning."

It was after ten o'clock. Christián hadn't been paying attention. Why was the boy awake still? "That's nothing to worry about."

"You have to get up early."

"It's all right. It's nothing." Cristián spoke more clearly into the receiver. "Is everything okay?"

"I've been calling home, but there was no answer."

Cristián was listening to him.

"Violet was supposed to pick me up."

"But she forgot," he put in. "I'll just come for you."

"I'm worried," his father said. "I'm afraid she might have done something."

Cristián was hearing every word.

"Something foolish," he went on.

His father said more about her not answering, but Cristián's mind whirled off. Violet, his father's wife, had tried to commit suicide almost a year earlier. You saw her now, how unhappy she was, and you knew this was possible still. It wasn't like her not to pick up the phone, and she never went out—she practically never left her bedroom. It was even a likely explanation.

"I shouldn't have taken this trip," his father told him.

"I'm on my way."

As a child, all Cristián really considered important to know about his father was that he'd come back from the war in the Pacific a hero, with captured flags of the rising sun and a Silver Star. That was enough. He was proud of this father of his, his real father. Cristián thought about it more these days because he'd become a father, and he loved his son. He'd been trying to remember the times they did have together. He wanted to learn whatever else, well, that a son should learn from his real father. Someday he would be an old man, and his own son would maybe have a son.

Cristián was renting a back yard house not very far away— East Hollywood, near Normandie and Santa Monica—so it wasn't like his father would have to wait for him too long, though it seemed like it. Cristián fell into a sleep of thoughts and meanings: his father's wife lived in the other bedroom to be away from him, and, Cristián learned, had for years, but the string she tied and stretched out to the doorknob so she could close herself in without moving from the bed, that was a recent innovation. His father demanded that she'd only had an accident, that Violet hadn't meant to take so many pills. Cristián remembered his father's face when he was telling him this. It was mad, daring anyone to challenge the power of his view. The expression right then, that was his real father, the father he did remember from his childhood visits.

As he turned onto Vine Street, Cristián seemed to wake himself up just as his mind began to play yet another game. It was as though he were remembering, not experiencing. Maybe only because he'd played around here not that many years earlier. There was a bar not too far this way, a club right there, another just a block over. That was a time before the woman and the son, before Cristián became a father, when, if he thought of his own, real father at all, he thought he might never see him again. It was only past ten o'clock, but Sunday night made it seem much later, like two, or even three in the morning. Or it was the new moon, the dark Hollywood sky completely smooth, cleansed of any natural blemishes.

Only a window of light inside showed from the small, Hollywood depot. Outside, the building went unlit. Not even the sign was illuminated. Nearby, against a fence, people mounded up against a chainlink fence, huddling into a gray mist above what seemed like a pile of dirty shop rags. His father was standing behind a city bus bench near the wide driveway and Cristián pulled up against the curb in front of him. His father kept back until a tall man walking close to the street, dragging his swollen right foot like a heavy stump, passed right between them, his eyes making contact with something very far in the distance.

"Thank you," his father said. "I'm sorry I had to bother you so late."

"It's not late," said Cristián. "I'm glad to help."

His father was wearing an untailored, golden suit—it hung on him limp and shapeless. It looked secondhand and dated, exactly like Hollywood. Cristián guessed his father thought he'd dressed himself like a proper businessman. Cristián grew up believing that his real father was rich since he lived in what he believed was an expensive neighborhood, on a hill overlooking Sunset Boulevard in Silver Lake. He was adult enough now to know that his father's only wealth was pride.

His father tugged at the heavy, squawking passenger's door to get it closed. This was the first time his real father had ever been in his car and Cristián was embarrassed. It was an old, eight-cylinder four-door whose interior was already worn out years ago. Prideful himself, Cristián didn't like it that his father might think he wasn't earning enough to own something better. He didn't think his father even noticed right now though.

"So," Cristián said, "where did you go?" The other subject was so obvious, and serious, so unavoidable, that it didn't need to be brought up.

"I had to go to Santa Maria," he said flatly. "I shouldn't have gone though. It wasn't that important."

"Santa Maria?"

His father repositioned himself onto the bench seat of the car. "It's north of Santa Barbara." He turned his head momentarily toward his son, then away. "I lived there when I was young, you know. We picked crops, and we had chickens."

"I didn't know."

"It's very different now," he said, looking straight ahead. "I hadn't been there since the thirties. Very changed, like everything else."

Sunset Boulevard was virtually empty of traffic. Most of the neon signs were turned off, iron gates locked in glass storefronts. When they stopped at a red light, a few men standing outside a cheap bar named Don Pedro's craned their necks at Cristián and his father.

"Friends of yours?" Cristián joked.

His father smiled.

"We bought a television today," Cristián told him cheerfully as they pulled away from the stoplight. "I guess we're finally feeling like we've got money to burn." He was determined to let his father know that he was doing well and was happy. "I left the baby drawing next to it. He's getting so big, I can't believe how fast he's growing."

His father nodded wordlessly, but with what Cristián took to be compassion. It made him convinced that what was growing between them, especially in this circumstance, was friendship, if that was the right word to use for a son and father. He even thought he might really begin to know this father, his real father, that from here on he would learn whatever it was he didn't, or couldn't, before.

"Those Dodgers keep on winning, don't they?" Cristián couldn't think of much to say. "They don't have a single good hitter this year, and still they win."

"It's the pitching," his father said. "The Dodgers always have pitchers."

Cristián turned left off Sunset, then right, toward his father's two-bedroom, Spanish-style stucco, the only house on the block with a turret jutting up at a corner of the roof, like some religious symbol. The streetlamps were on, but the asphalt directly beneath them seemed to absorb all of the pallid offering. More than dark, it was ominously still, so quiet that when they both opened the unoiled doors of the heavy, old car, the dissonant squeals echoed like gothic moans.

As the two of them stared upwards at the building, only the glittery fabric in his father's sloppy gold suit caught any outdoor light. At the top of the long cement stairway, a yellow aura, deep inside, stained a sheer curtain. The rest of the house was as dark as the evening's moon.

"Do you want me to go up with you?" Cristián asked.

"Please," his father said. Then he stepped. His movement was authoritative, unfaltering up the height of the steps. Cristián kept up a pace behind, and though both breathed harder at the top, neither he nor his father felt winded.

"Do you want me to go in with you?" he asked.

His father had slipped a key into the door lock. "Yes," he said, and he opened the door. He went in without hesitating, angry and muscular, turning a corner around a table, then through the kitchen, and into his office. There his father stopped for a moment and looked down the hall toward his wife Violet's bedroom door.

The office was musty from a time long past. Old papers gathered like dust on a wooden desk, whose peeling veneer was textured by black grime. A heavy, gray adding machine with a curved handle sat useless in a corner next to the one new object on the desk, a small, pocket-sized calculator. A tarnished brass lamp took up the other corner, a bright bulb in its socket the only operating light visible, its sticky yellow glow the overaged color of the shade.

"Should I go with you?" Cristián asked.

"No," his father said, not looking at him. "Wait here."

Cristián's father went angrily toward the door with a splinter of light at the bottom. When he opened it, that white light screamed out, burning Cristián's dilated eyes. He squinted, waiting to see more.

Suddenly his father reappeared at the door, closing it behind him. He carried himself just like he had since they'd arrived— defiant, bold, mad. He went over to his desk, to a slotted metal letter-holder, and picked up a stack of unopened mail. He picked up a letter opener with an ornate, dull silver handle. He slit open the side of a legal-sized envelope—he was practiced, and he did it skillfully, with a young man's dexterity—and reached for what was inside without letting go of the opener.

Cristián almost held off until his father had finished reading. "So? It's okay?"

He glanced away from the letter. It was the face Cristián recognized as his real father's. "She's fine," he said.

"I guess I'll go on home then," said Cristián.

"Thanks for picking me up," his father said as he sliced open another envelope. "I'm sorry I had to bother you so late."

"It was nothing," Cristián told him.

THE PRIZE

Mondays I won't go to Chino's because he's too crudo, hung-over, to cut hair. I won't go on Fridays after four because that's Bud time and he can't concentrate. Saturday and Sunday he's drinking, and though I get to have a beer along with him, I worry too much about my hair looking good when he's done with it, vain as that sounds or not. I've learned these lessons about Chino through close to ten years of personal experience. I call him for an appointment any of the remaining hours and days, never too early, not too late. When the whites of Chino's eyes aren't veined pink, when he's talking about the catfish he pulled from his personal spot on the river—he'll show me the fish, wrapped loosely with foil in the freezer section of his refrigerator—that's when Chino's an artisan. I can run my fingers through my hair when he's done, pleased, and walk out like I stole a twenty-dollar haircut for the seven he charges.

Facing the mountains, Chino's shop is in a Southwestern-theme motel called El Río Bravo—textured white plaster, fake vigas, red tile overhangs, long-hinged wooden doors painted turquoise, the same color, peeling off and fading away, as the window trim and the drained pool in the center of the court. Big made-in-America cars still puddle oil in the slots in front of room doors, but, just as the motel is in a decline, and old, they too are without hubcaps, dented, mud and dust slung all over them.

Chino's is the only business operating in his row; a tailor shop next door was abandoned a year ago, and management never has tried to clean it out inside. Chino recently moved from down the line some to a larger motel room, and he's been in the process of moving out or moving in since he's been here. Not that you can tell the difference. There are two broken wooden chairs on the porch, one good though rusting chrome one, and cardboard boxes, and a gutted stereo speaker, and a pushbutton car radio and portable TV set, their innards exposed to the elements. A life-size cut-out of a blond girl in a bikini, her backing a little bent by abuse and crinkled by damp weather, leans underneath Chino's handpainted—his own hand—black sign in small letters: barbershop.

It's Wednesday, minutes before one o'clock.

The sign in the window says closed, and his motel door is shut securely, but I park next to Chino's white convertible anyway. The sign never changes, and though its ragtop still goes up and down, the convertible doesn't run, and even though I don't see the car he drives, I'm confident because Chino's never stood me up.

I squint through the cloudy glass, and he's there, lights off, by the coffee table, above some steaming food. He's waving me in, but he goes to the door as I'm opening it anyway.

"I almost didn't have time for lunch," he explains.

"I'm glad somebody I know's got so much business," I say. "But you're gonna have to knock down a wall to make room for all your customers pretty soon." It's a tight squeeze inside. Half the motel room, now partitioned off, is his bedroom, and this narrow, visible part is for his business. He's been doing the remodeling himself, and has been for months. Pieces of wood and plastic molding jut and poke, carpenter's tools are piled and heaped. I sit on the frayed, lumpy couch in a tangle of an extension cord, which is on top of a few sections of a Juárez newspaper, which is underneath a pile of more recent editions. Rumpled newspapers and magazines inhabit his shop like cats in an old maid's home. You have to dig yourself some space.

"I'll only be a minute," Chino says, his mouth full. "You hungry?"

"No, no, you eat, take your time."

In the darkness, Chino looks even blacker than he is. His teeth and eyes illuminate his face like automobile grillwork at night, and the white plumber's outfit he wears radiates against his skin, as though a testament to laundry detergent. Chino has on a black hat—"I'm the one your mother always warned you about"—and the bill of it dips and sweeps around his hands. These hands balance half a Big Tex hamburger bun, folded like a tortilla, loaded with barbeque meat, the whole of it scooped into a see-through tub of pico de gallo.

"You're sure?" he asks again.

Watching his enjoyment I'm not, but I say I am. I root around for his naked-girl magazines. It's the only place I get to see them anymore. Though most are the well-known ones, occasionally I encounter speciality mags like this one called *Bottoms Up.* Its centerfold is a line of young women—twelve, I count them—bent away from the camera, their hands pressed to their symmetrically parted knees, their shapely moons ruler straight across the glossy double page. My imagination soars to the process, as a photographer, and it's such a bizarre, comic fantasy—lining them up just right, framing the shot, talking it over, squeezing them together—"Candy, sweetheart, could you bend your knees just a little bit . . . a *little* more . . . there it is!"—it puts me into a good mood.

"My God, Chino," I say, "how do they find them?"

Chino's gotten up and switched on the lights and drinks soda from a two-liter bottle in the refrigerator. He comes back to see what I'm talking about with the indifference of experience. "They're everywhere," he tells me sagely. "You only have to know where to look." He seals the foil around the meat, picks up the bag of extra-large buns, and goes over to the pressed-wood vanity, opens a drawer, its paper mahogany veneer revealed, and shoves around its contents to make room. He stuffs the puffy bag of burger buns there, and then the meat. Then he looks over at me, shaking his head, stares at what he's done, and takes back the meat from the drawer.

"One of those days, eh Chino?"

"One of those last nights," he says. He slides the foil package into the refrigerator. He tosses his hat on top, turns on the 24-inch console color television between the vanity and the refrigerator, and stares blankly into it as it warms up.

I decide to visit the toilet before I get under his bib. This room is as packed with his life's junk as the rest of the motel room. The sink next to where I stand has overflowed cigarette butts and stained food wrappers and empty beer cans—must be a case or so—but it doesn't really look remarkably messy in the context. I've left the bathroom door open. "Last night?" I say, nodding at the sink.

"Oh no, I only save them."

After I flush, Chino spins the barber's chair in my direction so I can sit. Then he turns me toward the television. It's such a tight fit in the narrow space that he's had to cut a V out of the vanity so the metal footrest can clear. He snaps the bib at the back of my neck.

"So what'll you have today?" he asks me. He lights a cigarette.

On the mostly purple TV screen, a couple from the Mexican novela are manicly kissing. "A little of her. She looks pretty good at it. Wait. Now that I think about it, I guess as long as you're asking, let me have two of her style, one for each arm. That'll be just fine, I wouldn't wanna get greedy."

"I'll see what I can do," Chino says. "You know, sometimes . . ." Chino's smile is sly, his pause like a drag off his cigarette. "Let me tell you something," he starts. Now he does take a hit on the cigarette. "This morning I was cutting a customer's hair, and I was thinking, after this I'm not supposed to have nobody for an hour."

I check Chino's homemade, cork appointment board. It's laid

out Monday through Sunday on the vertical, and, starting at nine a.m., stretches across in half-hour segments until six p.m. Chino has fuzzy polaroids of most of his customers sitting in his barber chair, and he tacks them in the spaces they call for. He has blanks from 11:30 to 12:30. Otherwise, the spaces are filled from 9:00.

"And you know, I'm glad about it today, because I'm tired. But I also know I am wrong. I can feel it, you see? I see in my mind I have another customer after this one, a walk-up, and I'm thinking how I should get out of here five minutes sooner so he won't come and ask. I can't turn down a customer if he asks. In my mind, I already see him standing there. But this customer, he likes to have his time here. Gets the shave, the whole thing. So I can't leave early, but I tell my customer, 'You watch, a man will be at my door wanting the next appointment. Any minute now,' I tell him. He laughs at me, thinks I'm making it up. But then there he is, like I said. And he's asking me if he can be next. 'See?' I tell my customer."

Chino's clipping my hair now. I'm getting my usual. He cuts between sentences. It's dramatic, and I see him as a character in his story. He's thin and tiny, Indio-like. I notice the elegant silvery streaks through his black hair, tied back into a chic, two-inch ponytail. He has gray, unshaven stubble all over his face. I notice how his palms are almost as dark as the back of his hands. His color amazes me because he's indoors all day.

"Now when I'm cutting this customer's hair, in my mind I see another one about to come, another walk-up. I can't believe it. I'm thinking how if I finish this one more fast, I can get out, eat, and then, after you at one, I don't got nobody til three-thirty. But then I realize no matter when, he'll come when I'm about to finish. . . ."

"Shaking the hair off the apron!" I jump in, excited. "Brushing little hairs off his neck!"

" . . . Yes, I know there'll be another customer, no matter if I hurry or go slow, this other walk-up will be here. And just like I knew, when I'm finishing, I look up, and there he is standing at the door."

I laugh. "You're a brujo, Chino, admit it!"

"It's what I'm saying. La brujería. Sometimes my mind can make something happen."

It's not really very logical what he's saying. Maybe he knows it too. But it's fun going along. "Shit, Chino, if that's how it is it shouldn't be no trouble for you to arrange those pretty women for me. With all your powers, at least *one* of them, a couple of margaritas with crushed ice on the side—it should be *easy.*"

His laugh is more controlled by other thoughts. He grips the top of my head while he snips my sideburns and around my ears. Afterwards, he steps in front of an impassioned TV dialogue about incest. Chino has equally passionate eyes.

"Let me tell you this other one. Last year I was in Juáritos, at a baseball game."

"You were pitching?"

"No, I was hurt, and I don't pitch anymore." Chino and I shared baseball stories since we both had played in league fastpitch softball, me here, him over there. I'd gone to a couple of games in Juárez a few years ago to watch his team play in a championship tournament against a team from Chihuahua.

"Too bad. What happened?"

"Forget that! Listen to what I'm telling you!"

I want to laugh at him for being so serious, but I resist.

"I was sitting with my friend, behind home plate, and we were losing three to one. Two guys had gotten on . . . well, it doesn't matter what their names are . . . they got on first and second, a bunt and an error, but, well, their pitcher, he's been doing too good since he settled down, and he's at the bottom of the order now, and the infield's in and ready, and he's struck out the last two."

I think I already know what's going to happen. Anybody would. But since it's so obvious, and he's telling it like it isn't, I'm listening for some unique twist. "It's bottom of the ninth, right?"

Chino nods his head, appreciative of my interruption this time. "We only got two hitters on the team, and that's how we got the run, two doubles in the first, but these guys, well nobody else has come close, and Heri, he's up, he can't hit. My friend, Jorge, sitting next to me, he says, 'That's it, it's three outs, let's get some beers.' And I say, 'You wanna make a bet?' He laughs at me."

"You saw it on the time delay, like a horserace, eh Chino?"

"I tell him he gives me fifty dollars and I put up five. I'm figuring that I'm gonna spend it on the beer anyway, you know?"

"Andale, Chino!"

"But really it's that I'm having this feeling. You know, like I been telling you about. So Jorge takes it. And so I'm sitting there, and I close my eyes."

Chino nods his dark head downwards and squeezes his dark eyelids, a hint of a frown, and touches his dark hands to his dark temples. I hear the TV above his silence. He looks up again.

"Jorge's laughing at me while I'm doing this, when *poosh!,* there it goes." Chino smiles big and proud.

"An easy fifty bucks. Or did he pay up?"

Since I appear to be missing the point, Chino hesitates to answer me. "I didn't make him." He goes back to cutting the rest of my hair.

I'm glad he's cutting my hair again too. I really have to be somewhere by two, and I don't want to get hung up here. "I'll tell you what, Chino. I'm broke, I need money. Make some money for me, all right? Make a big sack of money for me. You think you could do that?"

"Sure!" he says.

"Well, you just do that then, and then we can split it. Just one sack, man. It's enough."

"It's a deal," he says. He steps away for a second, and he squints with his eyes closed again.

"Andale, Chino! Big bills, no smaller than twenties!"

He shushes me quiet, puts his hands to his temples. It seems to me he's also got a grin, but maybe I'm interpreting. After some long seconds, he comes back to my hair.

"I'm talking a big sack, Chino. Like those ones for bushels of onions."

"Okay, you got it," he says. "But don't forget, we split it right down the middle, even."

"You can count on it," I say. "I wouldn't cheat you."

Chino's clipping the top of my hair right now, and I can't really see him, not even in one of the mirrors. "You can't cheat me," he tells me. "It makes bad things happen. You can't play with la brujería."

"Of course, I know."

He's just about finished. "I'm gonna do it everyday for you. It might take me a few weeks, say by the next time you have to come in."

"A few weeks is nothing for a sack of twenties."

"Good," he says. "I promise, I'm going to concentrate on it everyday for you. And if you get the money, you let me know. I'm going to trust you to tell me too. I'm not saying where it's going to come from. Only someplace like you've never gotten it before. It might be by a check in the mail, some relative you haven't thought of, something like that, but you have to tell me, we have to split it."

I don't even think about it, I'm so sure. No easy money's ever come to me, and if Chino can make it happen . . . even though I know he can't, he won't, it won't happen. "Andale, Chino. Make us both rich. I know you can do it." He hands me a small mirror. "Looks great," I say, checking the back from its reflection in the big mirror behind me. He unsnaps the bib and lets my cut hairs roll down the front and onto the floor. Then he picks up the powdered brush and sweeps my neck. I stand up, dig in my pockets, and count out seven dollars. "Thanks. We'll see you next time."

"Everyday I'm going to concentrate," he reminds me. "You call me when it gets there."

"Everyday I'm gonna look outside my front door, Chino. I'm already counting on it. We'll both buy new cars."

I get in my current one. Looking in the rear-view mirror, I run my fingers through my hair, pleased. I pull out, I drive away. Then I remember something. The prize. I applied for a prize. I did it so long ago, seven, eight months ago, I'd forgotten. I didn't expect to win. Not because I shouldn't, because I arrogantly believe I should, even pisses me off to think I won't. Except the prize isn't only about the work, how deserving. It's more about being in the right places, knowing the right people, doing the right things. I live in El Paso, and Chino, who I like, cuts my hair for seven bucks, and most of the time I scrounge for any work I can get. I'm not appropriate, I am not winner material. For years I've suggested to myself that I move. Then, not living here anymore, living in the right place, knowing the right people, living the right life, my past here would become exotic and exciting, like I'd been in the wilderness. Of course, I don't entirely believe that either, which is why I'm afraid to leave. It's my home, where all my family is, and it's comfortable.

But then again I do expect to win. Maybe they'll get it right, I'll get lucky and this time someone out there will choose me, make an exception, because I *don't* live in the right place and the rest, or despite the fact, or because they like my work. It's what I believe in, what I depend on. That's how I'd do it, if I were giving the prize.

I'm driving down Mesa Street, and I'm turning on Rio Grande, then I'm on Copia, and I'm thinking I can call Chino. I'll tell him the prize doesn't count.

I don't have to do that though. It *doesn't* count. I know it, and I don't have to explain myself. If I win, it won't be because of Chino but me.

And probably I won't win. Chino can't make me win.

I should hear about it any day now though. If I win, I have to make sure that Chino doesn't find out. And if he finds out, screw him. He drinks too much, and my hair's easy to cut, and I'm easy to please.

I think I'm going to win. I really could use the money.

A week later, on Wednesday, Chino calls me at home. Chino hasn't called my house in years. Not since around the time when I went to those ballgames in Juárez with him. "I've been concentrating everyday," he says, "and I wanted to know if anything happened yet."

"Not yet," I say. Do I tell him to relax, not work so hard? But I don't want him to think I'm hiding something. Do I tell him about the prize, how it doesn't count? But I don't want to tell him something he won't find out about if I don't bring it up at all. "You're not doing a good enough job of it, Chino. You're losing your touch."

"I'll keep trying," he says. "Let me know if something happens."

"Andale, Chino. Hey but if I find a dime on the street, I ain't reporting it to you."

It upsets me that Chino called. I think I won't get my haircut at his motel room anymore. I want to win the prize, but I hate all this worry. When I'm out in the day, I rush home to see what's in my mail.

On Friday night of the next week, Chino calls again. His eyes are pink, his ponytail is falling apart, the tails of his white shirt are hanging out, he's working on a twelve-pack of Budweiser in his refrigerator. I see all this through the phone, without squinting. "If anything, I'm losing money, Chino. Now that I think about it, maybe you're sucking money from me, not to me."

"I try to remember everyday."

"Well, there you go! Whadaya mean you *try to remember?*"

He laughs unreasonably. Then he gags, coughs, catches his breath, and his voice comes back deeper. "You better tell me. You have to split it with me, you know. You can't get it all and not let me have my share."

This really pisses me off. I can't think of anything funny or

clever. "Chino," I say, "I gotta go right now. I'll get back to you."
I hang up the phone.

I'm sure I will win the prize now. Nothing in my life has ever
been simple, I've never gotten any easy money, so it makes
sense.

Or I can put it in terms other than money. Most of the people
who have won the prize think of it this way since they're
already rich, own houses and new cars, and they've never had to
scrounge for a job.

My best hope is that the news comes late. That I don't find out
for a few more weeks. Then I won't have anything to explain to
Chino. So when the letter arrives, my heart whimpers. Here I
am, I tell myself, supposed to be excited about winning this
prize, and instead I feel sick to my stomach. Suddenly, I've made
a decision. Or it comes to me. I don't know which, but it's mine,
from the inner me or from the out there, and it's got me, it's my
liberation from Chino's spell: I won't tell him, and if he finds
out, I'll tell him I didn't hear about it until later.

I open the letter. We regret to inform you. I'm not really
surprised, I tell my cynical self. As they like to say over and over
to us, Who ever said life was fair? All I have to do is go across
the river, imagine how miserable everyone over there is, and
realize how lucky I am. Or I could go blind, I could be para-
lyzed, I could be wandering the streets hungry, cold, filthy,
muttering and paranoid. Those people don't even complain. It's
all true, I know it. I could be dead. Life is too short to worry
about petty prize politics, and I'm doing what I'm doing anyway. I also think of Chino. I could call him and point out to him
how he didn't make it happen. But I remember those few
minutes earlier. My decision. What if I had decided to go along
with Chino? Would the letter inside have read differently?

No way. No.

A week later, I call Chino. "Nothing, not even some
scratched-up pennies in a parking lot. You're not doing your
job. Are you concentrating right?"

"I can't understand it. I'm doing the best I can."

I feel him smiling through the phone. I see him. "Shit, Chino, I'll tell you what, think smaller. Could be that's the problem, you know? Maybe if you like just go for a box of ones."

"It's an idea."

"Or I'll tell you what. Remember the pretty woman I asked for? Just one of those. With a good body though."

He laughs. "So you want an appointment?"

"I can't even afford you now. Not for another week or two at least."

"Let me know," he says.

"Andale, Chino. We'll see you."

TRUCK

In the center of the carpenter's shop was the table saw. As always, or almost, Martínez was holding a piece of wood against the fence, his straw cowboy hat a little low on his forehead, a cigarette slanted out the right side of his mouth, his eyes slit onto a bevel cut he was guiding through. A few of the men, carpenters and laborers, had hopped up and sat on the work table which L'ed two walls. Others stood near the radial-arm saw, a couple leaned against the drill press. Two more men hovered near Martínez, so full of admiration their expressions verged on love. Since Martínez had once been employed in a cabinet shop, he was the star of the show, the man called on for the fine jobs, when patience and delicacy were more important than speed and strength. These two men near him were especially impressed by his skill.

The table saw was loud, even louder when it was cutting, and nobody bothered much about talking with it engaged. But when the power was shut off and the motor wound down, the contrasting silence was dramatic. Modesty being another of Martínez's virtues, he liked to take the hushed moment at the center of the shop to remark on his just finished product with self-deprecation.

"It'll have to do," he pronounced, the cigarette between his lips waving up and down with each syllable. He held the cut piece there, eyeballing the length as he savored a drag off the unfiltered butt.

Blondie, the foreman, known jokingly as el mero güero, was at his wooden desk at another corner of the shop. In fact his blond hair was mostly gray. "Moya," he called, waving Alex over. Carlos Davis followed a step behind.

"You wanna buy it?" Blondie asked. He liked Alex. "It's almost new."

"It's a .357 Magnum?" Alex asked. Carlos was big-eyed over Alex's shoulder.

".44 Magnum. If you don't know the difference, you don't know."

"Can I see it?" Carlos asked.

Blondie's head went back and his eyebrows lifted, meaning no way. He didn't need to respond with words, and he seldom used them, a result, probably, of his not knowing any Spanish and working with so many men who knew so little English. He'd worked for the city over twenty years, and this was his last week. He handed the pistol to Alex. He liked Alex, liked his work, but he didn't trust Carlos. A few of the other men wandered over, including Martínez.

"I guess not," Alex told him as he babied it in his hands. "Sure wouldn't want it aimed at me."

Martínez—nobody used his first name—reached for the gun, and Alex passed it on. "Go right through two or three walls, I hear," he said. "Puts a hole in the man the size of a football, I hear."

Blondie nodded, indifferent to the information. "Good protection," he said. "I just wanna sell it."

"Not today," Alex apologized.

"I own a Remington shotgun," Martínez said. "It'll put a hole in the right places too."

"Year, well . . ." Blondie stared back at his desk, at a pile of work requisitions. "This one's for you," he told Alex. "A partition at the Armijo Center."

"Just me and Carlos?"

Blondie nodded. Then he shook some keys off the desk. "I'm

going ahead and giving you this truck." It was the truck the shop had been promised a year earlier but had just got the week before. If Blondie hadn't retired, it would've been his to drive home. The new foreman didn't need one because he already had one.

Alex could feel Martínez's sigh of disapproval. He'd spend the rest of the day talking about what a mistake this was, how one of the other carpenters deserved it more.

"One thing," Blondie said, pulling the hand with the keys back to keep Alex's attention. He glanced over at Martínez, who was listening closer than he pretended, before he spoke. "Well, you know, or you should by now."

●

After he and Carlos slid plywood and 2x4s onto the bed of the truck, Alex picked up a skilsaw and a cord and some nails, then loaded them and his toolbox. It was a long drive from the city's yard in the rural Lower Valley to the Segundo Barrio. Alex, who was always in a hurry, was about to get on I-10. "N'hombre!" Carlos told him. "Go the long ways, make it happen slow." He'd dragged out the last word like he was talking about sex. Alex grinned and nodded and cruised North Loop, whiffing the damp smell of horses.

Carlos was excited about being in the truck—maybe the newest auto he'd ever been in, besides a police car, and it was close to two years old. "You see how I told you?" he said. "I told you about Blondie, how he'd listen. He knows how you're the best carpenter. He knows. He knows about that metiche Martínez too, how he talks pedo behind your back . . ."

"Forget about it, man," Alex said, cutting him short. "Let's forget about that dude."

Carlos had a habit of going too far, making fights. Not that he wasn't right about Martínez. And Blondie did honor Alex with one of the trucks—Urquidi drove the one-ton for the large jobs which most of the men went to, but now he and Martínez would be treated as equals for the smaller, two-man jobs. Still, Carlos exaggerated, just like he did about what a great carpenter Alex was. His exaggerations confused Alex as much as his confessions, like the one about stealing from the shop. A block plane, a Phillips screwdriver, some needle-nose pliers. Things did get lost, and probably other men had taken a tool or two. Carlos wasn't exactly wrong about this. But if Alex was sure it wasn't exactly right either, he didn't say so. He couldn't resist the admiration, seeming smart, or skilled, or whatever it was Carlos saw in him, and he didn't want to be a disappointment. And then, even though he was eight years older than Carlos, who was twenty, Alex carried a private respect for him. Alex might stand up and say he could hold his own, but Carlos had been raised real tough and done real bad, and that, like having been to war, was a strength that was always veiled and mysterious, envied by those who grew up on the easier side of the highway. All Alex had done to be this great carpenter was work for his cousin's construction company. He wanted this city job because it was steady—he was married and the father of two daughters, one not even a year old. It was Carlos's first job ever.

Carlos had grown up on Seventh Street. He came up behind one of the turquoise-framed screen doors, with only one light bulb, in that gray brick building, its seventy-year-old lintels and thresholds tilted and sagging, the building across the street from the one painted sapphire, next to the ruby one, a block away from the one whose each apartment was a swath of brilliant Mexican color—the whole street woven with shades as bold and ornate and warm as an Indian blanket. Across the street from the Armijo Center, at the Boy's Club, Carlos stabbed a dude when he was eleven. Across from there, under the mural of Che Guevara, where all those gang placazos are sprayed in black, he soaked red bandannas, shut his eyes, and sniffed until his mind floated away like in a light wind.

"That's some stupid shit," Alex told him. "Make your brains turn to hamburger."

"Already I know now," Carlos said, serious, "but I didn't then." His lips bent sarcastically. "If they turned into tacos, that'd be something else, eh?"

Alex had been driving real slow down the street listening to Carlos, even went past the Armijo by a couple of blocks before he U-turned around.

"Park in the front, güey," Carlos said. "You got the city sign on the side. I wanna show off for my bros."

"It's a loading zone." Alex parked in the lot beside the building. He didn't want to mess up. That's what Blondie had meant: Martínez was behind the scenes saying how Alex was no better a carpenter than Carlos was his helper. "My grandma could do as well, and she's got cataracts," was how he'd say it. That the two got along was evidence of even fewer skills, since Martínez especially didn't like Carlos. The truck was Blondie's way of backing Alex.

Carlos shook his head displeased, pissed-off that he didn't get his way. "It'd be *bad* parking out in the front like we own the place."

"We ain't rock stars driving a limosine," Alex said, at moments like these wondering why he ever tried to work with the guy.

While Alex went through the glass front doors, Carlos hung back, doing a slow, unhappy strut outside in his chinos and white T-shirt. But once he did push the doors too and saw nobody else was around, he quickened his pace and dropped the attitude. They unloaded the material and tools and even flirted with the secretary while they worked—she was married, but she was all right. They built a partition to close off a small, lockable room for basketballs and pool sticks, ping-pong paddles, and the like. They didn't hang the door because it wouldn't be available until next week, but framed and plumbed and anchored and sheeted the wall with plywood, even fixed a couple of other things the secretary pointed out. All of it was done in three hours. Alex *was* fast, especially compared to the other city carpenters. It was all they were expected to do that day.

"Fucking Martínez," Carlos said out on the hardwood basketball courts. "That old dude would still be chopping the tree or some shit. His camaradas would be right at his culo. Oh, Mr. Mart-*tí*-nez, you do it so *good*. Maybe he'd still be hitting on a nail. Tac. Tac. Tac. Fucking put a dude to sleep, like to dead."

Alex had borrowed one of the basketballs. He'd played on his high-school basketball team, once in a while on the asphalt courts on the grounds of Austin High School with some old friends—he was shooting better now than he did back then, and he'd been good in high school.

"Andale, güey!" Carlos was shaking his head under the hoop. "What don't you do good?"

Alex was feeling fine because of his play, and of course the compliment helped. So fine it made him think of those things he didn't do anymore, that he'd left behind. He'd been doing right and that wasn't wrong. But he'd missed out too. He didn't get to shoot hoops often enough, and he'd forgotten how much fun it was messing around for no reason when—maybe even *be-cause*—he knew he should be doing something better. He got all his girlfriends because he made baskets. His wife, who was the best-looking, sweetest girl he met in high school, first smiled at him because the ball swung in the net.

"Let's go to lunch," he said.

"Let's get some beer," Carlos suggested.

"Let's go to lunch and get beer too," Alex said.

●

They went down the street to the Jalisco Cafe and ordered the special and two beers each. It was still real early, and Alex didn't think it was a good idea to go back to the Armijo with nothing to do.

"Maybe we should just go back to the shop," Alex said.

"N'hombre! We ain't got nothing *there*. Better we do nothing *here*. How am I not right?"

It was one of these subjects that Alex didn't feel like arguing about. And Carlos was right—if they went back, they'd have to sit around bored, look for Blondie who probably wouldn't be around, even chance having to explain themselves if someone bigger came by.

Carlos told Alex about a shade tree they could park under, but first he made him stop at Mena's Bakery. Alex assumed it was for some cigarettes. Instead, Carlos came out with two quarts of beer.

"Are you crazy?!" Alex said.

"Yessir, I am the crazy dude, at your service." Carlos unscrewed the cap from one and passed it to Alex. He was already having fun.

"We can't do this," Alex said.

Carlos put on his cholo slouch, his head drooping sideways and back. "It's not chiva, not even mota. It's not nothing, güey, just some *beer.*"

Alex shook off his worry. He even felt ashamed for being afraid to do something as harmless as this. What kind of man was he becoming? It was no big deal. Who couldn't handle a little beer? And once he settled down and relaxed, he even liked it.

They kicked back under the shade tree for over an hour, then agreed to drive a long route back.

"Over there," Carlos said. Alex stopped the truck by a small grocery on Alameda. Carlos took a five from Alex for the peanuts that would disguise their breath.

He came back with a cocky smile and two more quarts of beer.

"No way, man," said Alex. "We're just going back. We can't walk in there after we drank these."

"I got the peanuts. And these were on sale." Carlos opened his. "Those dudes won't see nothing different in this dude."

Alex fought off his first impulses, even criticized himself again. Then Alex went ahead and opened the beer and drank and started enjoying himself—not quite like Carlos, who was chugging the bottle in a hurry. But Alex slipped into such a calm about it he drove with his mind on all kinds of things he'd wanted to do that he'd forgotten about, and he drove not thinking of much else other than this until he realized he'd driven too far, way east of the city complex. He both laughed and got mad at this lapse, looked both in front and in the rearview mirror. No cars were coming, and he turned left into the empty field on the other side of the street to turn around.

●

"What a stupid move, güey," Carlos said, irritated. He was more drunk than Alex. He was a sure bust—everybody would see him and know. "That pinche Martínez is gonna be out here to get us and be laughing in our face. What the fuck you do this for?"

They'd tried everything to get it out, but half the tire had dug itself into the sand. They'd tried putting rocks under it, chunks of wood. The tire spun, spraying sandy dirt.

"We ain't gonna get this truck no more," Carlos complained. "You lost us this truck."

Alex didn't disagree, or argue, or offer a word in defense. Like Martínez, Carlos was far away. Alex felt his feet leaving the ground, his arms cocking, the ball rolling off his fingers. As it spun away, arced, the touch of the ball stayed with him, and he felt the pleasure of it stretching the net, and clinging—a long time or short, depending on how he'd remember this, just like a first kiss.

P A R T   T W O

WHERE THE SUN DON'T SHINE

Usually Sal enjoyed his breaks between jobs and he acted like some kid who had legal ID and enough money to buy his partners a few rounds, a short to take a pretty barmaid for a ride, and a few quarters to lag at a circle. But not this time. This time took too long, and his unemployment money would run out soon and his daughters wanted some new clothes for starting school and his wife was getting worried because she was pregnant. Sal had even stopped going down to the Bar de Los Angeles. Instead he sat around his house and watched TV.

So it felt good when he got on at a luxury condominium, its structural steel just coming out of the hole, on the edge of Beverly Hills. It was a big job, twenty above and four down, and he could get at least nine months out of it, more if they liked him, and, if they liked him enough, more still at some other rich high rise they could transfer him to. That had happened to him before, because the big shots usually liked his work. All the men said that he should be a foreman, that he'd make a great foreman. It wasn't just wishful thinking on his part to think good things about this job.

And it was even better than that since down at the bottom of the dark hole, D-level of parking it would be, Sal's first five minutes were filled with shaking the hands of old carpenter and laborer buddies from other jobs. It was a lot easier, among good friends, to lift his boots out of moist, ungraded dirt, to drive doubleheaded nails in the heat of 250-amp lamps, and Sal settled into the job quickly. And it wasn't long before lunch break was just another time to sit around with the guys and talk about the mysteries of sex, the high cost of everything, or the incompetence of men in every trade but their own. Or the poor way the men with the shiny white hardhats made the men with the scruffy orange and blue and green hardhats work.

"I remember that job downtown," Augustín said, "and they wouldn't give us a morning coffee break. Sal says, 'I was looking for a job before I found this one!' and sits down with the ironworkers on this pile of rebar. So this foreman goes, 'That sounds good to me!' and heads to the office and everybody knows Sal's gonna get his check. But this guy sits there like nothing in the world bothers him and gets back to work only after the ironworkers do. And nothing, not a thing happens to him! A week later we're all taking a coffee break."

"Why don't we get a morning break no more?" Sal asked the union steward, cutting through the chuckles that surround him.

"It's not in the contract. The company doesn't have to give us a break if it doesn't wanna."

"That's bullshit."

"That's the times. Too many hungry men on the books. The company figures that they don't hafta go outa their way being nice."

Sal shook his head with disgust, knowing that the man spoke the truth, and soon he was back in the hole forming columns and walls, helping his foreman lay some grade marks for the first slab. No matter what, he needed to get healthy first, and he got along good enough with the foremen, all except the general foreman who nobody got along with, who for some reason hated just about everyone's guts, especially, rumor had it, those that didn't begin at lily pink lips. He was a hard man to disregard since he made a special point of watching and check-

ing over everything the men did. But Sal promised his wife he'd
ignore it, though he didn't like it, though the other men already
talked, because they knew Sal and anticipated another one of
his memorable confrontations.

"Down at that Figueroa Street job," Rudy was telling the
apprentice Jamaal, "Salvador was decking out this ramp that
curved, and this redneck foreman come up to him and told him
he was doing it all wrong. Salvador didn't pay any attention to
the shit and that got him really pissed. So they started saying
'Fuck you!' to each other and calling each other names and
came to blows. The whole jobsite stopped working to watch
that. Salvador kicked the shit out of him and they both ended
up in the office. We got to fuck around until quitting time, and
the next day that foreman didn't come back. They told us he got
transferred."

"It musta been a hundred degrees that day," Sal explained.

"And when Salvador got rehired a few days later it was in the
eighties, the cabrón," said Rudy.

Two weeks went by as well as possible. Sal was getting a lot
of the job's overtime, even the double time, and he and the
general foreman rarely spoke to one another, even so much as to
say good morning or good night. Then, in the eleventh hour
twilight of a very long, humid day, Sal, this man, two laborers,
and two other foremen were fighting to push a cement hose into
a long, narrow dirt opening so they could pour an odd footing.
They'd been battling with it for a good forty minutes and sweat
made the dank, hole dirt smear them in more places than their
clothes and body, and now Sal was translating the general
foreman's instructions into Spanish for the two laborers.

"It's not that they don't understand what you want," Sal said
as patiently as he could, "and not that we're not trying hard
enough. It's that it can't be done this way."

"We've got eight yards of cement waiting on us and a driver
who wants to go home and this has to be done tonight. Now are

we gonna stand here and talk or do you wanna get the job done?"

"Tell him how you want to do it," Benito told Sal in Spanish. Elario nodded in agreement.

"I have this idea," Sal said with contempt disguised as modesty. "You wanna hear it?"

"Jesuschrist!" the general foreman fumed, stomping away from them.

"What is it?" the labor foreman asked Sal.

"We take some wire and we feed it through the hole, then we tie the wire around some rope, pull the rope through, then tie the rope to the hose and pull it through."

"Do it," the carpenter foreman said.

While they stood around, ten minutes later, listening to the cement slop in, filling up the footing hole, the men relaxed and talked and Sal thought he'd try to break the ice with the general foreman. And so he asked, good-naturedly, "Are you buying the beer tonight?"

The man looked at him, scowled, walked over to the scaffold stairs and stepped up three metal flights to the office trailer.

There was a time when Sal wouldn't have let something like that pass by, but the union books were full, the wait was long, and he needed hours to keep up his medical benefits. And he'd promised his wife. For once he would say nothing, he would leave it to someone else. All the men had the same problems with this man, he reasoned, so why not let someone else play hero for a change? He wouldn't let it bother him.

And so he practiced. When an ironworker working above him with a torch and goggles showered him with glittering hot slag, Sal held in his rage and walked away from his own work area and waited until the man finished, and then he asked him to be more careful. He didn't say anything when the ironworker did the same thing an hour later to another carpenter, though he felt better that the carpenter, who screeched, also told the steward. It was, after all, the steward's job to watch out for safety. And then finally the ironworker was done working this level, and it'd be a week or so before they'd have to worry about him above them again.

And he didn't say anything when a foreman had the carpenters help the laborers move about fifty very heavy form panels, misloaded on C-level, down to D-level and all the way over to its opposite side, though it was another hot, muggy day, though a small caterpillar laced the dusty air with fat black exhaust as it graded the dirt, though the company didn't supply fans to ventilate the stagnant pit.

He even controlled himself a week later when they were working on their second hour of double time, and he'd been watching the pour, patching and fixing the columns that leaked and blew out. The general foreman was stewing because of all the blowouts and he was right to be, and soon they started pouring the last column of the day, which was now evening. It looked like the column would be okay, and Sal told Elario and Benito to keep their eye on it and holler to stop if they saw anything, because they pumped from the deck above and couldn't see and he needed to take a walk. He went to the toolshed to put the ramset away, even though that was really a laborer's job and his to watch the pour, and when he got back, all smiles because it was the end of another long day, he took out his hammer to tap the plywood and see how much was in it, and, stepping forward, sank his boot in an ankle-deep mush of fresh gray concrete.

The general foreman was screaming so much at him that Sal stopped listening, and he helped Elario and Benito shovel the yard or so of cement away, telling them in Spanish not to worry about it, it was nothing, it was too dark, maybe it just popped out right then like the labor foreman said, that he should have been there, that the mother should have been built right in the first place.

They all talked about what it was that made the general foreman hate Sal so particularly after that, because it wasn't just that incident, which might make the man think Sal was a fuckup, and it wasn't the one prior to that, which might have made the man look bad and Sal disrespectful. It was something else, and everyone had an opinion.

"It's your drinking," said Augustín. "He's a Mormon and Mormons don't like people that drink. You gotta stop drinking with us Sal. You gotta stop getting drunk!"

"Augie's sorta right, Sal," said Rudy, "but it's not beer or whiskey, it's women. It's that secretary who's been hanging all over you after work. The pendejo's jealous cuz he thinks you're getting some of his own private stuff. It's ever since you took her home that night and brought her back the next morning. Come on, Sal, tell the truth, you are getting some, aren't you?"

"She had car trouble. I took her home and brought her to work the next day because her car was being fixed."

Nobody completely believed that one.

"It's that the old dude is white and Sal's brown," said Jamaal.

They all laughed about that one, mostly because Jamaal said it and they'd never heard him say much before.

"I think because Salvador speak Spanish and he don't," Benito said in English, trying to agree somewhat with Jamaal.

"The guy's under a lot of pressure," said the carpenter foreman. "They wanna rush rush and he's worried. And he thinks you don't care enough. He's like a football coach, you know?"

"I'll tell you what I think, Sal," offered the labor foreman. "I think you're better than him and he knows it. I think he's afraid to have you around here. He's got a hardon to get you."

Sal did have his own thoughts. He believed it had something to do with the men sitting with him before work and at lunch and after work, and laughing, and talking, and his getting along with them as white or black or mejicano. He thought the man sensed that Sal didn't care to be a boss, that he liked laborers as much as, or even more than, the superintendents. But what he said to the other men, what he gave as his exclusive opinion on the subject, was, "He's such a miserable sonofabitch that the more I ignore him the more I like this job and the longer I stay. Other than that he can stick it where the sun don't shine." And that made the men laugh.

So Sal went on with his work, ignoring the fact that the general foreman wasn't letting him have the overtime, not saying anything about the small irritations thrown his way, like never having a laborer to find material or to bring him a tool, or getting all the dirtiest jobs in the dirtiest places, or about his getting a new partner every day and a half or less, his having to start at the beginning with each of them, telling them now this is a column clamp, and it goes around like this, and we have to work together, and when I set my pin in you have to make sure you can get yours in, and we'll put nails in at these measurements, and the rest. Instead he thought of the pretty dresses he was buying for his pretty daughters, the happy face of his wife when he got home to a sirloin steak in a cast-iron pan with onion and chile and tomato staining the apron that hugged her round stomach.

It was all to make a decent living, even Efren had to make a decent living, and that's why Sal didn't say anything bad to him about the column he fucked up and Sal was sent over to fix. The tall, spindly column, which was beside the driveway ramps and exposed to the Mercedes coupes and sedans that would eventually drive up and down them, seemed twisted at the top, and when Sal looked it over he discovered that the clamps were biting wrong so he and Efren took them off, about mid-form, and put them on again. But that wasn't the problem. He looked it over once more and checked the square. That was okay. He looked over everything he could think of, climbed up and down the scaffolding, back and forth across the planks, and from the top he pondered, staring down forty feet at the unfriendly dowels staring back out of the hard cement below him. It was a bitch of a problem, and he was almost stumped, but just to make sure, he asked Efren to tell him, one more time, exactly what he did when he built it. And there it was. He heard what the measurements were supposed to be, and figured out that Efren had managed to cut the panels fourteen inches at the bottom to almost sixteen at the top.

Efren was so relieved to know what was wrong that he ran off to the shitter, and Sal began unbuttoning the column by himself. He'd noticed the general foreman watching him for a while, but Sal didn't think much of it because the man so often watched him work. Sal's mouth dropped open when the man walked across a steel beam and hopped onto the scaffolding.

"So now what the fuck you doing with this damn thing?"

Sal began to explain.

"You mean you been working on this damn thing all day and yesterday and you don't got it cut right?!"

Sal was speechless. He'd been there two hours and figured the man knew that. He knew the man knew that.

"What the fuck kind of carpenter are you?! You think I pay you to be an apprentice?! You're no goddamn carpenter!"

The man often got hoarse and his voice was just starting to break up now. Sal blushed with anger. He swallowed. He said nothing. He heard his wife's voice. He listened to that. He listened.

The general foreman screamed and Sal didn't say anything. The men watched from below, waiting for Sal to push him off the scaffold, incredulous that the man knew nothing of Sal's pride and temper. But Sal didn't say anything, and the general foreman stomped back across the beam to the deck and screamed even louder that he was getting Sal's check, to pick up his gear.

Sal climbed down. He didn't talk and the men didn't talk to him. He picked up his toolbox and loaded it on his shoulder and walked. He heard Rudy say to someone, "Fucking Salvador's gonna kill that man, he's really mad now, he's gonna kill him."

Sal went to the Bar de Los Angeles and drank and stayed late and picked a fight with two cholos and took home a bruised face and the next morning his wife shook him to wake up.

"You're gonna be late! Your lunch is made. Go take a shower."

"I'm not working there no more."

She sat on the bed. "What happened?"

"We had an argument."

"You can go apologize. Go tell him you need the job."

"I already hit him," he told her.

"Why, Sal? You promised. You promised me!"

PARKING PLACES

John Veloz, a plumber, was getting out of his truck parked not quite in front of his duplex apartment. He and his wife Maria had just moved in. It was after work.

Vic Carrillo was watering the plants and flowers around the front of his duplex. He and his wife Helen had lived here many years.

The front doors and windows of both couples' apartments were so close to the activity of the street that it seemed to be as much a part of their lives as a loud television set.

"Hello," Vic said to John.

"Hello," said John.

"Welcome to the neighborhood."

"Thanks."

"I think you'll like it here. It's very quiet."

"That's why my wife and I chose it."

"We were glad to see you move in. If you need anything, just let us know."

"Thank you," John said appreciatively.

When we went through his front door that day, John felt very good about finding this place to live. He told Maria about the friendly neighbor across the street and said wistfully, "Who knows, maybe someday I'll buy something here. Maybe things will get so we can afford to live here permanently." That made Maria very happy, and the two embraced hopefully.

The only source of irritation that John and Maria encountered in the neighborhood was the parking. Though her car was no problem since they had a spot in the duplex's two-car garage, his truck was another thing. Because many other people lived in the old, odd-shaped duplexes and triplexes and multiple complexes that weighed down this hilly section of Los Angeles, there were many cars, and then there was also the fact that parking was permitted on only one side of their narrow street. Yet John was lucky in a way since he went to work earlier than most and came home earlier because of that. Only once in a while did he have to park a block or more away.

One day Maria told John to come to their front window. "Look at this," she said suspiciously. "The minute that car left, Vic Carrillo put theirs in the space."

"Pretty smart," said John.

"Do you know that that other parked car next to it is theirs too?"

"Really?"

"That means they have two on the street and one in the garage."

"It must be nice."

"They must watch from their window."

"They've lived here a long time."

"You're right," she said, almost apologetically.

The Carrillos and Velozes found that they got along very well as neighbors and even found a special kinship because of their similar Texas roots. They liked each other so much that finally Vic and Helen asked John and Maria over to dinner. And what a dinner: the best chili from Terlingua's cook-off, young corn on the cob, a big salad with bright red tomatoes and ripe slices of avocado, inch-and-a-half steaks barbequed over dried mesquite that Vic saved for special occasions, and, for dessert, homemade peach pie with homemade vanilla ice cream on top.

"This is so delicious!" Maria raved.

"I'm so glad you like it," Helen told her.

"You guys didn't need to go to such an expense for us," said Maria.

"It's nothing," Vic told her. "We like to eat good."

They all felt stuffed.

"So just what exactly is it you do for a living, Vic?" asked John over some cherry liqueur, something he'd never tasted before.

"I was an electrician in San Antone. Then I got a chance to take over a contractor's business here."

John didn't ask, even though he was dying to hear the rest.

"We like it in Los Angeles," Vic went on. "Lots of opportunities. We almost bought that place you live in, for instance. I kind of wish I was smarter then. We'd have got it dirt cheap compared to today's prices."

"You own this place, is that right?" Maria asked.

"It was my daddy's," Helen told them. "He bought it when we moved out here. It was an investment for him. Then when Vic and I got married, he gave it to us for a wedding present."

"How nice of him!" said Maria.

"Rich Spaniard," Vic laughed.

John restrained his jealousy. "So you keeping busy?"

"In these times? No way. The fact is I haven't done any contractor's work in five, six, already maybe eight years. I worked for the city a while to keep busy, but I didn't like it. Hell, we can live comfortably off our property. I own the place next door and that place next door to you. Property income's the only way to go, I'll tell ya."

The next morning, a Sunday, Maria asked John to make a trip to the market to buy some coffee since they were out. Without really thinking about it, John took his truck. Now it just so happened that John had been parked in one of the two parking places the Carrillos always made sure was theirs, and when he returned, with coffee and a bag of pan dulce he bought at the bakery next to the market, his space was gone, and the Carrillos' car was in its place. And since it was the weekend, there were no empty spaces nearby.

"I was only gone five minutes, ten minutes at the most!" John was screaming as he came through the front door. "The way they act you'd think they owned those parking places too!"

"They've been here a long time," Maria said judiciously. "It's just a habit with them. People like us come and go and they're staying."

"There's no reason for it," he said more calmly. "I was only gone *five* minutes. Why couldn't he leave that car where it was? Nobody else can park in front of his garage like him. He could park there if he wanted to. He didn't have to take that space from me."

"Somebody else might have come along and parked there. Then neither of you would have had the space. Have you thought of that?"

Though they tried not to talk about it, from then on John and Maria kept their eyes on the way Vic Carrillo maneuvered his cars around so that he and Helen would have both of the spaces directly in front of their duplex. If they were going to use the newest car, the one in the garage, it was simple, but if they wanted one of the other two then Vic had to move the one out of the garage to the front of his driveway, keep it running, start and move the one he took from the street, slip the new one in the old one's slot, then back the old one where the new one was, in the driveway. John and Maria particularly liked to watch Vic take the car farthest from his driveway, because then he moved all three cars so that an older car and the driveway would surround the newest car, which guaranteed that no one could park in front of it and possibly back into it. It was quite a spectacle when Vic and Helen came or went, and most of the time John and Maria got muted chuckles from it.

Meanwhile, there was their friendship, and John and Maria

felt obligated to have Vic and Helen over to dinner too. So
Maria cooked pinto beans and melted jack and cheddar cheeses
in it, steamed some rice, made her own flour tortillas, and
ground a salsa from fresh chiles and tomatoes. John picked up
two six-packs of Michelob and cooked carnitas on his back
porch.

"You both are eating so little," Maria fretted toward the end
of the meal.

"It's very good," Helen assured her. "It's only that we seldom
eat pork, and Vic can't eat chile anymore."

"Another beer?" John asked Vic.

"No thanks. I'm filled up. You go ahead though."

John did, and the four of them sat quietly around the living
room.

"Guess what?" Vic said. "I'm taking a job with the city
schools. I couldn't resist it. I get bored sitting around, you know
what I mean?"

"Yeah," said John. "I've been out of work for over a month
now."

"I'm sorry to hear that."

"Part of the trade, I guess."

"I hope it doesn't last too long for you," said Helen. "It's too
bad my father isn't still alive. He always knew people who
needed plumbers. Good plumbers were the hardest for him to
find when he had his business. They were just as hard for Vic
when he took over. Good plumbers are rare."

John's unemployment lasted some time, and since Vic now
had a job, he often would leave one of the spaces in front of his
home vacant and John would park his truck there. For some
reason, leaving it there gave him some weird kind of pleasure.
John loved to open the curtains and see Vic's car parked in the
driveway in front of his garage. He loved imagining Vic and
Helen living their lives looking out their front window, miserable without one of their parking places.

One Saturday morning John and Maria were forced to take his truck because he was getting the radiator in her car boiled out. John didn't want to, but Maria was insistent.

"You're obsessed!" she told him. "You can't do anything without thinking about that parking place!"

"*He's* the one that's obsessed!"

"Well, you're as bad as him now."

"Okay, okay," he conceded. "It's just that it's not fair. I just hate giving it to him. I hate knowing he's gonna jump out of his house and move that car."

"We have to take the truck, John."

And it wasn't long after that John was loading his truck for the last time with their belongings. They were moving. Though John's employment outlook had improved and Maria had taken a job as a bank teller, they decided it would be better for them in a different neighborhood.

"Well," said John to Vic. "Guess that's it. I guess we'll see you around."

Vic, who'd quit his job, was watering the lush plants and colorful flowers in front of his duplex, the ones that almost reached over and kissed his two cars.

"Sure thing," said Vic. "We'll keep in touch."

RECIPE

You have to feel never married. You have to wear an almost new football jersey. It has to take place in East L.A. You have to think about the possibility before it happens.

You should think you'd like to be a writer. You should go to poetry reading at a college with this on your mind. You should know no one there. You should take a seat away from the lump of audience. You should stay away from the lights directed at the poet as he reads, watch his brown face become white as photographers flash even brighter lights. Two young women should sit a row in front of you. They should be attractive. In a while a young man should sit a seat over from you. He should be handsome.

During a brief intermission the young man should ask you if you are a writer. You will shrug, shake your head without conviction, and say you're an ironworker. He should be surprised that you're an ironworker and a writer. You should ask him if he's a writer. He will say he has lots of ideas. He will say he does maintenance work at the college. He will introduce himself. His name has to be Pablo. You should shake hands with him.

He should tell you that he's done some work in construction, that his father was a cement-finisher, and you should tell him that it seems to you that there's a lot of work, that he looks strong enough. You should look at the young women who retake their seats in front of you. You should smile at Pablo. He will ask the light one if he could look at the copy of the poet's book. He will ask her if she's a poet. She will say she has lots of ideas. Pablo should smile at you. Pablo will suggest that she get the book autographed. She will say she's going to, after the reading.

You should not pay too much attention to the second half of the reading. You should think about how pretty the light one is. You should think that the dark one is pretty too. You will notice that Pablo looks at the young women. You will believe that the young women aren't concentrating on the poet either.

After the reading Pablo will ask the light one if she liked it. She will say very much. He will say his name is Pablo and that you are his friend. She will say her name is Monica and her friend is Josie. He will ask them if they'd like to go to a party. Monica will say are you serious? and Josie will say where is it? He will say of course he's serious it's a friend of mine's it's not far from here. He will draw them a map and they will all laugh at his directions. Monica will want to think about it. She will take her book over to the poet to have it autographed. Josie will go to the restroom.

Pablo will ask you if you want to go to the party. You should smile and say sure. He should smile too. You will say that you'll follow him there.

Outside on the auditorium steps it should be new moon and the wind should be cold. You should be looking through glass doors at the bright room where people will be gathered around the poet. You will look at Monica. You will think how pretty she is. You will read what the poet wrote in her book: a Mónica, que te llegue mucha suerte con tus poemas. Pablo will say that you're a writer too. Monica will say really? and you will say no, you're an ironworker. You will wish you said yes. You should still think Josie is pretty too.

Pablo should pull up to you in his car as you are getting into yours and he will tell you that he's going to stop at a liquor store and you should ask him if he thinks they'll come and he will say he hopes so. He should buy a six-pack of tall beers. You should buy a jug of a sweet rosé wine.

At the party you should shake hands, say happy birthday, say no to beer and drink three glasses of wine very quickly. You have to feel that you've slipped back into time, back into high school. You have to feel you've leaped ahead in time. You have to notice the punks. One should be very pale and his skin should look laquered. He will have his hair cut into a flattop. He should be a Chicano. The female punker should have short platinum hair and bright red lipstick and thick sweeps of skyblue eyeshadow. She should seem to have no complexion. She will always wear a full-length black coat. She should be an Anglo and her girlfriend has to be a Chicana, a chic chola. You should be smoking a joint while you are talking to an older man wearing a red silk shirt with a piano keyboard stripe circling it. Fingers should be printed on the back side playing some of the keys.

You should be sitting on the sill of a broken-out window that looks onto downtown L.A. and your feet should creak the old wooden deck. You will ignore the dude leaning over the railing wasted on downers and beer and you will talk to the fat dude who smiles and drinks beer and asks you which buildings you worked on. You should tell him with typical ironworker's pride. You should be petting a dirty cat. You will still be drinking the wine and you will be smoking the fat guy's marijuana. You should not feel surprised when you turn around to see Monica and Josie walk in the door. You should not say much about them to the fat guy who looks at them hungrily.

You will watch Pablo already making a move on Monica. You should be grateful when Josie comes and sits next to you and smokes and is drinking the wine you brought. You should nod in agreement when she says the view is beautiful.

You will watch Pablo dance first with Monica. It has to be the Doors. It has to be an uninterrupted album being played on an

FM station. Josie will be sitting very close to you. Her black hair will be very close to your shoulder. You will wish it was the auburn hair of Monica. You will watch Pablo dance with another young woman who is dressed in a 1950s party dress. Then you will watch Monica join in and you will smile along when Josie tells you Monica had already gotten jealous. You will wonder if Josie would like to dance with Pablo too.

Soon Monica will be wearing Pablo's jacket. Pablo will say to you that he wants to be a writer. He will say that he wants to be up there. He will mean his name. Monica will say she wishes she could get a poem published. Pablo will ask her if she knows any by heart. She will say yes and be embarrassed. He will tell her to go ahead, that we four will be the only ones to hear. She will be coaxed into it. It will be a poem about lost love. It will be bad but Pablo will say it's good and Josie will say she thinks Monica writes beautifully and she will look to you to say something untrue and you will say you wish you could write poetry but it's hard when you're an ironworker. They will laugh. You will too.

For a while you will be standing next to the female punker. You will have wanted to talk to her and finally you will ask her if she's in a band. She will say no and ask you if you play for the L.A. Rams. You will say no and say that it was just that you thought people who dressed like her were in bands. She will say she just thought that people who wore new football jerseys played for the L.A. Rams or maybe were P.E. teachers.

By this time you will be feeling the wine and the marijuana. You will be sitting on a couch and Josie will be next to you again. You should be deciding whether you should sleep with her, if she will sleep with you. You should kiss her and feel her warm leg against yours, and when you touch her you should feel her responding. She will touch you.

You should leave together. As you twist down a narrow street you should almost sideswipe a car and that should awaken you. You should say no to Josie when she asks to drive. You should stop at a bar. It has to be called "One For The Road." It has to be a strip joint. It has to be run by Korean barmaids who are topless.

Josie will say that it's okay, she will stay, she doesn't mind. She should say she's never really been to one. You should say you didn't know. You should order bourbon and water. She should order gin and tonic. You will both be embarrassed at first. You will watch a stripper bend in every way and you will watch her reflection in many mirrors. The dominant music has to be the Rolling Stones and Rod Stewart.

You will begin to listen to the story of Josie's life in Spanish and English. You will begin to like the way she looks. At moments you will confuse her with the stripper dancing naked on the table next to where the two of you talk. Josie will be telling you about her marriage, about her husband, about her divorce, about her daughter, about her sadness and disappointment. You will have more drinks than her.

When you return from the toilet a man will be sitting beside her. She will look unhappy. He will be asking her to dance with him. You should tell him that she is with you. He should look at you like he doesn't care who she came in with. He will sit closer to her. You should stand near him, say okay man, time to leave. He will say nothing to you. You should feel excited. You should feel the liquor like a strong god and you should reach at the man's shirt and be pulling him away from the table. He will jump at you and you should hit him twice before his bottle smacks you on the neck. Before he can kick you you will see someone leading him past the red velvet curtain. Before a Korean barmaid says anything you should say that you're leaving, you're leaving. You should tell Josie you're all right, you can drive, you're all right.

You will drive home quietly down Brooklyn Avenue. You will not be pulled over by the police.

At your apartment you will turn on the stereo. You should find the station you listened to at the party. She will ask you about the photographs on the wall. You will tell her that one is your son and the other is your daughter. You should tell her that they live with their mother. She should say that they are very cute.

You should offer her some cocaine. She will accept. She will ask you if you've known Pablo long. You will say you just met him tonight. You should ask if she has known Monica long. She will say that they grew up together. She will say that Monica was always so pretty. You should say nothing. You should wonder if Pablo's sleeping with her. You should wonder if Josie wishes she was with Pablo. You should imagine Monica's auburn hair near you.

You should kiss Josie. You should go to bed with her. You will not feel like a good lover. You will like her body only in the abstract. Soon you will be making love to her. You will orgasm and you will ask her if she did. She will say yes. You will both fall asleep.

You will wake up. You will make love to her again. This time you will enjoy it. This time you will know she did too.

As the sun rises you will look at her. She should resemble the first girl you ever fell in love with. You will wonder where Pablo is. You will think that in time you may get your chance with Monica.

When you both get up you should tell Josie to stay over the weekend. She should stay much longer than that.

PHOTOGRAPHS NEAR A ROLLS ROYCE

At night, standing in the middle of the street in front of the building I call home, I can see into another apartment, through its smearless picture window, a chandelier sparkling above a grand piano and men with crystal goblets stirring with white wine. If I turn around and look into the apartments facing that one, I see, between the louvers of another kind of glass, other men playing poker under a bare kitchen light, drinking Bud in the can, listening to Radio Trece-La Mejicana. From where I stand, the calm blend of Pedro Infante and Mozart is strange, though it still remains true that the Mercedes and Cadillacs are the ones parked in the garages, while the Chevys and Fords of the sixties and early seventies squeeze into the open spaces on the street.

We live on the east side of our complex, which seems right since the tenant next to us is a nervous type involved with the business, which is to say the film industry, and his apartment, a mirror ditto of ours without the furnishings, is westside luxurious. We're decorated by the working class, though I've been unemployed for quite some time, a state of today's economy which I try to make the best of since it does offer its pleasures— every morning I pour some extra water through our Mr. Coffee for another cup to read the sports section with. I go over every word of it now, every detail about the Lakers, struggling this year after their championship last season, about the Dodgers's possible trades and the new kids from Albuquerque and San Antonio and Garvey's new team and Cey's bitterness, Fernando's million-dollar screwball. I don't care much about the new spring-to-summer football league, about who thinks Larry Bird might be better than Magic Johnson (no way), but unemployment means I have time to read about the Angels, who I didn't care much about before. I also go through the "Style" section, which is about movies and movie stars and television, and I tell Gloria if the TV critic says there's going to be something good on that night. I read the rock critic too, since I like to know what music to hate and why, and so that even if we don't ever go out, which we don't, I feel like I'm still hip to the LA music scene.

After the paper and the coffee I invariably look out the window and into Ralph's window across the way. Ralph is my oldest son David's friend. David's almost five, Ralph's eight, nine or ten—we don't know which because he's given each as his true age. He and his older brother and his mother live in an apartment situated on the hill like us, though in a newer building with stucco and sheetrock, not the hard, textured plaster, inside and out, that was common in the less prefab days of construction that designed our building. Each apartment has one exceptionally large window in the dining area which face each other, and both large curtains are usually open to the daylight, and because of that we've come to know of each other from the distance as we share meals at our separate tables. Ralph and his brother like to wave, and David waves back. Sometimes, from the decks in front of the windows, they yell at each other across the lot that divides us—an ivy-covered piece of the hill that makes the decks, both old, not the safest place for kids to play since the fall is a good fifteen to twenty feet. There's an ugly little building at the bottom of the hill where the ivy ends, and we both can see a corner of its green tarpapered roof, and from our windows we view each other's lives through the right

triangle of smoggy air that butts into that ivied soil, and then
through those glass windows. It's more than enough distance to
keep adults from knowing each other through words and conversation.

Yet Ralph and David became friends, despite the difference
in ages. We don't know why, and we stopped asking. Ralph is a
well-mannered boy and he likes to play with David. David also
has plenty of toys, and Ralph doesn't. We aren't rich, even when
I'm employed, and have never been, but Ralph is poor. His
mother takes a bus to her fulltime job at the downtown Burger
King, and his father is still in Nicaragua. His older brother is
fourteen, likes the Dodgers and has talked to Pedro Guerrero
twice when he came across him in the neighborhood streets,
where he spends most of his out-of-school time. Ralph is alone a
lot, a circumstance that resembled my own so much that when
he started coming around everyday after school, or earlier if he
didn't go, which he often doesn't, we opened the door and the
boys would play until an hour after sunset, or later if the lights
in his apartment were still not on, usually until his brother came
for him.

Ralph and my son played so well together that Ralph started
to feel like family, so we fed him and took him on little trips—
making sure he called his mother and got permission—to the
zoo, to Hollywood Boulevard, to Olvera Street for a sentimental
festival, to Griffith Park. He's run errands for us, and when
Gloria's gone to the store he's walked back carrying a grocery
bag. For Christmas we decided to buy him one of those small
footballs with an L.A. Raiders decal on it. It cost two dollars for
one and three for two. We gave the other one to David. We
think it might have been the only present Ralph got besides the
very small plastic replica of E.T. his mother gave him. He
wasn't only surprised when we gave him the package from
under our Christmas tree, he was utterly grateful, with expressions that Hallmark makes its living on. I'd been thinking about
taking him to see the movie *E.T.* since he hadn't seen it yet, but

we had all seen it, and that money buys some food. I wanted to take him though, and I promised myself I would.

●

We always talk about going out, though neither of us waxes nostalgic about all the times we went out before marriage and children, when we were a mere couple who often did night-clubs, which is where we met. We hit it off so well because we both liked the same rock'n'roll, restaurants, and movies. Later, both of us agreed that we'd traveled here to meet each other, that Los Angeles had been cold and fake until it became the L.A. of lights and dance and sunshine. We made love, but we weren't from here—eventually David was born and we were married.

David was two when we moved back out here. We wanted to stay in New Mexico, where Gloria's parents live, but the money just wasn't there, and I was doing okay when we lived here before. I thought, we thought, that this would be the best place for us.

Like I said, we haven't gone out since we've been here. Not alone, only the two of us. It's hard for us to find a babysitter. We've moved three times and we don't know many people, especially ones that are married with children. A girl down the street has babysat after school, when Gloria had to go to the doctor, but she can't at night. We hate to ask the neighbors because we don't know them that well. And now our youngest is only six months, and that's a hard age for someone who's not family to take care of, even for a few hours.

But we made an attempt after this one morning. I'd read the rock section in the paper, and the critic was raving about Saturday night at the Club Lingerie when the best bands from East LA would be doing a two-set performance. The East Side Review, he said, would feature the hottest music in L.A. at the moment, like Los Lobos, and from the past, like Cannibal and

the Headhunters. I wanted to go, and so did Gloria. We ran
over as many options as we could—like asking that teenage
girl's mother, or the neighbor who just got back from Mexico,
with much immigration difficulty, who might need a few extra
dollars. When we thought of Ralph's mother, it was only a
question of how many hours.

It should be said that Gloria wasn't as confident as I was that
she'd agree to it. Ralph's mother was obviously not simple. She
liked to drink and dance, and we've seen her a few times
moving inside her apartment to loud rumbas and later outside
on her deck with a boyfriend. She's a big, tall woman, hefty,
strong looking, and dark, very dark, like Ralph. Her hair is
tinted red, for what looks like fun. But she's also timid, and the
two times she came near our door for Ralph, she never got next
to it or knocked when it was closed. She only called his name,
and not too loudly, definitely not with anger, just meekly
matter-of-fact. The time Gloria went with her and Ralph and
David for a Christmas show in school—Ralph was in it, and
asked several times that we all go, please. I said no thanks, while
Gloria thought the invitation was too cute to be turned down—
she told me that they barely talked and that Ralph's mother
seemed to want to stay secretive about herself and even her
country. The little they did say to one another, which came out
strained and brief, was about Gloria's New Mexico, how each of
them liked it in Los Angeles, and how well Rafael—it was
Ralph who wanted to be known as Ralph—was doing and how
fast he was learning English, whereas she didn't think she ever
would. We thought that that had been the reason she was shy,
that we speak English in our home, unlike our parents, but after
Gloria was with her that night she came away thinking it was
something else, though she had no idea what it might be.
Through Ralph, we gave her pictures Gloria took at the Christmas show. Later, when Ralph let it be known that the pictures
weren't, in his words, bright enough, we decided that this is
what made the world go round.

Still she was the clear first choice for babysitter, though we both wanted her to agree to it only if she really didn't mind, and really did not. Gloria went over to ask, not plead, and to allow her any easy way out. If she accepted, then she was to understand that we would pay. It would be her decision where.

I wasn't surprised that she said yes, but I wanted to celebrate. That she might be a little later than seven—we decided that from then to the Cinderella hour would be the best we could get, and enough—was nothing important. And Gloria said the woman seemed honestly willing, not the least bothered. She even said that it was the best Saturday for her because she wasn't going out dancing. And she would stay at our place, with Ralph, which meant David would be happy. So we were out the door—Where would we eat? What kind of food? God, a night *out*—and parking our Chevy Nova on Sunset Boulevard, between the Berwin Music Complex and Maxim, where a red carpet exits the entrance of the restaurant and crosses the sidewalk and ends at a curb where patrons get out and let valets do the parking. We were getting out of our car to buy advance tickets for the show. I even brought my camera—the day felt eventful—and I told Gloria to stand in front of the ivory Rolls Royce we parked right ahead of. David sat on a bumper and Gloria held the baby and I shot two angles hurriedly, stealthily, afraid someone would suspect me of stealing something from the car. I was glad we posed so fast too because not a moment after I took the second picture a beautiful woman in a pink and white cashmire outfit rushed from the building and into the Rolls like she was afraid fans would torment her if she didn't. Stevie Nicks? Kim Carnes? We were excited and the first to buy tickets, and I took a photograph inside of the bar of the empty Club Lingerie like I was a photo artist.

The next day I told Gloria that she could buy some new rags if she wanted, that we should go for broke and have a night of it. I somehow felt like it might be our last of this kind, I don't know why. She said no and I didn't argue. We made plans so that it would work out just right. Gloria taught herself to express milk from her breasts with one of those pumps and she worked at it hours to get a large bottle full. She bathed the baby and David and went to the laundromat and washed clothes. She ironed her best pants and blouse and polished some stylish boots. She washed her hair and set it while I cleaned the house, vacuumed, emptied trash, washed dishes, and put all the children's toys away. It even seemed like fun.

I worried about how much to pay Ralph's mother. The going rate would have been about seven or eight dollars for five hours; ten would be good. But three an hour was below minimum wage to my mind. Would she think we were insulting her if we paid the rate, patronizing if we paid too much? She would be in our home, which has furniture. Gloria told me they had very little. What would she think of these pochos going to dinner and a nightclub while she, who's older than us and works with teenagers for the same money, watches the kids with all the toys she can't afford to give her children? I asked Gloria, but I decided, despite her reasoning, to give Ralph's mother fifteen bucks before we left because I'd feel better if she thought I was a big spender, however right or stupid it might seem.

When I went to the store to buy beer and some soda and potato chips so everybody could party while we were, I ran into Roberto, who I worked with at a job about a year previously. Roberto is from Salvador, is ten years older than me, is very religious, and enjoys drinking beer, so I bought an extra six-pack of Bud. He'd been working on his car, already drinking some, and we sat on the curb by his car and near his place and started talking about the times. He wasn't working either, but he wasn't collecting any unemployment. He was in a mood that I wasn't. From the street I could hear a 76ers– Celtics basketball game on someone's nearby television and I was with it until I cracked my third beer when I realized how much he'd been talking and I hadn't. I guess they aren't the best of times, I told him, not good at these things. He was still going on, telling me about how he got here and how hard it was for him to leave his country and that they'd killed his brother and his brother's family and they were after him. The mierdas were everywhere, both sides are filled with mierdas, he said, shits who will kill for all the good and bad reasons in the world. There is no meat without blood, he said, but why the blood of children?

Well I'd heard this before from him and gotten mad along with him, but this time it hurt. I felt bad for having listened to the game, for sitting on the curb unemployed, drinking beer. I've worked for a living, when I could, when it was there. I don't like being unemployed, and I didn't decide where I was born. So I told him we were going out tonight, Gloria and I. I felt American about it. I made myself sound sincere and deserving, determined to live the life I understood.

Though I'd changed my mood some when I got home, Gloria's peaceful happiness made me hold back. She was writing out a list of things to tell Ralph's mother—where the diapers were, the baby's milk and water, the food for them, the toys, the names and phone numbers of the places we'd be, to let David go to bed whenever he wanted. I went to our bedroom and looked around. I wanted to put things away since I knew Ralph's mother would take a tour. Anybody would. I hid some cash that I had in a top dresser drawer in a bottom one, under clothes, not because I didn't trust her, only because I don't trust anybody. I don't know. I took down our miniature El Salvador Libre flag—we went to this demonstration in MacArthur Park right after I met Roberto—and I slipped it under the clothes and on top of the money. I didn't want to wage an ideological war in my home with someone I don't know or haven't talked to, and one time Ralph told me his father was in prison back in Nicaragua, that he was a bodyguard in Managua for the president. Ralph has told us many things that conflict with one another, and for a while he told us that his father lived right there with him. If his mother's husband had been with Somoza, though we knew she had her boyfriends here, I believed the least I could do was not possibly antagonize the woman who was going to care for our children that night.

We were ready at six-thirty. Everybody was dressed and David was satisfied with Ralph coming over. I counted the dollars in my jeans and made sure the tickets were in my pocket and said what I said, that the show started at eight-thirty. We figured to be home by eleven-thirty. I turned on the television to kill time, and I had the curtains open at seven so I could watch over at Ralph's for the lights. I asked Gloria several times whether or not Ralph's mother said she got off work at seven or got home around seven. We watched the national news, which not inappropriately had a feature about the Central American countries in turmoil and how all this might affect the United States.

At seven-thirty I decided to go out and bring back some food. The important thing was to get to hear the music and have a couple of drinks, for Gloria to get away from the baby for a few hours. I could see Gloria wasn't taking it too well and I insisted that she not give the baby milk from the bottle to see how he liked it that way. I drove over to this new restaurant across the street from the grocery store. I drank a beer while I waited and ate the warmed chips the owner offered me. I was trying to figure out if I should go to the show by myself. I was mad that we were so dependent on a stranger, that we didn't have a string of friends and acquaintances like on TV shows, or family like at home. I started thinking about being unemployed.

I could see from my car driving back that the lights at Ralph's apartment still weren't on. It was eight o'clock. Gloria suggested at the dinner table that I go sell the tickets. I said we should all go. She said she wanted to wait. I waited too.

●

I think it was pretty stupid and impractical of me not to sell those tickets. Money is money. Anyway, somehow, I figure we had a good time preparing for our night out. It made some average days more interesting, and I got two decent photographs of Gloria and my boys next to a Rolls Royce. The other one didn't come out.

That night, at about ten, Ralph had dropped by looking for his mother and seemed surprised that she wasn't with us. We didn't understand what that was all about either and chose to wait and let the explanation come without questioning. It didn't and hasn't yet, already months later.

There were some changes for a while. Ralph didn't come around and for weeks the curtains stayed closed at his place. We talked about whether or not we were mad at Ralph's mother. We really weren't—we don't even know her—although Gloria still thinks she should have known better. I guess for the first week I expected her to apologize or at least send Ralph over to. I did get angry at Ralph one day when we passed him playing in the street with some friends. He was ignoring us, so I asked him if he didn't know how to say hello or what. The next day he came by. At first we had mixed feelings about his visiting again. But we fought it off. Ralph and David are little kids.

Ralph doesn't drop over quite as often as he used to though, and sometimes when he does it's at late hours and we send him home, wondering if he thinks we're getting back at his mother through him because he acts so hurt. We're not. It's just that nobody ever comes to take him home like before.

I put that flag back. From now on I leave it where it is until I don't want it there at all. You can never be sure what people think and I've learned that there's no point in hiding what you believe to be true. I also start a job tomorrow and I hope it lasts. Today I brewed more coffee and then melted some chocolate in it. My feeling is that the Lakers are better than the 76ers, that the Dodgers are going to do fine without Garvey or Cey. I'd rather think about these things when I look through that wedge of L.A. air that distances us from Ralph and his mother's apartment.

THE DESPERADO

On her way out she slammed the door and the boy wauled like Tucker'd never heard before. He picked him up but he fought and squirmed in Tucker's arms convulsively. He spoke to the boy calmly, though he didn't feel that calm, telling him that everything was all right, she'd be right back. This was the first time she'd run out on Tucker like this, the first time he wasn't gonna be able to hand the boy over to her if he got to crying. It was the first time Tucker and his son had ever really been together, alone.

"Your mama's gonna be right back," he was saying. "She'll be right back, you'll see. You don't gotta cry, boy." His son's wail was steady.

All this was very hard for Tucker. It just wasn't in his nature to take care of crying babies. He told her that all the time, and she'd always been good about this end of it. She said she didn't trust Tucker with their son most of the time anyway, and though somehow he didn't like her saying that, he didn't have to worry about no crying babies, and that was good enough for him.

"Come on, boy, settle down. This ain't the fuckin end of the world." Tucker held him tightly, so he wouldn't kick out of his arms. He was fighting his urge to scream at the boy to shut up, the urge to spank his ass. But he knew the boy had something real to cry about, and that restrained him.

Tucker tried to think of something to make his son happy, so he set him down beside the plastic blocks he played with so often. The boy stiffened himself, throwing all the fear and hurt of his tightened muscles into smacking his head against the dusty hardwood floor of their rented house. Now he had something really real to scream about.

Tucker let the boy cry in the middle of the living room and went to the kitchen for a beer. He cracked one open and threw the tab on the floor near the trash bag and went over to the table. He considered rolling up a joint from the bag of weed he'd skimmed from several of the pounds he'd moved this morning. It was good reefer and it cost mucho. He'd considered it his chance, the only way he'd ever get them their own piece of sky. Of course she didn't believe him. She said it was too much risk. He said these dudes wore gold, that in a year they'd be sitting pretty.

The motherfuckers were probably somewhere near California by now, Tucker thought, sucking on his beer. He didn't feel like smoking any of the weed, not right this minute. The boy was still crying. Tucker drank some more, most of the can.

It seemed to him that the boy must have just about worn himself out because he let himself be picked up. He was in an out-of-control stage of crying, wheezing and gasping spastically, a weak and small sack of flesh.

He held onto the boy. He felt uncomfortable, but the boy's arms around his neck squeezed out some instinct and Tucker felt like a father, in that unexplainable sense. "We'll be all right now." He caught himself talking in the plural. "You're gonna be all right now." That didn't make it much better.

Tucker walked his son around the house, rocking him, rubbing the boy's back. Tucker was relieved that the boy was finally going to sleep, though he still whimpered in an easy sort of way. Tucker was hoping that the worst would be over once he got him in bed, that she'd be back before he woke up.

He walked his son into the bathroom so he could see if the

boy's eyes were closed. He stared at the both of them in the mirror. He'd never seen himself holding his son before, never let himself feel his own flesh press against his own flesh, and he never let anyone else see him doing this either. It seemed so mamalike, and that just wasn't Tucker's style.

And he wouldn't let himself experience it, no more than he would stare at himself in a mirror any longer than he had to. He took the boy to the bedroom and put him on the bed, where they all slept together, except most nights, when the boy woke up crying and Tucker got up and slept on a secondhand sofa in the living room so he could get some uninterrupted sleep. The boy was out fast.

Tucker didn't really want to drink more beer, but that's what he got out of the refrigerator. There was nothing better to do, and he wouldn't leave his boy alone in the house. He wouldn't be that irresponsible, even though he knew she'd be back very soon.

This time he did roll a joint, and he lit it up. It was good weed. He thought about eating some downers so he could relax, but getting all fucked up on some ludes or something to escape would be even worse than some baby whimpering for his mama.

He was gonna take care of his son. That was something he was gonna do right. He wasn't gonna give her no reasons for running out on him. If she was to do it again, or he left her, he didn't want her to be saying that he didn't take care of his son. At least not truthfully. He smoked a joint.

He smoked and thought about ways of getting even with those scumbags from L.A. He imagined football-size holes in their chests. He imagined himself and some of his Mexican friends doing a job on them one evening when they'd forgotten he was alive. Then he thought more realistically, thought about just kicking their asses, getting his money back, or even the weed. He knew he'd never see them again, that he was gonna have to kiss it all off.

Tucker walked into the bedroom to watch his son sleep. He stretched himself out beside the boy. He felt bad that he was sleeping so hard, though it was natural for him to be so upset. She'd run out on him too. He wondered when she'd get back. It occurred to him that she might not. He rolled onto his back and stared at a crack gouging its way through the wall, a thin veneer of plaster continually peeling away at the banks of the widening crack, working slowly, like the Rio Grande. He closed his eyes and saw himself standing near the river, under early morning stars buzzing neon like the Hollywood burning in his imagination, laughing along, loading their Trans-Am with beautiful colas of marijuana, making this exception for these rich kids who'd come through before. He saw himself turning down the dial of the radio, tuned into ranchera music from Juárez, his boot pressed hard on the accelerator of his six-cylinder Falcon, following them past the exit for their motel on Mesa Street, following the taillights that got more distant on the interstate, saw himself shooting at the chips of red stupidly, his Colt whapping harmlessly into the black desert air.

His adrenalin shook the bed. The boy stirred. Tucker patted his son's back, praying the boy wouldn't wake up, not yet. He wanted to know where the fuck she was. He wished he hadn't slapped her. He wished the boy hadn't seen him slap her. He remembered how quiet the boy was when they were fighting. He remembered that he didn't cry then. The boy was back asleep. Tucker decided he too could use some winks. He tried to sleep, and after a while he did.

He woke up to his son crying. She told him that babies always do that when they wake up. Still, this wasn't in Tucker's nature. He picked him up out of bed and walked with him. At least he wasn't crying in the same way he had been. He still wanted his mama, but he didn't have the same desperation.

Tucker went into the front room and turned on the television. He flicked it around until something he liked struck him. A western gunfight. A marshal and his deputies were shooting it out with some outlaws in a rocky canyon. Tucker watched attentively. Even his son was distracted by it, though only for a few moments. He laid his head back on Tucker's shoulder and cried. Tucker knew who was gonna win the fight, but still.

He went into the kitchen and got another can of beer. He stood there, fiddling with the tab, feeling disgusted. The boy took a piss in his paper and plastic diaper and some of it ran down his leg and against Tucker's shirt. Tucker was just not in the mood. What could she be doing? he wanted to know. And what if she didn't come back?

Tucker put the boy down by the television and pulled the diaper off and left him there naked.

The beer wasn't tasting good. He wanted to get out, just get out, get away from this dump, get the fuck away.

But this was his own baby, his own son, his own flesh and blood.

He threw the almost full beer can against a wall near the table with everything he had. It hit the thick plaster with a bloated thud, spraying beer up onto the ceiling, slicing a crescent out of the wall. The boy, drawn away from his own misery, quieted until almost all the beer had gurgled out of the can. Then he cried, hard.

"I'm sorry, boy. I'm sorry. It didn't mean nothin." Tucker was serious. He didn't know what had come over himself. The boy was looking at Tucker in fear, but also for comfort. "It didn't mean nothin, nothin at all." Tucker picked his son up. He walked him around the room, back and forth, through several TV breaks in the movie. The boy was settling down. Tucker couldn't.

"Let's see what we can eat," he told his son. He looked around the kitchen, but there wasn't shit. That was one of the things she'd been yelling about. He'd told her that there wasn't any money. Then she'd brought up his dope deal. He'd thrown some money at her, then slapped her. He shouldn't have. She'd been right.

The boy seemed to be enjoying the search through the kitchen. He was smiling, pointing to things in the cupboard. Tucker found two slices of white bread and took some margarine out of the refrigerator. The boy knew what was going on, Tucker figured, because he was reaching for the tray the margarine was in, seemed excited about the bread going in the toaster. "Yeah," Tucker said, trying to imitate the sound of his son's enthusiasm, "this is gonna be for you."

Tucker felt easier now that the boy had stopped crying, didn't feel like he was just going through the motions. He would be strong when he grew up, thought Tucker. He'd learn a few things.

He carried his son over to the picture on the upper half of the parts store calendar hanging on the refrigerator. "See, those're clouds in the sky, above those mountains." The boy, interested, put a small finger onto the cloudy blue sky and smiled at Tucker. "Yeah, that's it! Clouds and sky!" He embraced the naked boy and led him over to the window above the sink. "Now look here," he said, pointing above the Franklin Mountains. "Can you see real clouds and real sky out there?" The boy looked off with him, and Tucker was sure he saw and understood. He stood there with the boy in his arms and lost himself in a fantasy he believed his son was lost in too.

It was too late before Tucker realized that the boy was pointing to the smoking toast. It was already burned black. "I'll hafta figure out somethin else for you to eat," he apologized to his son. But the boy wanted toast, and when he realized that there was going to be none, he cried.

"You can't have none now!" Tucker screamed. "There's no more!" And the boy cried so hard with hurt and fear that he pissed all over Tucker again.

Tucker left his son back by the television. The marshal was riding the outlaw back into town. He was wounded, but he got his man.

Tucker threw off his wet shirt and pants. He didn't feel like looking for other clothes and he didn't feel like listening to the crying. He went outside, slamming the door just like she did, hoping that then he wouldn't hear that boy inside. He wanted to know where the fuck she was, how she could leave knowing the boy needed his mama.

DOWN IN THE WEST TEXAS TOWN

The sun was sucking up the thin juices of the desert earth until a lazy effluvium floated above the motionless river named the Rio Grande, sucking until the naked mountains named the Franklins seemed to scream out in silence, sucking until the back side of the man named Danny had become a cracking hide. The sun burned; the heat was all, consumed all—even the whacks of a twenty-eight-ounce framing hammer swatting a sixteen-penny nail one time two times and three through the ridge board and into the peak end of a rafter, even the rippling buzz of an electric saw chewing through woodflesh, even they fell short of cutting through this insatiable heat.

"Alfuckinmost!" the Texan was yelling at no one in particular.

Danny was dropping his hammer back into the sling at his side and was slipping off a red bandanna he had tied around his forehead to wipe away the sweat that still clung to his face. He'd nailed his last two-by into this skeleton roof; the half-inch sheeting was all that was left and Peppy—who preferred the English mispronunciation of the Spanish—was pulling those up, though not without a strain and a gripe. Danny didn't move to help him. He liked this moment too much, liked standing there, watching, each arm looped around a rafter, his boots bent over a joist. He liked it because it felt dangerous but safe—and being closer to the sun, to the heat, being still in it, quieted something within himself.

At the other end of the roof, not too far from where Peppy began tacking in the plywood, the Texan unhooked his bags and threw them below into the dirt. It was breaktime.

"All right!" Peppy wailed, fidgeting with happiness. "It's time to go home!"

"You been fuckin home all day, Peppy," said the Texan. "The resta us are just gonna cool down some. You can stay up here, maybe work more on your suntan."

"Pinche culero!" Peppy laughed.

Danny climbed down from where he was and walked around to the shady area off to a side of this house they were framing and headed for the five-gallon water jug. He waited for Nigger—who got his name because he was so prieto, dark—to get his fill of water as it trickled down from the spout and into his open mouth. Impatient, Danny grabbed a coke bottle that was lying nearby, lifted the lid of the cooler and listened to it bubble full after he submerged it into the icy water.

"I can do better than that," Nigger boasted, and he lifted the cooler like it was an oversized mug and drank from the rim while water splashed and drooled down his face and chest and into the dirt.

"Git your face outa that water!" the Texan yelled. "God only knows what kinda things been sloppin between those lips, and *shit,* you don't *never* brush your teeth!"

Danny joined the Texan and Peppy, then Nigger came and sat, making it a circle.

"Ernie's got some really good stuff," Peppy was saying to the Texan. "I mean really good, ese. Dark brown. It gets you really high. . . . Just a little bit"—he took a pinch of sandy brown dirt from the circle's middle—"just about this much"—about an eye drop full in the palm of his other hand—"and about five of water"—he pinched up some more of the dirt—"like this"—and mixed it with what was already lining the wrinkles of his dark, chapped palm—"and you get off real bad."

Peppy sat there in the silence, growing big with the thought that he'd had it, that he could tell about it now, could draw interest in it, growing yearnful enough that a few rays of wishfulness radiated from his smirk and brightened up the shade they sat in.

Danny took a couple more cold swallows from his bottle of water. The water tasted good, he thought. It was nice to be away from the heat too, to feel cool inside. Sometimes it was better to avoid the heat. Sometimes it felt very good.

"It was *so* bad," Peppy went on, "that Ernie had to cut it down because these dudes OD'd on it. But even cut you can get off like . . ."

"Quit talking about that," Nigger whined, stretched out on a dusty patch of desert. "It makes me feel sick."

"Well here," replied Peppy, sprinkling the dirt over Nigger's chest. "Stick this shit in your arm!" He cackled at Nigger and looked over at the Texan who grinned without enthusiasm. "You know," he added, still giggling, "one time Nigger bought a half of dirt. Dark brown dirt, just a little darker than this." Another handful from the inner circle, only a little wet.

Nigger rolled his head.

"How'd that happen?" the Texan asked Nigger. "Didn't you even look at it?"

"No," he muttered.

"Why the fuck not?"

"I just didn't."

The Texan's wince was a blend of disgust and understanding.

"Let's hump this bullshit. It's only gittin hotter."

●

Danny and Peppy were squeezed between sticks of lumber and beer cans and electrical cords in back of the Texan's dented up '62 Chevy pickup. They'd finished the job an hour and a half later and were headed out in the direction of the place the Texan called home.

Peppy, who liked to complain whenever possible, fumbled for a comfortable seat in the back of the pickup and grumbled to himself, until finally he bitched out loud. "That gabacho is a real judio."

"Whadaya mean?" Danny chuckled.

"The fucker's only gonna pay us sixteen dollars."

"He told you that?" Danny'd expected low wages—it was hard to get a job, and he had trouble keeping them—but not this low.

"That's what he says, ese." Peppy stood and banged arrogantly on the back window and then leaned himself around to the driver's window and barked out something to the Texan.

"That sure isn't much, man. You sure?"

"Well . . . he's gonna get us something else too."

Danny nodded. He'd ask for his payment in coin.

They turned off Dyer Street and onto another. Peppy yelled at the Texan and pointed to an auto parts store, and the Texan skidded the truck up against the curb on the street opposite it. Anxious, Peppy hopped out of the car, with a belligerent smirk. Danny waited on the business alone in the back; the Texan and Nigger, both smoking cigarettes in the front seat, quietly listened to a country music station until suddenly Nigger opened his door and puked on the curb, about three retching convulsions. Moments passed, then Peppy came scampering into the street from the parts store in his way—a kind of flat-footed, short-stepped, stiff-legged, stooped-over prance. Nigger, his door open in anticipation, shoved his head into the gutter again.

Peppy kept coming and as he reached the Texan's door he threw his feet high in the air toward it and farted rapaciously. "God*damn* you're a disgustin mexikin!" the Texan yelped. Giggling, Peppy dashed around the front of the truck to Nigger's open door. "Here, hold this," he said, handing him the brown paper bag from the store, unconcerned about Nigger's condition. Peppy pulled out a bright blue bandanna from his pocket and snatched back the paper bag from Nigger, whose face was wrenched with sickness, then, joining bag to rag, looked around nervously, but also with that smirk, and let the hissing within the bag soak the rag throughout. The Texan barked out something from the driver's side, and Peppy sneered with a chuckling contempt. Then he mashed his face into the rag and wheezed in the fumes. When Peppy finished, Nigger imitated Peppy's performance. They all drove off to a bar for a few beers.

●

They bounced into the front yard of the Texan's rented house about five pitchers and a dozen games of pool later. Driving into his front yard was not a show of disrespect; the curb was recessed just for this. And the yard—the rocky dirt lot with large chunks of gravel driven in here and left undisturbed there, keeping the dirt turned mud after a rain from being an undrive-able slop—the yard seemed more suited to the days when horses were hitched to a post and boots were scraped on a mud-sling before vittles. The house, the shack, was a simple job—a narrow rectangle with a left-to-right lean-to roof, the paint on the wood siding so ancient that it made it hard to guess what the faded rust color once really was.

Inside it was cramped, the swap-meet furnishings stuffed or crammed into a corner or against a wall, and the remaining path through it cluttered with baby toys and needs. The three non-belongers took a seat after they said their hellos to the Texan's old lady, who was spoon-feeding her baby boy. The Texan was already on the phone.

"Do you think you could do another whole for forty?" he asked with abject concern, sort of squinting down at the telephone dial and speaking with calm determination. "I can't do it all myself. Could you do half? . . . No, I'm ten dollars short. . . ."

The Texan seemed emaciated, anemic, his eyes a droopy and saddened blue-green. "Okay. Orale." He hung up the phone dispassionately. He kept a distant gaze in his eyes, a distance of time and place.

"So wha'd Ernie say?" Nigger wanted to know.

"He's gonna call back."

"Another whole?" The three of them had agreed to divide up a whole and a half. Danny had to sit it out, he had to resist.

"He's gonna see if he can do a half."

Peppy and Nigger sat, nervous. The Texan's old lady sat wordless at the kitchen table with her legs crossed, her baby fed. She never said much, and when she did say something it took the form of a private conversation that only she and the Texan could make absolute sense of.

The Texan paced evenly, in a way that didn't resemble pacing exactly, but which was nonetheless. The baby, who had just learned to walk, danced across a dingy rag rug from one man to another until one would pick him up or tease him or make a ridiculous face which would momentarily convince the baby to stay.

The heat hung in the room. Danny was uncomfortable. He felt parched, like his flesh was a tight-fitting jacket. He felt dizzy, felt like he was still up on that roof pounding nails.

"Anyone ready for another beer?" the Texan asked, looking inside the refrigerator. "There's only three, but maybe if we all spit a mouthful Peppy'll get a glass." He laughed and took out three cans of beer. Then he got out a glass from the cupboard and put a share of each can into it until it was full. The phone rang.

The Texan listened, grunting his presence to the other end of the line. "I'll be back," he said, dropping the receiver hard, and before the jarred bell inside the telephone had stilled, the screen door slammed once and again on a rebound and the Texan was opening the door of his pickup.

"Is there mota?" Peppy asked the Texan's old lady.

"On top of the television there should be a tray with some."

Nigger played with the baby. He played affectionately and the baby squealed with happiness.

Peppy and Danny shared a joint. Nigger didn't want any. Neither did the Texan's old lady.

●

"You don't like chiva?" Nigger asked Danny. Nigger was subtle about it; if Peppy would have asked, which he already had a couple of times, it would have been why can't you do some heroin with us, ese? You're a man, aren't you? You can handle it, can't you?

"I don't do it."

"You never do it?"

"I already been in the joint for a while."

Nigger considered that. "You shouldn't mess with it no more, dude."

"You don't like it no more?"

"Shit yeah I like it. It's just expensive. A dude shouldn't never get started, you know?"

"How long you been into it?"

"A few years. It's that I'm used to putting it in my vein." He paused, unhappy. "It just fucks you up too much. It fucks everything up too much." He thought this over. "But it feels so good." And he closed his eyes, imagining.

Danny let the heat take him over. He let it lift him, send him back to the roof, closer to the sun. It was so hot that he could barely stand it. He could barely stand it.

●

The air snapped as the Texan burst through the door hurrying to the kitchen table where he dropped the gleaming silver object. Peppy and Nigger flung themselves close to him to be by it. Danny's heart pumped thunderously. He felt himself backing away, then approaching, awed, fascinated, scared, tempted. His heart raged. He saw the room through a dizziness which tested his equilibrium. He tried to watch, he wanted to watch, but for him it was as dangerous as staring at that sun.

Nigger and Peppy waited. The Texan organized. A glass of water appeared upon the table. Then the foil was unwrapped, and a soup spoon received brownish dust.

"It looks good, man," Peppy said more seriously than necessary as he eye-dropped the water into the spoon.

"Just git it in there!" the Texan sniffed irritably.

The baby played behind Danny. The Texan's old lady stood near the men, vibrating as imperceptibly as a rattler's tongue. Danny's heart pounded. He considered: He felt an unmistakable rush. The very air resonated.

Peppy struck a kitchen match against the box it came in and guided its sulphur-smelling flame to the burner on the stove.

"Willya quit the fuckin around!" screached the Texan. "Light the damn thing!" He was waiting, prepared, a bandanna loosely tied around his bicep.

"I can't get it, ese. It won't light."

"Let me see them matches," he said more calmly, but then exploding—"son of a *bitch!*" He snatched the matches away from Peppy, lighting one match, then a second. The burner came on, its tiny choreographed flames rolling into a circle, and the mixture was readied.

The Texan sucked the juice up into the syringe and put out his arm. His face was twisted in nervous anticipation. His starving arm reached out, and his eyes took aim—the needle roamed around a purplish vein that swelled up, stalking it muscularly. And then it struck, and the syringe purled toward emptiness. The Texan responded as in reflex: his eyelids cascaded shut, tranquility flooded his desert baked face.

Serene, he yanked the bandanna from his arm and walked toward Danny. "Let's go check on that other job," he said.

"The other job?"

"A remodel on the eastside."

"Vámonos pues."

He threw a glance at his old lady which said see you in a while. Danny followed him out the screen door while Peppy and Nigger took their turns. The baby cried to go with his daddy but the screen door slammed and the Texan's old lady latched it to the door jamb and consoled the child. The two of them watched the Texan and Danny drive away.

Danny had the window down on his side of the truck. He let the cool air pour in and dry the perspiration that had beaded up on his forehead and around his scalp. Relieved, he relaxed his arm on the window's frame, but it was burning hot, as hot as the noon sun, so he quickly took it away, though not before he let out a little yip of pain.

The Texan shook his head sympathetically. "I hate this fuckin heat. I hate to do anything in this fuckin heat."

But Danny liked the heat. He preferred the heat. Danny needed the heat.

He rolled his window up, telling the Texan that it was to keep himself from burning his arm again.

L O V E   I N   L . A .

Jake slouched in a clot of near motionless traffic, in the peculiar gray of concrete, smog, and early morning beneath the overpass of the Hollywood Freeway on Alvarado Street. He didn't really mind because he knew how much worse it could be trying to make a left onto the onramp. He certainly didn't do that everyday of his life, and he'd assure anyone who'd ask that he never would either. A steady occupation had its advantages and he couldn't deny thinking about that too. He needed an FM radio in something better than this '58 Buick he drove. It would have crushed velvet interior with electric controls for the LA summer, a nice warm heater and defroster for the winter drives at the beach, a cruise control for those longer trips, mellow speakers front and rear of course, windows that hum closed, snuffing out that nasty exterior noise of freeways. The fact was that he'd probably have to change his whole style. Exotic colognes, plush, dark nightclubs, maitais and daquiris, necklaced ladies in satin gowns, misty and sexy like in a tequila ad. Jake could imagine lots of possibilities when he let himself, but none that ended up with him pressed onto a stalled freeway.

Jake was thinking about this freedom of his so much that when he glimpsed its green light he just went ahead and stared bye bye to the steadily employed. When he turned his head the same direction his windshield faced, it was maybe one second too late. He pounced the brake pedal and steered the front wheels away from the tiny brakelights but the smack was unavoidable. Just one second sooner and it would only have been close. One second more and he'd be crawling up the Toyota's trunk. As it was, it seemed like only a harmless smack, much less solid than the one against his back bumper.

Jake considered driving past the Toyota but was afraid the traffic ahead would make it too difficult. As he pulled up against the curb a few carlengths ahead, it occurred to him that the traffic might have helped him get away too. He slammed the car door twice to make sure it was closed fully and to give himself another second more, then toured front and rear of his Buick for damage on or near the bumpers. Not an impressionable scratch even in the chrome. He perked up. Though the car's beauty was secondary to its ability to start and move, the body and paint were clean except for a few minor dings. This stood out as one of his few clearcut accomplishments over the years.

Before he spoke to the driver of the Toyota, whose looks he could see might present him with an added complication, he signaled to the driver of the car that hit him, still in his car and stopped behind the Toyota, and waved his hands and shook his head to let the man know there was no problem as far as he was concerned. The driver waved back and started his engine.

"It didn't even scratch my paint," Jake told her in that way of his. "So how you doin? Any damage to the car? I'm kinda hoping so, just so it takes a little more time and we can talk some. Or else you can give me your phone number now and I won't have to lay my regular b.s. on you to get it later."

He took her smile as a good sign and relaxed. He inhaled her scent like it was clean air and straighted out his less than new but not unhip clothes.

"You've got Florida plates. You look like you must be Cuban."

"My parents are from Venezuela."

"My name's Jake." He held out his hand.

"Mariana."

They shook hands like she'd never done it before in her life.

"I really am sorry about hitting you like that." He sounded genuine. He fondled the wide dimple near the cracked taillight. "It's amazing how easy it is to put a dent in these new cars. They're so soft they might replace waterbeds soon." Jake was confused about how to proceed with this. So much seemed so unlikely, but there was always possibility. "So maybe we should go out to breakfast somewhere and talk it over."

"I don't eat breakfast."

"Some coffee then."

"Thanks, but I really can't."

"You're not married, are you? Not that that would matter that much to me. I'm an openminded kinda guy."

She was smiling. "I have to get to work."

"That sounds boring."

"I better get your driver's license," she said.

Jake nodded, disappointed. "One little problem," he said. "I didn't bring it. I just forgot it this morning. I'm a musician," he exaggerated greatly, "and, well, I dunno, I left my wallet in the pants I was wearing last night. If you have some paper and a pen I'll give you my address and all that."

He followed her to the glove compartment side of her car.

"What if we don't report it to the insurance companies? I'll just get it fixed for you."

"I don't think my dad would let me do that."

"Your dad? It's not your car?"

"He bought it for me. And I live at home."

"Right." She was slipping away from him. He went back around to the back of her new Toyota and looked over the damage again. There was the trunk lid, the bumper, a rear panel, a taillight.

"You do have insurance?" she asked, suspicious, as she came around the back of the car.

"Oh yeah," he lied.

"I guess you better write the name of that down too."

He made up a last name and address and wrote down the name of an insurance company an old girlfriend once belonged to. He considered giving a real phone number but went against that idea and made one up.

"I act too," he lied to enhance the effect more. "Been in a couple of movies."

She smiled like a fan.

"So how about your phone number?" He was rebounding maturely.

She gave it to him.

"Mariana, you are beautiful," he said in his most sincere voice.

"Call me," she said timidly.

Jake beamed. "We'll see you, Mariana," he said holding out his hand. Her hand felt so warm and soft he felt like he'd been kissed.

Back in his car he took a moment or two to feel both proud and sad about his performance. Then he watched the rear view mirror as Mariana pulled up behind him. She was writing down the license plate numbers on his Buick, ones that he'd taken off a junk because the ones that belonged to his had expired so long ago. He turned the ignition key and revved the big engine and clicked into drive. His sense of freedom swelled as he drove into the now moving street traffic, though he couldn't stop the thought about that FM stereo radio and crushed velvet interior and the new car smell that would even make it better.

WINNERS ON THE PASS LINE

In an office swivel chair, Ray Muñoz faced his jobsite and a pane of fixed glass. He'd missed a few days of work without explanation and the field superintendent was due anytime. He would be expected to say something. Only one of the foremen had even brought up his absence this morning, asking with an uncomfortable laugh whether Ray had tied one on or what.

The majority of the men were huddled in pairs and small groups near the coffee truck next to the gate, holding styrofoam cups and sandwiches and burritos, the steam from which quickly became indistinguishable from the overcast sky. Ray could hear a couple of them near his window talking about the leftovers they still had from Thanksgiving, about Christmas, about the sex in the movie last night and about what they were probably going to do today at the job. They were sitting on a stack of large but not full sheets of plywood waiting for the foreman to start them to work. When the time came, Ray rocked in his swivel chair and watched the wobbly manlift roll up the cable line to the eighteenth and the nineteenth floors where most of the men unloaded, and then to the roof where the lift clicked off to let two laborers load several empty oxygen and acetylene bottles. He saw the operator pull the cage door together when they were finished and the counterweight rise as the manlift coasted down where stragglers were waiting for the next trip up.

Ray thought about how only a few years ago he believed he'd be wearing leather bags into retirement. Never did he imagine a chair and a secretary. He worked construction with callused hands that made the tools feel like they had grips, hands that held so many nails and hammers for so many hours they stayed clenched like fists in his off hours. But they earned him a living, not a rich one, but enough not to be ashamed. He remembered how his wife changed his thinking about that. She told him he should stop thinking like he'd just crossed the border and couldn't do better and to remember the where of his birth, to think about the miracle of possibilities on this side. He knew she was right about miracles because he could touch her with his palms and fingers, always cut and smashed and lumpy with splinters, always dry because of cement and rust, and they could still record the sensation of such a contrary texture. That she fell in love with him should have sent him back faithfully to Mass every Sunday. There was no other explanation: she'd been to college and still married him and lived his life of wages and alcohol, rented apartments and, when children came, rented houses which would never have been homes otherwise. Houston was her idea. He never would have left El Paso. But she was convinced there were opportunities and she was the smart one. And soon there was a new truck, then a new house, and finally, when he got this job, a savings account he planned to surprise her with someday.

His secretary peeked through a crack in the door. "You're here," she said as though he never was. "Sorry I'm late. I'm making some coffee right now." He didn't say anything to her. He'd fired his last secretary six months ago for not typing well enough and being on the phone too much, but the real reason was that she'd been coming on to him and that was too disruptive to his life. He'd already had his youth, was what he'd decided, and this new world, Houston, had offered him winning dice: while his childhood friends were still struggling near the border, he'd become a superintendent in a major construction company. He was on a roll and he didn't want to complicate the betting.

He should have known better. Looking back, it was easy to see. Just as his wife had started teasing him about that secretary, she'd been telling him about all the women she worked with at her job in the federal building, about all the fantasies and even affairs that began at their more than an hour lunch breaks with lawyers and government administrators and sometimes diplomats. She even told him about the one she met who spoke— besides Spanish—French, German, and even some Russian. He just never suspected, probably because he was so preoccupied with his new status. He just never suspected that she'd moved with the times too.

●

Before the phone call, Sylvia Molina had been methodically packing their luggage, neatly folding all the clothes that she and her husband and their youngest son might need. She'd been thinking about the things she had learned growing up, because this certainly was not one of them. Vacations were a time when her father got to sleep in and nap in the afternoon and talk about it happily if it was a gift from the job, or worriedly if it was because he was unemployed. She could only remember taking a trip once, to Durango, when her grandmother on her mother's side died. Her father's parents were from this side and lived with them.

"Are you just about done?" her husband asked.

"Uh-huh."

"And Jimmy . . ."

"Is already over at Peter's." She said that strongly and it even surprised her.

"Is everything okay?"

She could hear the department store's Christmas music in the background. A voiceless Noel. "I'm a little nervous. I don't know why."

"We'll have a good time. Look, I'll be home in an hour, maybe two. I gotta go."

Sylvia hung up the phone guiltily. Everything mental told her that the trip was going to go well. A weekend in Las Vegas before her husband got bogged down with the holidays and then inventory. They'd catch a show, gamble, have a few drinks, eat out. Neither of them had been there before. And it was she who'd wanted to do something exciting.

Excitement, she believed, must be a word belonging to her generation. Her mother had never mentioned the concept to her. What might pass for it in their home came through living next door to Mr. Rodriguez, who would often come home drunk in the middle of the night and would sometimes try to get in his locked front door instead of sleeping in his car. Mrs. Rodriguez would scream at him and the neighborhood about whores and the devil, diseases and lice. Then there was Rudy Rodriguez, their oldest son, who had brought police cars to the street more than once, and Mike, their next oldest, who was a football star at UT-Austin and even tried out for a pro team. She didn't remember her sisters seeming too concerned about the feeling of excitement either. The older one married when she was twenty, and the big thing in her life was a wedding ceremony and reception and her first baby. She never wanted to leave El Paso for even a drive. Her other sister went to college to get married but ended up a schoolteacher and, as far as she knew, was still a virgin.

Sylvia herself had chosen security when there'd been a choice. Her husband now hadn't been her boyfriend then. But he wanted to marry her and had a degree from college and a good job with a future, which was the life she was leading today. He was already a floor manager at a major department store in Huntington Beach, they were paying off a mortgage on a four-bedroom house in an almost new development only a mile from the ocean, and they lived on a stainless street where there was no concept of race or creed and where the gloom of unemployment and bad times she heard about over the color television seemed as distant as Mexico. Though they were by no means rich, they could make all their payments on time, and for her birthday her husband had even bought her a microwave oven she never asked for or wanted.

She didn't often think about the boy she didn't marry. She was in high school, which he'd only been to for two years before he dropped out. He lived wherever anybody would let him if he didn't have money, and sometimes that was in the county jail. He told her he loved her but she probably would have let him even if he hadn't said it. That was a winter night when a windhard hail broke out the windowpane in his rented room off Montana Street. He got up naked, his eyes the only part of him that seemed to have to adjust to the black wind, water cresting his cheekbones and rolling down his back, and he took nails and a hammer from his workbags and made a shutter out of an empty dresser drawer he disassembled with his fist. It was still cold but they were laughing under his blankets because he said there was nothing to worry about, they still had two more drawers with nothing in them.

●

Ray withdrew all the money from his account. It was, by accident, a thousand for each of their ten years. Not much by Houston standards, but enough to make him feel gold-plated when he visited back home, and it might have been only the beginning. It had crossed his mind more than once to put it down on some land—he imagined building a house near the river, planting some trees, raising thoroughbreds, starting up a ranch not unlike the one his father spent his life working on— but he never kidded himself about how far away he was from that. He didn't know what he'd do with it now. He'd been considering a swimming pool, but he always recalled the lean, unemployed times when he wished he'd had enough of a cushion to wait for the better jobs. Good and bad construction workers, including superintendents, came and went for lots of reasons, and he'd taught himself not to be surprised when he was handed an extra check on pay day with "layoff" stamped on it. This time maybe he could have kept the job, but he didn't offer the company's field boss an excuse for his time off because he didn't want to talk about his wife and children. He didn't know how to explain such things because he'd never learned how and it never occurred to him that he might have to. Layoff checks were to be expected. They always made some sense.

He took the money from the account and cashed his checks. The ten thousand he wanted in hundred-dollar bills. He agreed that he was acting a little crazy but it was a decision as certain as the cash would be in his pocket and the bank manager spent several hours making sure he got it once Ray assured him that he knew exactly what he was doing.

He drank only one beer on the airplane. He sat next to a window in the non-smoking section and no one sat next to him. Sometimes he shut his eyes, but he didn't sleep. When he opened them he'd see the wing of the airplane shudder. There weren't enough clouds to look at, and the earth seemed only slightly more alive than one of his hundred-dollar bills. Thinking like this shamed him somehow, and he prayed he'd be forgiven such a huge ingratitude.

●

Sylvia relaxed considerably when she saw the green road sign that told them Las Vegas was 175 miles away. She'd examined her map too many times and her husband had noticed. He'd wanted her to go to the auto club and get a new map and make reservations through it because that was what they paid for. But she insisted that she could do it all herself. Everything about this, even calling for hotel prices and making reservations over tollfree telephone lines, even marking out the simple route on a map, had become like a statement of independence for her, a muscling-up in challenge to what in any mind was a contented, idyllic life. And she took it very seriously. She was determined to have things go her way, to direct the flow of events without suggestions or advice or cautions. She was doing this with "her" money, alloting a certain amount for the hotel, food, entertainment, gas, a certain amount for her husband to gamble with, a certain amount for her gambling. She'd figured all this as a debit in her bookkeeping, but she also figured that her winning would verify something, would mean something, though she had no idea what. Winning was her hope, and though she pretended otherwise, she clung to it religiously.

"Do you see that sign?" her husband said to their son. " 'Eat Gas.' Those oil companies think of everything."

The boy was fidgety and Sylvia told him to go to sleep and when he woke up they'd be there, even though she knew that if he did she'd pay by having to stay up late with him. She could have easily left him at home with the older boy, but she wanted him along for an excuse. With him, they'd have to do their gambling separately, in shifts. She gave her husband another reason for taking the four-year-old along.

"It's great to get on the road, isn't it?" her husband asked her. "And in a big, comfortable car. Who would have thought? Think we'll see Frank Sinatra?"

She smiled. She never doubted that she made a good choice marrying him. He was ordinary in the best ways, watching football games on Monday nights, taking the children to amusement parks every month and her to a restaurant every week or so. His pride would show when they went back to visit their parents, and when someone asked him where they lived, he would say down the street from Carlos Palomino, though in fact they had no idea where the fighter lived, only that it was supposed to be within the same city limits. His small exaggerations like that made up for his unstartling existence, kept him in touch with his neighborhood friends still linked to the less affluent, working class suburb he grew up in. He was a good man, and, most importantly, he loved her.

"It's pretty here," she told him.

He chuckled at her. "I guess."

"In a different way. It's still open. The sky looks like El Paso's."

"I guess I see what you mean. I guess."

●

Ray came to gamble, but instead he wandered through casinos and lost money, betting randomly at dice tables the house favorites like the hard ten and hard four and any craps, and, while at the roulette table, the single numbers and always the double zero. Each time he played a twenty-dollar bill from his paychecks and each time a dealer or a croupier would turn his green paper into red chips which would be eased away and clicked into perfect stacks. He was aimless enough even to play the dollar slots, and when he won sixty dollars, his first winning since he got there, he tinkled and spun away the time until every silver dollar was gone on a triple and double and single line play. When he decided he wanted to sit and drink he settled on seven-card stud with a ten dollar buy-in and alternated between whiskey, his Houston drink, and rum and coke, his Juárez drink. He tried to fill flushes when he had three of the same suit and the high hand showed the same face cards, and he would raise with a low pair under and a low pair up and invariably lose to a full house or a flush. During one hand, he stayed in on three raises each on the last two cards when he had a chance of a high straight, and lost to three nines. After this he simply played drunk, seven rounds worth, waiting for more cards that never came to drop in front of him, losing three hundred dollars more. When he finally stumbled through the tall heavy doors of the casino and stood underneath the heaven of hundred-watt bulbs above the main entrance, watching old men with young women exit limosines with two-hundred-watt shines, with the bells and tingles and shuffles, the melody of all this ringing between his ears like a phrase from a song he heard on the car radio when he walked into work, it occurred to him that he didn't have to do it this way, that he could win.

He lay down on the bed of his hotel room, listening to the television he'd left on while he'd been out. The movie was *Lawrence of Arabia* and the voice he heard was Anthony Quinn's. He didn't feel drunk anymore, but very alone, and sad. Those days he'd spent in his empty house were angry, and he'd paced, opening drawers and cabinets like he would find something, waiting like he knew what he was waiting for. He'd cried like his youngest son and he only slept an hour or two at intervals throughout the day and night. He wanted to feel alone, but in the morning newspapers scuffed sidewalks and cars would drive off, children would walk to school. In the afternoon he could hear a neighbor's soap operas if he went to the right window in his house, and a meter man passed through his back yard. In the evening the cars would return and there'd be football, basketball, rock'n'roll. From midnight to dawn a digital clock whirred. He was in this new world and he could be hidden, but not alone. Here he was. He turned off the television, letting the darkened room loom with images of the wooden steps outside his office, with a picture of his wife changing her clothes near him, of his children boarding an airplane for a stay in El Paso while he and his wife sorted things out, of his own childhood there, the dirt baseball diamonds, the dirt driveway where he pulled the engine from his first car, the girls he loved so purely, the candles he lit on holidays, the stupid fights he won and lost, his marriage and the move from El Paso and his mother's tears, his father's bony handshake—all as distant and dry as that blue sky, as a story he could tell his children who could speak only English.

He heard voices in the hallway. Young men persuading young women to go in. When their door closed, their existence muffled away, and that was good to him. He had even been about to fall into sleep when he heard something that squeezed his heart until he stood up, frightened, and held still for several seconds. He nudged his shoulder into a wall and heard the hymn music coming from the room next door, from a television or radio. Jesus, the lover of my soul, sung by a choir, accompanied by an organ. He went back to bed relieved. He couldn't take any more surprises and for a moment he thought he'd gone over the ledge. He felt very weary now, even thought he would get some sleep, and he stayed on his back, in the center of the king-size bed, getting up many times throughout the night and morning to drink and to piss, expecting sleep any time, resting in the dark.

●

"What's all this stuff about El Paso?" her husband asked.

"I don't know," Sylvia said like a thief.

"Are you homesick? Is it Christmas? You could go there this Christmas if you want. It's only me that has to be around home this year."

"No."

"Because you don't have to stay home. You could take the boys back with you."

"I don't want to go. I didn't realize I was talking about it that much."

"You could stay those two weeks school's out. I could get an airplane and spend the day."

"I don't want to. Honest. There's just something about Las Vegas that reminds me of it, that's all."

Her husband sighed and fell onto the bed. "You were talking about it before we got here," he reminded her.

Sylvia didn't argue because he was right. She felt embarrassed and wanted the subject changed. "We can all see the Captain and Tennille," she proposed.

"I don't know why you're acting so weird about it. Wanting to be with your family is as Mexican as having babies."

"Let's eat dinner and everything."

"All right," he yawned, stretching on one of the two hard beds in the bright hotel room.

"We'll go make a reservation at that booth we saw in the lobby and you take a nap."

"Good thinking," he said, yawning again.

She took her son's hand and the room key and went out the door and said hello to the two maids, a Black and an Asian, who stopped talking as she and the boy passed almost running.

●

Once Ray made the decision to win, he knew the first thing to do was to have control, so he began by observing the play at dice tables and cards without drinking or gambling. He passed many innocuous hours and finally took a seat at a seven-card stud game and tested his will. He set a two-hour limit on himself. He didn't play when he got bad hole cards, and when one of the players was on a winning streak he didn't stay in if he had a weak though solid hand. When he held a good hand he bet moderately and raised only the last two deals. When he left the table it was with forty dollars more than he had when he sat down.

Later that evening he removed his envelope with the ten thousand dollars from his safe-deposit box at the hotel and walked it to a Texas Hold 'Em table which required a two-hundred dollar buy-in. A simple game, each player getting two cards down which he combines with five cards the dealer turns up on the middle of the table, it is also a game of big winners and big losers, and this one was for particularly high stakes, even by Vegas standards. Already a second row of spectators strained to see over those in the first row, who snuggled against the metal railing that partitioned them off from the players, all of whom showed a minimum of a thousand dollars in green twenty-five-dollar chips and red five-dollar ones.

Ray took the seat at the top of the oval and counted out five thousand dollars, which were quickly transformed into chips for the dealer by a young woman, and his swell of stacks beat all but two of the players, an obese New Yorker with a slobbish cigar and a bag of green chips, and a slit-eyed, deep Southerner who hid under a cap and peered above several highrise-like piles.

Ray played conservatively in the beginning, in order to follow the betting. He quickly discovered that there were really only three serious gamblers—the Southerner, who bought a few hands with large raises and was challenged only one time by the New Yorker, whose two pair beat one, and a Hollywood movie type who lost with average hands, but whose pocket was so full of hundred-dollar bills he didn't seem to worry about it, and an Arab who would never show his cards.

After two hours Ray was about eight hundred dollars down. He had won a hand, dropped out of three, and paid to see two. He'd drank one shot of whiskey early to settle his nerves and it must have worked because, even though he was behind, he felt a confidence he hadn't remembered since he married his wife, since he accepted the job as superintendent. It was something that only happened to a person a few times but which was as palpable as silver dollars in the pocket: he belonged there, an equal to the best, his hidden status hovering over him like a fawning lover. He knew, and he was certain they knew, he was going to walk away a winner.

His chance came about an hour later when he got two tens underneath, spades and diamonds, and the first card the dealer showed was a seven of hearts. The guy from Hollywood bet unusually high, five hundred, and only the Arab and the South- erner, besides himself, stayed. The next card was a two of spades, and he stayed in for the next five-hundred-dollar bet, and for the five hundred more the Southerner used to scare away the other two.

The dealer turned a ten of clubs and Ray met the South- erner's next five hundred with a thousand-dollar raise. When the Southerner notched it up another, he matched it and shoved in all the chips in front of him.

"Let's play 'em up," the Southerner smiled when he called the bet. The table was excited, but no one moved. Ray didn't really understand what he was supposed to do.

"Let's see what ya got there, friend."

"Turn 'em up," suggested the New Yorker. "He wants to negotiate."

He showed his tens. The Southerner had two hearts. It was three tens against a possible flush.

"I'll give ya two to one on the pot," offered the Southerner.

Ray didn't even think it over. He shook his head confidently. Jack of hearts.

"Fifty-fifty," said the Southerner, who'd stood up to see.

Ray shook his head again.

Two of hearts.

The Southerner was immodestly happy and the spectators breathed loudly as he pushed his chair away and reached in for the pot and, nearly hopping, stacked his mound of winnings to new heights. He talked voluably to the players sitting beside him and gave an unsporting stare of triumph at the loser.

Ray counted out four thousand dollars more. He felt more dazed than defeated, weak-kneed but standing. He was more disappointed than angry, not at the Southerner or himself, but at the deeper injustice of things. It did not make sense. It was not fair.

He thought that maybe he should pull out right then as the cards were being dealt around again. If he backed out, he could

WINNERS ON THE PASS LINE

spare himself more loss. That would be the sensible thing to do considering the realities of unemployment, even in Houston. And chances were that he would be wearing those work bags again. He felt blurred by his insecurity, but in this fuzz he made out a queen on the table to match the queen-four in his hand.

He stayed in, as did the Arab and the moviemaker, as did the Southerner, who seemed to be playing this one for fun while he continued to reorganize his chips. After the dealer turned up a four and an ace, Ray upped the pot by five hundred on his two pair, and all stayed.

The dealer turned over another four and Ray made it another five hundred. The Arab dropped out, the moviemaker saw the bet, and the Southerner raised it another five hundred.

The last card was a king. Ray bet another five hundred on his full house, figuring the Southerner to play for that. The moviemaker considered the stakes and his chances, then threw in his cards.

"That plus five," said the Southerner carelessly.

Ray saw that and bet the rest without hesitating.

"I gotta see this one, amigo," the Southerner said. "Let's see what you can do."

Ray matched his queen-four to the table's queen-two fours.

The Southerner could barely contain himself. He flipped over a king-four and hugged the chips to his corner, crying for some racks to put all his money in. The New Yorker laughed. The other players felt no happiness for him, though they showed no signs of pity for the loser either.

Ray walked evenly to his hotel, contented only by knowing that in this defeat he had not been a fool because they were such strong hands that he couldn't have played them any other way. He couldn't say that about many losses. He'd done this gambling to win, and someone else had the better luck, and only luck. It was not always so simple. His wife, for instance, had left him for a richer man who she'd fallen in love with.

He was not sure what to expect next because he was taken by an unusual mood. Late by work standards, it was still early in

Las Vegas. He turned off the lights and opened a window to a windless, cold, desert, a range of mountains and below a tall, arching sky. He listened for something but all he got was some hotel machine and puffs of traffic. It was maybe okay that he lost, even justice of a kind. It was fresh like the cold air, like the winter air in El Paso.

Ray Muñoz closed his eyes on the bed. He waited to shiver with some strong emotion. Instead fell asleep in the chilled silence of the sanitized hotel room.

●

"I don't see how people can do it," her husband said after his night out alone. "It goes too fast and hurts too much."

"Did you win?"

"In a sense. I stopped contributing to the cause."

Sylvia looked away from him.

"You know, I think they've got it rigged, because when I played the dollar slot machines I won right away, on my first pulls. Something like thirty or forty dollars. I thought I had it made, but I never won again after that."

"Is that all you played?" she asked, angry.

"No, I played some blackjack too. It's something, this place. There's so much happening. This man that sat by me was playing twenty dollars a hand and was winning for a long time, but when he started losing he started betting more money. That's how it is here, easy come, easy go. I think the guy was drunk. Did you know that all the drinks are free? Anyway, I couldn't take it. I don't think I can take winning or losing, though it is fun to watch. I wandered all around the casino and counted all the money that other people lost. That felt better than losing all mine."

"Mine," she said seriously.

"Ours," he said automatically. "And I can't waste it. Maybe if it was money someone gave me and told me I *had* to gamble with."

"I did," Sylvia said.

"And then again I doubt if I could do that," he laughed without hearing her. "Hey, we're gonna have to take the baby to the circus shows they have at night. There were these stunt motorcyclists driving inside this ball and it scared the pants off me." He yawned. "I tried to win him a stuffed animal while I was up there. How long's he been asleep?"

"A few hours."

"Too bad they don't have babysitters. It'd be fun to have a drink together." He pulled her down on the bed and even touched her breasts.

"He'll wake up," she said.

He rolled off. "I guess I'm a little drunk already." He looked at the television screen. "What're you watching?"

"I just found it an hour ago. It's a program on how to play the casino games."

"They think of everything, don't they?"

"It's exciting."

"It's not worth the risk though."

"Do you really think that?"

"Yes. I really don't think you can win. Las Vegas exists because people lose. The only money I'd like giving them would be to own a piece of it."

She turned off the television. "I've already seen it twice."

"Leave it on. Maybe there's a Frank Sinatra movie."

●

Ray slept twelve uninterrupted hours, got up and drank water at the bathroom sink, and slept three more. When the sleep was over, and he shook the blood loose in his veins, he felt what he least expected, like he'd won.

He counted the ten crisp hundred-dollar bills he still had. He counted seven twenties he had in his wallet.

His plan had become very simple. He would go back to El

Paso and see his children, he would talk to his brothers and sisters, listen to his mother, visit his father's grave, and, no matter what happened tonight, he would go home a winner.

●

Sylvia stood under a wide archway that divided the hotel lobby from the casino. For two days she'd seen and heard this, but now she was by herself, awed by how quiet it really was and how alone it could make her feel.

She wanted very much to age past this stage in her life. She didn't think it was right of her and she felt guilty and spoiled. Had she not been so fortunate, had she made different choices along the way, she knew she would probably want nothing more than what she had, and she would have undoubtedly settled for less.

She had no idea what her purpose was in this. She didn't know what kind of answer this would present her with, what she would do with it. She only knew that winning would be an answer, and that losing would be an answer. She didn't know which would be preferable, and still she was determined to win.

●

That evening Ray turned the thousand dollars into chips and leaned into a craps table. He played intelligently, and when he didn't feel right, he didn't place any bets. He waited for the dice and a hot hand. He was up, but not making a killing.

Sylvia had not been doing well. She took cards for blackjack and lost, she layed chips on red and black numbers for roulette and lost, though both by the inconclusive nibble of small wagers. She was more short of time than patience or money. And though she had been afraid of craps because the betting was so complicated, and though she was aware that she could just as easily spend her fortune waiting on the click of a ball at a spinning wheel or the snap of a laminated card on a baize table, she knew it had to be the padded tumble of dice.

At first Ray didn't find anything too special about the attractive woman who came to stand across from him, and it was only because he didn't want to bet on a few rolls that he noticed her choosing the poorer odds on the table, like the field and the hard-way numbers. So he watched her, and then he stared at her, and he did this until he felt he had to, until the casino had become nothing more than a faded backdrop of noise and light and color to her. Like the sight of a pretty girlfriend long forgotten, she flushed him with such a strong emotion that it didn't seem a memory but an awakening as conclusive as the one he'd left his hotel with. He stared, certain he didn't know her and never had.

Sylvia had very early become used to men's eyes, and had learned that even though she couldn't ignore them, she could walk away from them. But rather than being distracted by this large man who gawked at her so childlike, she became more focused and sharp. His unwilled admiration was the warmest luck she'd played with all night.

When she was offered the dice by the stickman, Sylvia was down to her last three nickel chips, while Ray was three hundred above his original thousand. When she accepted the dice and bet one five-dollar chip on a pass, Ray put four hundred on the same and then the full extent of the double odds on her point of four, which she threw on the next toss. He put up a thousand on another pass while she let her ten dollars ride and threw a ten. He backed his thousand with two more on the odds, which, like the four, paid two to one. She rolled two times before a four-six combination appeared.

"Winners on the pass line!" the stickman barked. "The table's got a shooter!"

Ray counted out five hundred dollars worth of the chips the dealer gave him in winnings and slid them over to Sylvia. "Please," he said. "Give it back only if we win."

She might have refused, but she was gagged by confusion. She picked up the dice and threw.

"Seven! *Big* winners on the *pass* line!"

Ray wouldn't take back the money he'd left her in the pass line area, and Sylvia considered setting the loan aside in the rack in front of her, but gave into it, to him, and played the line. She had become the one watching now, watching him, and never had she felt so in control and out of control at the same time.

Ray bet on her pass with certainty and when she had a point he took as many come and odds bets as he could get, and she shot lots of numbers. Sylvia let Ray's pass line money ride and made her point three more times in a row, which multiplied into winnings of four thousand dollars. Ray quit when he counted close to forty thousand, and it took racks to carry the chips to the cashier's window.

"Thank you so much," Sylvia said uncomfortably, as though she were standing under her front door porch light. She held out the money she owed him.

"I want you to keep it," he told her in Spanish.

She believed that he was not making some haughty or suave or even the slightest of an insincere gesture. But she did expect him to say something about a drink or food. She'd already thought of how probably she'd have to say no, say something about her husband and son who were waiting, but he did not ask, and it did not seem because he was so overwhelmed by his winnings.

●

Sylvia checked to see that her husband was asleep beside her and listened for her son's breathing in the bed near them. She touched herself slowly. At first it was her hand and then it was not. At first she made her stiff fingers tingle across her skin, and then her palms flattened and her fingers softened and bent. Sometimes the hand would even reach her face, her lips, her eyes. She was warm and unlonely. She felt young and she liked the familiar cold air settling above the blanket. She knew that she could not leave the window open long, but she let herself enjoy every moment it was.

●

In bed much later that night, Ray was thinking again of Sylvia. He had not cheated on his wife in those ten years of marriage, and though as a young man he had a better than average share of dates, he had not had that many lovers, and those he did have he looked back on as much in defeat as in conquest. Maybe he'd be different this time out. He thought of Sylvia and he felt her as though she were next to him on the vacant side of the bed. He felt her without moving, sexually, and he liked it very much.

●

Sylvia and Ray stared at one another as he came into the restaurant for breakfast. He'd chosen the place randomly and seeing her again, by chance, inspired some strange confidence in him.

Sylvia didn't want to draw him into a conversation so she looked away. Sitting there, patiently waiting for her husband to eat his meal, tested her until she realized that Ray wasn't going to say anything. Then she felt very alive.

When her husband finished, Sylvia stood, glancing at Ray self-consciously. Her son scooted the wooden chair away from the table noisily and ran out to the other side of the glass door and smashed his face on it to see back inside. He made faces at Ray who smiled at him from his table.

"Big tip or little?" her husband asked her. "Maybe we should save some to make up for all the losses. We still gotta get home." He left twenty percent.

She couldn't let herself look at Ray on her way out, but she

walked down the restaurant's aisle worried about her appearance. When her husband caught up with her, she still couldn't
think of what to say.

"Are you feeling okay?" her husband asked.

"Just sleepy is all."

"Too much action without the old man last night, huh? You
can nap on the way home."

She took his hand.

"You sure you don't want to go and visit the family for
Christmas?"

"No, really, I only wanted to do this. And I had a good time. I
always wanted to know about Las Vegas, and now I do." She
squeezed his hand.

●

Outside the restaurant, on the famous Strip, Ray couldn't help
but notice the flat plain of black asphalt that belted the under-
lying desert, couldn't help but realize that the miracle of these
steel and concrete casinos and hotels and restaurants were
doomed by the wind and the sun and the sand, couldn't help but
feel good that he was moving around in this impermanent place
like a winner.

PART THREE

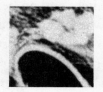

THE SEÑORA

The view from the señora's building was handsome—below its height on the Franklin Mountains sat a wide, manly expanse of land, from the buildings downtown, over the river to Juárez, past its colonias, to the emptiness of the Chihuahua Desert. In the day, in the summer, the land below never budged, and the blue sky would hang above it without end, everywhere, while in the evening the same sight was an ocean mirroring a black, starry air above it. No doubt it was this which attracted the señora to the spot here on the mountain so many years ago when she was young, when she and her husband, who survived only a year back on this side, moved north, wealthy from Mexican mines. So maybe her building wasn't the most plush in the city, but expenses weren't spared either. This could have been a matter of chance—that is to say a matter of history, because it was built in the days when property and labor were especially easy to come by—though it could equally be argued that for someone of her wealth and position, life had always been cheap in El Paso.

Maybe cheap, but never easy. Anyone who had lived here knew this. Jesus knew, and Jesse had learned it. They both knew this woman—the señora was all they ever called her— wouldn't for one moment let them think it could have been another way. Not that they would mention this to her, not that she'd have to remind them of it, or even bring it up once. Not that they thought about it all.

They did think about her, though. Maybe for the obvious reasons. Like that Jesus, a national without documents, often got work from her, both here and on her ranch in New Mexico, and that his wife, who was also undocumented, was her maid. Like that Jesse rented one of the guest houses, in these times called a furnished apartment, for practically nothing, even when he paid, which he hadn't every month because the señora didn't always notice. But there was more to it than that. They thought about her because it would be impossible not to.

●

In the four months he was a tenant, Jesse seldom came out of his apartment. When he did, he always had a shirt off and dark glasses on. Since there was no one around to ask him what he was doing in El Paso, why, how, no one but Jesus made a question of anything, and his was only where Jesse was from. California, Jesse told him, the Bay Area. And even that was answered with a caution Jesus could read. But despite first appearances, Jesse was gentle and soft-spoken, friendly toward Jesus, who was as kind as the name of the village he'd come from, La Paz.

"Coffee?" Jesse asked with a leg outside his screen door. His shirt was not on, and a blue tattoo of an eagle spanned his hairless chest.

"Of course," said Jesus, pleased. He rested his roller in the bucket of white paint and wiped his hands on the brown cotton pants he worked in. Then he adjusted his paint-splattered Houston Astros baseball cap and waited at the steps near Jesse's door.

Jesse came back and stepped outside with two mugs of hot instant coffee he'd already sweetened. "You keep going as fast as you are and you'll paint yourself out of the money." The arm with the black widow tattoo held out a mug for Jesus.

"The señora told me when I finish with this she has more for

me, like the rooms inside, and some other things too." Jesus had
been defensive ever since he perceived that Jesse didn't approve
of the wage he'd accepted for the work.

"It's hot," said Jesse.

"I think it's just right," Jesus said, referring to the coffee.

"I'm talking about the sun, the heat. That it's already hot."

"Oh. Yes. A little." He hadn't thought about it.

They drank the coffee under the wooden eaves of the building while the chicharras, the cicadas, clicked on and off like
small motors.

●

It was always quiet when the señora wasn't there. She wasn't
physically loud when she was around, but even her unseen
presence filled what was silence otherwise. So the noise she
made the day she died wasn't surprising. Both Jesus and Jesse
heard it from the beginning and neither thought anything
peculiar about it. She was throwing a tantrum at a nurse—the
woman, anyway, who wore a white uniform. The señora fired
her, screamed at the woman as she was helping the señora into
the wheelchair. The señora told her to get back in her car and to
go and to not come back. The nurse obliged and drove down
the unpaved alley, popping her tires off the rocks, dusting the
air. The señora rolled herself across the rocky path until she got
to the smooth cement sidewalk. Neither Jesus nor Jesse moved
to help her, instinctively knowing better. When the señora got
to her door she began screaming about that nurse still having
the keys. She stood with her cane, and then, standing on her old
legs, heaved that cane into the glass panes of the door. That's
when Jesus came over. He couldn't understand all she was
wailing about in English, but he broke out a square of glass and
reached inside and turned the deadbolt. When the door still
didn't open, the señora tensed again and screamed more. She
was not sweating, but she was breathing with a loud hiss. Jesus

couldn't get it opened, and the señora hollered. That's when Jesse came over. He positioned himself, then kicked the door. It splintered the jamb and sprang into an arc. The señora did not thank them as she went inside, and left behind the wheelchair and the two men. She screamed and complained from within her home. Jesus and Jesse returned to what they were doing, which is to say Jesus rolled white paint onto the plaster walls and Jesse went to the other side of the screen door where he couldn't be seen.

●

It got hugely quiet. Jesse stepped out of his apartment, and Jesus looked over to him.

"We better see," Jesse told Jesus.

"Yes. It's what I'm thinking."

They entered the señora's home, the mahogony and crystal and silver sparkling with cleanliness. She was sprawled on her rug, the stem of a rose in the carpet's pattern seeming to hook between her teeth. Her eyes were closed, but an ornery scowl kept the señora from looking peaceful. The combination suited her death. There was nothing at all sad about seeing her like this, and neither man felt a twinge of sentimentality. They simply respected the finality of it.

Later, after people had come for her body, Jesus tried to finish the section of wall he'd started, while Jesse went back to his apartment. In those hours, the chicharras, hundreds of them, drilled without pause at the sky. They were the reason the memory of that day became so inexhaustible, and they were what both men, in their separate lives, talked about from the moment they moved on and told this story.

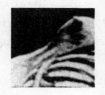

BALLAD

The truth was that Cowboy Mike Duran had been getting miserably sick. So sick he'd finally let a doctor have his way. He'd allowed himself to be strapped to a soft bench, and he'd stared up into the wormy black patterns of the acoustical tiles. The laboratory was new and clean, crisp with the aroma of fresh plastic, alert with the intelligent stares of computer screens, their invisible grids always accommodating more and more fluorescent numbers and letters. As Mike Duran's skull penetrated the machine's cylinder, the radioactive hum he heard, and swore he felt, reminded him of television, and that made him think of Texas. Mike Duran thanked God for union benefits, because he knew this was not any ordinary office visit.

Mike wasn't surprised that the test didn't discover anything. The doctor had wanted to find out what the trouble was, but all Mike wanted was a prescription for pills. For Mike there was no mystery whatever—it was death, and that was not going to show up on an x-ray, no matter where some doctor thought it might be. Of course this was not an opinion he offered openly. It was only that the sickness, the thoughts that came with them, convinced him of this overwhelming fact. Pills, strong ones, were the only hope that these thoughts would go away, despite that fact, though not immediately. At first they simply redirected the more specific pain in his head to an overall disgust and nausea. In other words, first he was sick, and then he got sick as he fought that off, and in either case he'd miss a day of work. Sometimes he'd take the pills—always much more than the recommended dose—and stay at the job. Usually when he did that it meant he'd lose the next work day anyway, because he'd have to recuperate from the combined exhaustion of work and over-medication. Sometimes he'd both take the pills and stay home, which often meant he'd lose two days. All of this had the obvious effect on his employment—he went through jobs. He'd get so unhappy or so unhealthy that, if he didn't get laid off, he'd quit. Which meant he was not always making money, which meant he felt pressured, which meant he'd worry, get angry about everything, and think that was why he got sick.

Nobody he worked with knew any of this. He only went to the union hall, signed the out-of-work list, and waited for the time to try again. In the trades, there were lots of reasons for a man to go through jobs, many good, many not so good. In either case, the discussion at the hall usually broke down like this: the job, according to a man who'd been there, was a bad one, run by assholes, designed by idiots, worked by suckasses; or, in the opinion of another man, the guy claiming that was such an incompetent he couldn't keep a job if the only thing he had to do in eight hours was sign a paycheck. It was often hard to know which was the truth, but reputation usually dictated which of those two views would rule the outlook at the hall, since every building that'd been started found men who'd stay to the end, who'd do it whether it was good work or not. Every job could be criticized, every job could be praised. But which-ever the case, a man who was at the hall, who was out of work, had to give a reason for this, a convincing one whether a lie or the truth, because that was the nature of the men who chose the trades as the way to make their living.

Cowboy Mike's reputation was solid. He hadn't always been sick, and over the years he'd established himself at jobs so large that many men had come to know him and his sweaty, honest style of work. There was no reason for anyone not to believe that he was absolutely sincere when he blamed the union and the times. His claim was that the union had gotten so weak that just about anything could go at a jobsite and nobody'd say a word about it. Contractors didn't have to worry about safety, didn't have to treat a man with respect, because the hall could, and would, always send another. He said he was tired of having some prick scream at him like he worked on four furry legs, and that he was tired of getting in arguments with morons who, as he put it, were so stupid that they thought everyone around them was stupider. Mike could go on, and often would, about what union was supposed to stand for, like dignity and security and craft, and about non-union. He liked to talk about Texas when he talked about non-union. How he used to work in Texas and was paid so little, how he'd have to have his own power tools at those jobs, and how at one some guy had plugged him into a 220-volt outlet and burned out his personal saw, which got him sent home without pay. He particularly liked to say this: non-union is you falling off the side of a building and the foreman running over screaming "You're fired!" before you hit the ground and workman's compensation goes into effect.

For him personally, it was more complicated than that. In his own local, Mike knew the officers, and in particular the business agent, an alcoholic and the most powerful man at the hall, played favorites, and took money. Cowboy Mike knew these things because he knew men who told him how it worked for them. And he'd seen transactions with his own eyes. For all his talk to the men, Mike Duran did not consider himself either a fool or a hero. Like anyone else, he wanted to survive. So in the morning and at the job dispatch window he played-up his knowledge to the BA, implying, never outright saying, he wanted in on it.

There were other details about Cowboy Mike Duran. Like, for instance, that he grew up without parents. His grandparents raised him, and there was no certainty that they were his blood. They never said so, and both were dead before he had the courage to ask them. He had no birth certificate. He knew of no other relatives. What he was told was that he was born in Texas, and growing up in an old, deteriorating neighborhood of Los Angeles, the state of Texas took on mythic proportions in his mind. Mike Duran, whose childhood was so confined by the smells and movements of old age, made his mother and father a knobless black-and-white television, and from that he learned his heritage, his personal approach to life. That was why, after his grandmother died, he took his only trip ever and ever since to Texas, first to El Paso, then up to Dallas, then down to San Antonio, the city where he met his wife. When he came back to L.A. married, he was driving a pickup with Texas plates, which he kept from then on registered there, and he was distinguishing a cowboy hat which, also from then on, he wore whenever he was behind the wheel. It was after this that he acquired the nickname Cowboy. And he liked that a lot.

Cowboy Mike Duran got into construction because he thought it was the only work that was still Western. He thought it wasn't much different than what cattlemen and trailer drivers, wildcatters and roughnecks did in the earlier days. They were drinking, brawling, whoring, hard-working men whose jobs tangled them up with the outdoors, men whose clothes were secondary to what was inside them, men whose independence was so dogged they'd do it alone if they had to, without cranes or dozers or backhoes, with two hands if it came down to getting the job done, and who afterwards would move on without a second thought to the next job. Cowboy Mike Duran, in so many words, was as committed to union about as much as he was to the belief that he was from Los Angeles.

●

Cowboy Mike finally felt better and came those days when he was ready to go at it again, and came a day when the BA waved him over to the dispatch window to tell him, with a wink, that he was gonna like this one.

He wasn't lying. It was a site for a sixteen-story highrise on Sunset Boulevard, at the real center of Cowboy Mike Duran's existence, where billboards were as bright as lights and as big as banks, where pastel restaurants had names like poodles and atmospheres like clubs, where body-conscious men and women dressed like famous actors, or musicians, or producers, or just plain cool and rich. It matched everything Cowboy Mike ever wanted—here he could be admired, his muscles veined with sweat, a real live Marlboro man across the street from where the largest cut-out one in the world never did more than hold a rope.

The job itself was like all the others. Three men, along with Mike, went out, and the three were laid off within the week. An old man, who was working on his thirtieth year toward a pension, got it because he was slow. A black guy got it because he didn't know the work, and the carpenter born in Mexico because he didn't speak English well enough. None of them were told this of course. What they were told was that there wasn't enough work. It wasn't smart to say anything else, to open things up to lawsuits, just as it wasn't smart to hint at the deeper truth—that the guys who ran the job didn't like old men, most blacks, or Mexicans who weren't laborers. If Mike would have been laid off, he'd have been the first to say something about these injustices, but, especially from within the barricading of the jobsite, employed, he also could admit to the logic of their thinking: a good crew was one that liked each other, and a good crew got the work out. Construction operated on schedules, and missing them meant losing money. Why shouldn't a company have the right to let go of any man it thought would cost it profits? The same logic explained why those men were replaced by others not from the union hall, who were not even union until they got a card from the BA, who obviously thought that was good enough for him.

The steward on the job, the man who represented the union hall and union principles, who was the only one who could hear a complaint and take it over to a foreman or super without any fear of being fired, was called Bud. He doubled as the job foreman. He was brother of the superintendent, Charles W. Hobbs, whose name was that of the company, Charles W. Hobbs Construction. Besides these two, there was a son of Charles W., little Charles or Charlie, and there were the other brothers Ben, Mack and Preston. The Hobbs brothers were born in San Angelo, and each had trickled west to Los Angeles, one by one, for the work that oldest brother Charles W. was getting more and more of. Hobbs Construction was union only when the job required, and this one did because the rodbusters, from the United Brotherhood of Ironworkers, wouldn't work any job beside non-union men, period. There was no way Charles W. Hobbs could find a non-union crew of steelmen who'd work a job this size.

The Hobbs brothers liked Cowboy Mike, and not just because of the Texas background he claimed, less forcefully around them of course. Cowboy Mike could work, and since he'd been on lots of highrises over the years, in most respects he knew more than anyone else on the job. That's why they let him work with anyone he wanted, doing whatever he wanted to do, though if a wall or deck or some columns really needed getting done, Bud or Charles W. would ask him, and Mike would have it ready for concrete on time.

Mike loved his work, and his outlook on life brightened each day that went by with him employed and healthy. He even made a special point of waving howdy to the BA when he stopped by and talked to Bud over at the corner of the jobsite when it'd reached street level. Mike figured the BA came around for a payoff. If he'd been sick, that'd be sure to fly him into a rage. But Cowboy Mike felt great, and didn't even care for a second that most—maybe all—of the crew took home two checks every week, one for hours that would be reported to the IRS, the other, from a separate account, for straight-time cash which wouldn't be reported by the company or the man who got it. This was something they'd never talked about to him directly, he figured because the BA was in on it and had told them not to be too sure of Cowboy Mike yet.

His one check cashed, and that was enough for him. Besides, he was having fun. Because of the job's location, photographers were often around taking pictures, and one time Mike, a healthy looking man, was asked if he wouldn't mind having some shots specifically taken of him. Of course Mike didn't mind.

The one he liked the most was the one of him with his shirt off, his cowboy hat on, standing with some of the guys drinking beer next to his pickup after work. That was the one he claimed was the best when it came out in *California* magazine, in a glossy photo essay titled "Men at Work." Along with a farmer, a steelworker, a butcher, and a firefighter, it was one of several pages of Mike Duran at the job. But naturally it was the photo on the cover that made the biggest impression. Cowboy Mike Duran, his face as strong as any Indian's, his body as brown as wet earth, all muscle and hardhat, bags and hammer, a cord stretched out and a worm-drive skilsaw near him, became every man who banged at it, who built buildings.

●

Then the sickness began making its comeback. He tried to exorcise it with a good attitude and over-the-counter pills in front of a morning cup of coffee. At first that worked, which it always did. A whole week could go by. Gradually the pain got worse when he woke up in the morning. He'd take the stronger prescription pill and a handful of the others to the job. He'd maybe sweat more on the job, but in his sleep he was worrying. Certain kinds of dreams would tell him the sickness was in the shadows. He'd think it was too much sleep, so he'd stay up later and watch television. He'd think it was too little sleep. He'd drink more, he'd drink nothing. The pattern was a routine: Cowboy Mike Duran got sick bad and started missing a day or two of work every other week.

Either way, in the pain or the relief from it through pills, Mike Duran would play-back his childhood. His grandparents were old, and they were always worried. What they worried about was never clear to him, and he never asked—he turned on the television. It was the only piece of furniture that was not chipped, whose varnish was not peeling away the same way he imagined his grandfather's skin was. He'd finally died when Mike was seven or eight, he couldn't exactly remember. And then Mike's grandmother stopped talking in Spanish, for his benefit. Mike stopped listening and talking at all. He made his own meals. Cans, of soup, vegetables, fruit. He cooked hamburger meat. She made beans. If he didn't have the TV on, he'd sometimes stare at a knot in the slats of wood on the ceiling in the same room. He could stare at that knot until it came alive. One time he saw it as a black snake, coiled. He ran into his grandmother's room and found her in her bed, a woman so much more weak than he, and he stopped himself from telling her. He was in junior high then.

This sickness was like that snake. It slithered through him slowly, fearlessly, raising its head each time it came on some new detail from his present. Its venom was bitter—he'd take pills— and that detail would numb, twisting, a frenzy of ugly meaning until it was overcome, when a calm, serene afterglow of remembrance would settle in. In those moments he would know himself with a clarity that he knew could only be death.

●

Hobbs Construction did employ carpenters who weren't relatives of Charles W., but, with the exception of Cowboy Mike, they were related to someone by friendship. Friends of family, however, were not family. Charles W. was the only one of them that couldn't be described as either dumb or lazy, and there was little doubt that his brothers' and son's working days would have been much less picturesque if the company didn't exist. Their friends covered for them consistently, and gratefully, to all appearances. A healthy Cowboy Mike Duran would say he didn't care about that either—it wasn't his money, and the worse they were, the better he looked.

Since his picture had been on the cover of *California* magazine, Mike was given more slack than could usually be expected. It seemed everyone was more pleased to see him back than irritated that he hadn't showed up. That was the biggest payment he'd received for his fame. If everybody's fantasy was to be recognized on the cover of a magazine, it was no less so for a working man whose only achievement was doing what just about everyone took for granted, and it was the same for Mike too, except that his health had taken away some of the pleasure he imagined was also supposed to be his. He'd have thought his life would change somehow, in some big way. Instead, he didn't make more money, nobody called him to make a movie, women weren't throwing themselves in his way as he passed by. He still got sick. Nothing was like he expected.

He imagined that if it weren't for the sickness his life would be a whole lot different, that he'd be some other person. Maybe he wouldn't be union, maybe he'd be an independent like he always thought a man should be. If only things had gone as well as that trip he took to Texas. That had been the one thing in his life that'd turned out like he'd wanted it to, the way it was supposed to. He'd come back with a sense of place, of people, of land, of past. Everything since had been a disappointment, and he was sure it was because of the sickness. It wouldn't let him have the kind of stories he wanted to tell.

Sickness was what made him begin to resent watching the Hobbs boys not working, reminded him of the many times he'd seen men get their checks, how they were the ones who didn't know anybody, had no daddy or brother or uncle. He thought this particularly the day Bud, whose belly was so large he could eat his lunch off it, and who was the same age as Mike, asked Mike to walk a beam soffit to hold a grade stick so that he and Charlie, who usually stood the stick up, could get a reading. Hobbs Construction was not the safest outfit he'd ever worked for by any stretch, but that was something he didn't care much about except on these days. He'd already taken three of the prescription pills and too many others, and he was unsteady on hard ground, and right then fat Bud wanted him, not little Charles, to walk a twelve-inch beam soffit for twenty feet. Below, the scaffolding and x-bracing, stacked two high, wobbled sloppily, unsecured, unleveled. The soffit's plywood rested on 2x4s on edge, because Hobbs Construction, which hadn't before worked a building this large, didn't want to spend money on more stable 4x4s, which wouldn't roll over if a man's step was wrong. On either side of the beam were open holes four stories deep where elevators would be.

Cowboy Mike Duran couldn't tell anybody about his being sick, because he could not. He wouldn't tell anybody about taking too many pills, about weakness and fear. He didn't know how to talk about these things. So he stepped along the beam, a black shaft of death on each side of him, a blue Western sky above. And when he did make it to the other end, he held that stick up for as long as it took dumb, fat Bud to read his mark, and then he walked back across without complaining. But when Bud signaled and yelled for him to do it a second time—because he didn't think his gun had been set up right—Cowboy Mike Duran thought about the union, Texas, and death.

●

He tried to ignore that snake, and he'd moved a chair around the room so he wouldn't notice it. He moved the television. None of it did any good. He ate TV dinners with it above him. His whole childhood it was coiled above him. Once he stared into its jaws and let himself enter. It was dark and frightening, but then that went away, just as time did. Just as time did watching a movie on the television. Good guys, bad guys, guns, horses, right, wrong. The West.

THE RAT

There was something nagging me about being in the city, and the rat started out as just another thing the day my wife said it got in. She'd opened the door with the baby in her arms and screamed about it clawing up our side of the screen. It took me a couple of minutes to understand, but after I did I went to the door with a plastic trash bucket and a straw broom. When I looked, the rat was gone. My wife was sure it was in the apartment, but she told me when she slammed the door it was eye level on the screen. I told her it couldn't be here inside but she didn't believe me and I wasn't positive I was right. The rat had chewed a towel we had stuffed at the bottom to keep out the cold, and shreds of it were on the outside, which to me was proof that it couldn't squeeze through the crack, though maybe it could once the towel was moved away. They can do a lot of things when they want to.

Under normal circumstances they don't mean that much to me. I mean rats exist, rats hang out in city basements and attics and once in a while they get into your place. Anyone could hear them scratching across our ceiling. I think the rain had upset them too because it seemed like I heard many little feet. We'd seen a couple of dead ones on the street outside our building that'd gotten run over by cars. They were on the move. I made sure all the openings to the attic in our apartment were nailed closed. I felt pretty confident that they wouldn't start dropping in on us from above, and I wasn't convinced that that one at the front door was inside.

Then we saw chewings next to the cast-iron grill in the living room where the gas had long ago been cut off. To me it was evidence that another one was trying to get in. But my wife said it was the same rat, and she swore she saw it in the kitchen too and she talked about the baby and how she couldn't leave him alone when she was in there cooking or cleaning up and that she tried to keep him in a playpen in the other room but he cried too much. I said okay, I believe you, and finally I did see one. It was in a bottom cabinet, below the sink. I tried to catch it with the broom and plastic trash bucket but it got away from me. I closed the kitchen door so it couldn't escape to another room and I thought it went under the refrigerator. Things inside spilled and fell as I dragged it into the middle of the kitchen and leaned it against an open wall and got onto the floor to sweep at the sticky dust of the machinery. But it was as though the rat had disappeared. I propped up the stove and looked underneath that. I took out everything in the bottom cabinets and dumped out drawers. Nothing.

I bought poison and fed it to dark corners. I went to a local market for a large trap but settled on four smaller ones for mice. I loaded them with cheese and peanut butter and apple pieces. My wife worried incessantly about the baby finding one. It kept raining and the roof leaked. We had pots that caught the big drips. An electric heater followed us through our rituals of sleep and food and diaper changes. I didn't want to move, and I told my wife that we couldn't afford to pay any higher rent so to quit talking about it.

When I heard the rat in the wall at the head of our bed I told my wife she had to go home and I had to be alone. I bought her a train ticket because the weather wasn't safe for flying or bus. She was on the train two days later. On my way home from the station the windshield wipers couldn't smear an image that remained of the baby's face asleep on the seat where I'd placed him. I'd kissed his warm, soft head and I'd said goodbye to my wife and kissed her. An old couple near us, sitting close together and wrapped in heavy coats, smiled at us nostalgically and they made me more conscious, fixed the time into a series of snapshots.

I went around the apartment picking up toys. Any day before this one I never would have noticed them. I'd sit down thinking I'd gotten them all and then I'd spot another. I'd hold it, squeeze it, and pile it in a closet with the others. When I did get them all, I sat disoriented. But soon I could make out sounds. The rain had been coming down for hours, and if I let it it could even drown out the thumping bass next door. I'd told the neighbors that if I heard the music once more they'd never listen to that stereo again. But all this made me understand that the neighbors were just people. The music wasn't loud.

At night, on my back in bed, I kept the curtains open. I liked the street lights and shadows, the mirror lit up by the city. When I was about to doze off, I heard the rat. It was gnawing something, like a stud in the wall. I wanted to bust that spot open to catch it but I contained myself. Instead of sleeping, I listened to the rat clawing and scratching up and down and I was close to certain that at one point it jumped on a shelf and onto the floor under the sink, which was on the other side of the bedroom wall. I listened to the wood trickle down from near the ceiling. I imagined that it was trying to make an entry and exit.

I got a large trap. I cleaned out the cabinet under the kitchen sink and I fixed it so that the rat couldn't get out of that area. Weeks went by and I'd often hear it, chewing and crawling. I'd hit the wall with a hammer I kept near the bed and I'd hear the rat scramble and be still. I'd try to go to sleep, but if I thought about it too long I got so angry I would lose hours and have to concede the bedroom and take the living room.

It continued to rain and the winds blew. A metal garbage can lid flew through a window of the neighbors' apartment with the thumping bass. The wind poured inside and tipped over lamps and the rain that accompanied it ruined the stereo receiver. A week later there was an electrical blackout and the whole neighborhood was free of music and television and light. There were fewer cars. It rained hard and I found a box of five votive candles and melted the bottom of one to a plate. It rained and rained.

A boy from the building, Martín, asked if it would be okay if he stayed with me until his aunt—he had no parents—got home from work. He was thirteen or fourteen. He told me they didn't have any candles at his place. He didn't say he was scared but we talked about the wind and the rain and the darkness. It was awkward at first. We sat at the table and watched the wax run down the candle. The dim white light was more than enough. I could see all the boy's features. I could see what he looked like as a baby and I could see how he'd look as a man. He was at that age. I cooked some eggs and toasted bread in the leftover butter and when he heard his aunt I gave him a candle and matches.

I liked the darkness and the silence. I liked it even more the next night. I was feeling better. I went outside when it stopped raining. There was lightning not that far away, deceptively above the tall buildings of downtown. The storm looked especially dark and threatening. For once the city seemed small and vulnerable, the hills and streets uninhabited. My own feelings were large and open and I sat on the front steps with Martín. Neither of us were cold. We didn't have much to say to one another, which was unusual because we talked the night before and in the warmer days had thrown around a football and baseball. When the rain returned we lit another candle inside and I fried more eggs and toast. He fell asleep on the couch and I used the phone. I told my wife I felt better and she told me everything was okay, the baby was doing fine. I could hear him near the phone, reaching for it, she said. I told her that I'd work this all out. I didn't tell her I considered going away.

In the bedroom the next night, the third night without electricity, I couldn't sleep and I realized it was not because of the rat. I jumped up and struck a wooden match and passed the flame to the candle. I went to the cabinet beneath the sink and opened it. I pointed the dim light into the space and I saw it, its bloodied snout caught under the u of metal. Its eyes were open but cold and a turned-up lip exposed its sharp upper teeth. It was as long as my hand and its fur was gnarled. I set the candle down and went for some pliers. When I returned, the candle was flickering. The tiny shadows it cast hopped around the dead rat unevenly, flashing the body like a police photographer. I squeezed the trap between the pliers and carried it to a dumpster. It was raining so powerfully that I held my head down to the left, looking away from the rat. At the dumpster I took one last gaze at the soft flesh dangling from the trap. The rain screamed down and I didn't fight it off. I released the rat and kept the trap. I went inside and took a warm shower in the dark. I put on dry clothes and went to bed with the heater turned up and the candle burning nearby.

There was electricity late the next afternoon. Martín came over anyway, asking if he could watch my set because theirs wasn't working. I watched a couple of shows with him and he went home. It was good having someone in the apartment. Another storm was overhead but it wasn't raining. There were no winds. I still occasionally heard clawings across the ceiling.

I woke up in the middle of the night swearing there was a rat under the sink or probably in the wall, so I tapped it with my hammer. Nothing. I wasn't convinced. I got up and switched on the lights in the kitchen and set up the same trap, though I'd heard that they can smell one that's been used and won't go near it.

I thought I heard another one there more than a few times, but it could have easily been my imagination. I was getting used to being alone, and it was probably better that I lived this way here, but when the sun started breaking through the clouds I decided my wife and baby should come back. The city was falling into its routine again too, the cars and buses and helicopters, all the sirens, the neighbors' new stereo. I think I might have even gotten used to that but they moved out a few weeks later.

FRANKLIN DELANO ROOSEVELT WAS A DEMOCRAT

That morning, the second day of what would be only three days of work, Bobby Diaz drove toward the freeway onramp still blinking from a sweet dream. It was a good tired to him because he liked to work, and he didn't figure he had anything to lose taking a job out there in Santa Monica, even if it was only supposed to last a week. He was trying to learn to live like everyone said he had to, by going where the work was and getting used to the drive. This morning he was ready. After dinner last night he'd filled up his truck with gas and bought batteries for his portable radio. This morning he felt like a million.

Back in El Paso a million still meant something. It was maybe the largest number a person like Bobby could count up to, and even then it was just about impossible to fix in the brains. Bobby Diaz drove innocently toward and then onto the onramp of the Golden State Freeway in the darkness—the sun poking at the horizon, the drone of an open window and his three-speed transmission a calming melody—when he saw what a small-change guy he was here in Los Angeles: all those cars, their lights like strings of rubies and diamonds, flashing, sparkling, glistening, all the cars within this wail and surge, this pull and push, made Bobby open his eyes large. He clicked on his radio to rock'n'roll and lifted his head and straightened his posture and drove the accelerator toward those headlights and taillights, the bumpers and tires and lines and lanes and signs, asphalt and concrete and steel. Bobby pushed it to the Santa Monica Freeway and within the million he steered and drove— this is what people do, this is how people get to work—and drove and steered to the San Diego Freeway and he pulled off on Santa Monica Boulevard and parked in a lot two blocks away from a jobsite, a ten-story highrise, where all kinds of cars and trucks, most much prettier than his faded truck, had already parked.

"So how was it?" Joe de la Garza asked him.

"How was what?"

"The traffic. You think I'm asking about your old lady? I would like to meet her though."

"Too fast, Homes. It moves out."

"I thought you boys from El Chuco were bad. Can't even take a little L.A. freeway?"

"Shit, man," said Bobby, "it took me a fucking half-day to make it home last night. Tonight I go the streets again. Fuck it."

"My house is ten minutes from here," said Joe.

"Your house costs eight-fifty a month too, Homes," Bobby came back. "And my rent is paid."

Joe didn't offer any of his thermos coffee so Bobby went to the roach coach for some and a danish. Joe accepted the offer of half the pastry. Joe wore a watch but the two of them waited for all the other guys to get to work first. They had to wait anyway. They'd built some stairs for the manlift yesterday and would build a landing today as soon as those thirteen 450-pound drums filled with concrete were rolled up and inside the cage for a brake test.

They waited until the foreman, Howard McCann, informed them that moving the drums was their job too. So they doubled planks and set pairs of them next to each other and began straining their milk. The elevator operator, an old man named

Frank Lopez, told them to be careful. He held up an ugly finger on his right hand.

"Five months ago I smashed it. It was a half-hour before we went home and I didn't think it was nothing. But when I got on the freeway it started hurting more and more. That was the longest traffic jam I was ever in. They took off my fingernail and bled it and said I crushed the bone. Then, to top it off, the very next day the company had problems and shut down the job. I got one day of work."

Frank insisted on helping because he didn't have much else to do yet, and the three men worked up a sweat, especially when there was an audience, like when McCann and the superintendent were standing around. And when two pretty women happened to be passing by, Joe rolled a drum to the bottom of the planks by himself, and, once all three of them got it up and inside the lift, moved it around and stood it up by himself, puffing out like a rooster. Once they were left alone, they went at it more slowly, taking breathers after each.

After all thirteen drums were loaded on, an inspector came with a clipboard for the brake test. A button on a remote control box he held directed the manlift to the top, another let it fall, and a third stopped it. The inspector said something about it having a proper two-foot skid and that was that before breaktime.

"You guys aren't going to vote for Reagan, are you?" asked Frank. The three men sat on the sidewalk watching the traffic pile up and then stretch out at the signal. Bobby and Joe talked about being Democrats.

"I don't care what they say," said Frank, "we're doing worse. Except for that one day, tomorrow I would be unemployed for one full year. Tomorrow to the day."

"You started today, huh?" asked Bobby. "We started yesterday. It feels bad being out."

"I started going crazy," said Frank. "I was thinking I really would go crazy. My wife works about three hours a day, and my son goes to college and works for the Pep Boys, but that's only eighty dollars a week. Unemployment called me in and told me I owed them money because I didn't report that one day I worked. I worked that one day the whole year. But I did report it. Only I reported it on the form for the next week when I got the check and I told them to look it up. And it was like I said too. I'll tell you something, there was as many people there then as there was the first day I went."

"Sometimes I think Reagan has some good things to say," said Joe. "I don't like the idea of the Russians telling us what to do."

Frank stared at Joe. "I've only liked two presidents," he said. "Franklin Delano Roosevelt and John F. Kennedy. Reagan's a lot of talk, and he's only for the rich. He doesn't care about the people."

"I just heard Reagan talk something about Roosevelt," said Joe.

"But Franklin Delano Roosevelt was a Democrat," Frank told him, irritated.

The three men unloaded the test weights after break, which was easier than loading them, but still not much fun since they had to be put in a particular spot where the superintendent wanted them. After that, Bobby and Joe went for material to build the landing. Bobby was a more experienced carpenter than Joe, even though Joe was almost ten years older, and so there were some difficult minutes early the day before as Bobby established that fact. Generally, when two men come together as partners, the older man is expected to lead, but Joe didn't know how to build stairs, and now that they were going to build the platform, it seemed to Bobby that the issue had been settled. He was wrong. Joe took out his tape. Bobby would have preferred following, but it was obvious that as much as Joe wanted to lead, he couldn't. Right off he wasn't sure what the "best way" was, and so he asked for Bobby's opinion. Bobby told him, then showed Joe when Joe asked him to, until he finally let Bobby have the lead back, no more words exchanged. Bobby didn't want problems with Joe because he hoped the job would last more than a week—if not right now, there was still a lot of work for carpenters coming up, and lots of times a company kept on a pair even during the slow time. So Bobby wanted to get along with Joe.

The day before, the two of them, working at Bobby's pace, had had a good day of it and got along so well that they slipped over to the 7-Eleven and got themselves a six-pack, which they drank at a distance from the job in Joe's car. At quitting time both the superintendent and McCann told them that they liked Bobby's and Joe's work and were surprised by how quick they were getting it done. Bobby smiled at Joe, and Joe smiled at the bosses. Today Bobby felt like he was working beside another man. Joe had stopped talking to him altogether and when the bosses came by he noticed Joe was on a first-name basis with both of them. So when Bobby asked Joe to take it easy, told him the job would get done soon enough without rushing, Joe's ignoring him meant more than quiet. The landing platform was built and decked before lunch.

Joe didn't try to persuade Bobby to come with him to the store this day. He didn't even suggest it. So Bobby walked over to the lunch truck and bought a burrito and some cottage cheese and an orange juice. He sat with Frank on the landing.

"So no more frijoles at your house after today," Bobby said.

Frank laughed. "My wife can make them taste all different kinds of ways and I have thanked God many times for that."

"Fucking Joe told me yesterday he couldn't even make his rent last month. I'm not doing so good either. I've been hearing about all this work that's gonna break for three months already. Everybody says in two weeks, in two weeks. It makes you nervous. I need money so bad I let go of my number at the hall and took this one. They say a week, but we better get at least a month."

Frank thought and said, "My son comes home and says 'Mom, I'm hungry, can't we have some meat?' I have to tell him he doesn't even know what hunger is. When I was young my mother put a handful of beans in some water and that would be our dinner. To feed the baby she'd pick out a bean from the soup with her fingers and put it in his mouth. Our stomachs would hurt sometimes." Frank pushed both hands on his stomach and leaned forward to show how it looked.

Across the street, Joe backed his car into a space. He didn't look over at the other two men at first. He was drinking a beer.

"Where's he from?" Frank asked.

"Arizona."

"Goldwater. That's why."

"I was at another job he was at too, but I didn't work with him before. I think he's mad at me or something."

Frank thought and said, "Franklin Delano Roosevelt was the only good president besides Kennedy. I still want to lose my temper if anybody says something bad about him. I don't know what we would have done if I didn't get a job with the CCC. They sent me away from that camp in New Mexico to Colorado. And during the war there was work in Los Alamos. I voted for him every time and I would have voted for him again. We would have starved without him. We would have starved, and this is the United States of America. I was born in New Mexico, you know, and so were my parents."

Lunch break was almost finished when Joe came over with a can of beer in a sack.

"Nobody'd ever guess what you got there, Homes," said Bobby, who hoped that in any case the beer would lighten Joe up some.

"Isn't it something what they're letting across the border these days?" Joe said to Frank.

But the beer didn't help. With the landing done, they had to put the railing on it, and Joe took quick charge of that. So Bobby humped material from the other side of the site while Joe cut and nailed. When Bobby got back from one trip he saw Joe standing with McCann talking over how he wanted it done. Bobby worried about him understanding, but short of insulting Joe he didn't know what he could say or do, so he let it go, hoping that maybe, no matter why, Joe would feel better and want to get along.

When they finished, Joe, wordlessly, went over to the super- intendent's trailer to find out what was next: plywood was to wing the building side of the cage door at each level so men wouldn't lose their hands there when the manlift was operating. Bobby and Joe went for the plywood delivered for this. That they went together Bobby took as a sign of improvement.

"More gravy, give me gravy," Bobby said, happy. He stacked one sheet on top of another and Joe threw on still another, making three.

Joe was still stern-faced and bossy.

"It'd be easier and better if we just cut two at a time," Bobby suggested.

"We can cut three at once," Joe said coldly. "And it's faster."

Bobby kept his eyes on him. "Why don't you take it easy, man? There's no reason to get all excited." It was also a lot harder on a saw and sawblade to rip three sheets at once, and the extra time involved in cutting two instead of three would have been about five minutes for the whole task.

"I can cut three," Joe repeated.

Bobby worked both the corners on his side to match and drove a nail so the sheets wouldn't move, then shopped around for a straight edge. Joe got his side ready and marked the width of the rip and did the same with Bobby's side and snapped a line. He picked up the power saw.

"You got to use a straight-edge!" said Bobby, not wanting to lay waste to some brand new plywood.

"I can cut with my eye. I cut straight."

"I'm gonna use the straight-edge, man," Bobby said, leaving no other option. "It'll look like shit if we don't. It don't take any longer to do it so it comes out good, and if you fuck up, there's no more plywood, and we both look bad."

Joe knew Bobby was right but didn't like it anyway.

So Bobby ran the saw, ripping two at a time, and, once there were six rippings, Joe went off with them to the top of the short highrise to work by himself. Once Bobby had cut all they needed, he carried what he could to the manlift. He yelled for Frank, who was at eight, to come down because there was no call buzzer yet. Figuring Frank couldn't hear him, Bobby left the material and climbed the stairs. Joe had already finished two levels and was starting on a third. Though he was working fast, the pieces Joe had hung weren't secured well. Bobby wished he didn't have to say anything.

"I know how much you wanna get on steady, Joe," he said as kindly as he could, "but we still got a few hours today. Let's work together. If we don't work together, we're down the road together."

"This is how I work," Joe replied, though he directed his words to Frank, who had stopped the lift to watch. "When I was a kid I worked at a hotel. I carried all the luggage I could and I would still hold the elevator doors open for the people I was helping. When we got to their room I'd make sure they had clean glasses and towels and if they didn't I'd rush out to get whatever it was without them asking. I'd get them anything they'd ask for and I did it as quickly as I could. That's because that's how I learned to do things. That's how I was raised."

Frank nodded his head. Bobby didn't think he'd be able to say anything to him the rest of the day. Bobby and Frank went down for the other plywood rippings and the foreman, Mc-Cann, already displeased about the railing, came back up with them. He shook the plywood wing Joe had put up and said it was no good, it wasn't how he told Joe he wanted it, and then he explained again. McCann walked across the silver Robinson-decking and took the stairs back down. Joe got more than quiet.

Bobby felt like a prick for having the mean thoughts he was

having about Joe, who, like lots of people, had his troubles.
Bobby had the thoughts anyway. He wondered how they could
work together for any length of time, and it got him down. He
figured that he'd just have to stick it out until one of those big
jobs due to break came up.

At the end of the day, Frank laughed before he spoke. "So
long as we're all Democrats!" The three men said their see you
tomorrows to each other.

Bobby wasn't sure it was the right decision to take a street
route to his home. Sometimes the traffic moved, and sometimes
it stopped, but at the beginning at least it was interesting. He
went past Century City, where all the tall work he might have
been on was, where all those men and women in business
clothes carried briefcases or drove polished cars, the glass of
them so clear and clean he could see the luster of the driver's
eyes. He drove through Beverly Hills and past the luxury stores
and the shoppers, those women who seemed as real and ap-
proachable as they did in glossy magazines. Bobby was tired,
probably from rolling the drums around, and he switched lanes
to avoid others making a slow left or right turn and began
losing his patience. He turned up his portable radio and listened
to rock'n'roll much louder than he usually liked it. Then he hit
some real traffic and inched along. He faced it as well as he
could, but when it finally started moving and some woman had
a change of mind and decided to turn left, even though she
wasn't in the left turn lane, Bobby opened the door of his truck
and stood up on the running board and used his voice to
substitute for not having a horn that worked. After he yelled he
noticed that people were staring at him and he sat back down
behind the wheel, shut the door, and turned down his radio.

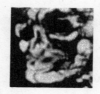

H O L L Y W O O D !

Santa Monica beach was clean and quiet. The sand was moist, the air cool, the ocean as gentle as a bay, and Luís was happy that he didn't have to pay for the parking.

"The sun's out," he said. "Just look what a pretty day it is."

"It's still cold," Marta told him, making sure he didn't get away with it. She was trying to wrap her sweater around their son Ramón, who wasn't about to cooperate and was about to cry because his mommy wouldn't leave him alone.

"He'll be all right," Luís said to ease her worry. "It's good for him just to get out."

"It's not good for him to catch a cold!" Marta was mad at Luís for insisting that Ramón wouldn't need any more than shorts and a T-shirt at the beach.

"He won't. Look at how happy he is." That was the kind of reasoning Luís liked to use.

Ramón was happy. His plastic grader tore through the sand, slicing out a smooth road for his matchbox-sized cars. He didn't seem the least bit cold.

Marta had learned long ago that she couldn't fight with Luís's logic. She lay down on the old blanket she'd never convinced him to replace, draped the sweater over herself, and looped her arm over her eyes. The sun was out. She felt pained.

Fishing boats bobbed on the near horizon. Helicopters battered the air. Joggers came and went along the wet part of the shore.

"If they worked like us they wouldn't have to run," Luís said of the joggers.

"At least they move to keep warm," Marta shot back.

"We've got the whole beach to ourselves. Think of what memories he'll have."

She scoffed. Ramón's cars vroomed and squealed and crashed into themselves and mounds of sand.

"The beach is so great," Marta shivered. "I can't wait to tell everybody at home what a great experience out first ever vacation was." It was Luís's idea to visit California in the winter because the motels were said to be cheaper and everyone said it was warm anyway.

"He's gonna remember this forever," Luís said. Just to make sure, he went over to his son. "You wanna go see the ocean up close?"

Ramón looked over to his mommy. He seemed to know, even at his very young age, that his daddy didn't always have the best ideas.

Luís picked Ramón up and carried him to the water's edge. "Now those boats out there—they look like the ones you have for your bath, don't they?" Luís felt pretty clever thinking of that. It was always better to describe things to a child in a way he could understand. "Those boats go around and catch fish so that people can eat. It's just like at home at the groves. Except instead of nuts it's fish, like sardines. You know, those fish from those cans your mommy puts in my lunch sometimes."

Ramón seemed to listen and Luís was sure he was getting through to him, and he was determined not to lose the momentum.

"And the seagulls, those birds that are flying around out there, see? See how big they are? Those are called seagulls and they go around and catch fish too, just like those boats, and that's how they live."

Ramón was listening. He was watching the birds.

"The ocean's just like the land. Animals live in it. Men make a living on it the same way I do working in the groves for Mr. Oakes." Luís thought this over and realized he didn't know how to explain himself any better. "The only important thing in life is hard work." That was somehow what he was getting at, and in any case he loved these kinds of statements, and he always sincerely believed them.

Ramón started fidgeting.

"You wanna get down? Okay. You should get your feet wet. These are nice waves..."

Now Ramón was crying. The water was very cold and the little waves scared him. He ran up the sand to his mommy.

"Why can't we go to Disneyland?" Marta implored Luís back at the blanket. "It can't cost that much. He would have such a good time, even if it is expensive. I could pay with that money I saved..."

"It's not the money."

"... Or we could leave a day or two earlier, and with the money we save by leaving..."

"No."

Marta rolled her eyes and shook her head. It was no use. Even though every little boy and girl dreams of going to Disneyland at least once, Luís had his ideas and this was one of them: it was better for his son to learn the important things first. What would a place like Disneyland teach him besides cartoons? Of course Marta didn't believe him for a second. She knew he was just being cheap.

A couple came wearing bathing suits and left with warmer clothes on. They didn't stay long. A teenage couple came carting a portable stereo with a cassette player. They listened to a tape of Tierra turned up loud and felt each other up. Luís finally couldn't stand it and told them to turn it down and to make their sex private. They left, but once he got a safe distance away the boy yelled something about Luís's mother. Marta laughed. Ramón wanted a hot dog because Luís promised to buy him one the day before.

"They do too sell hot dogs up on that pier," Marta told him. "I saw that man coming down the stairs eating one."

"No they don't," Luís insisted. "Besides, we brought these sandwiches."

"You already told him you would!"

"Hey, look at all the birds landing around us," Luís said to his son, changing the subject.

Ramón stopped whining and looked. They were seagulls and pigeons. They waited in segregated clumps.

"Let's feed them! We can feed them some of the bread!" Luís pinched off chunks of the white bread from his sandwich and threw them at the birds. They squawked and flapped their wings and moved in closer. Ramón watched ecstatically. Seagulls hovered in the air and Luís tossed the balled-up crumbs so they'd catch them there. More gulls flew in from the ocean and more pigeons from the pier, and Ramón threw them pieces of his sandwich too.

Luís tried to show Ramón how to tear little pieces off the bread so he wouldn't go through the sandwiches too quickly, but the boy had already lost control. Pigeons were almost crawling on the blanket, and it seemed all the ocean's gulls waited by him while he talked and laughed, letting the pigeons eat from his hand and making sure each and every seagull got something.

Pleased as he was, Luís was also relieved when the last sandwiches were spared by three high-pitched beeps, and then music and song, which distracted Ramón from the feeding.

"Look!" Marta pointed. "They're making a movie over there on the pier. See the camera?"

Ramón went back to the birds. Luís looked at the filming area skeptically. Marta demanded that they go see it up close. Luís, watching his son take out another sandwich from a plastic bag, gave in to Marta's wish and waved the birds away.

It was a commercial for A&W root beer but Marta didn't

care. This was Hollywood! There were film people standing by electronic machines and under wire cables. There was a fat director, dressed in a casual velour suit, shooting scenes with his noisy hands and arms. There was a cameraman, who wore a cowboy hat, sitting on a rolling lift. And there were handsome young actors and beautiful young actresses and a punk style woman dabbing them with makeup.

"They're all blonds," remarked Luís cynically.

"Those two men on the roller skates have dark hair," Marta corrected him. "And there's a black man."

"Boys. Those are all boys."

First came the beeps, then the music, and then the action: cute, barelegged actresses drank from a can of the soda and expressed amazement and pretended to sing the jingle that screamed out of a speaker in front of them. Other actresses jogged to a stop and one of the actors twirled on his roller skates. They all moved toward a park bench while the camera aimed down and away from the crowded park bench.

They watched the actors do this several times before Luís made the move to another area behind the rope. He didn't like standing near the shirtless blond longhairs with tattoos who, according to Luís, didn't do anything more than smoke marijuana and drink beer.

After a while Luís stopped paying attention. He watched a man below him driving a tractor across the sand. He watched a truck collect the trash from the barrels on the beach. Then a uniformed guard was standing next to him telling him something in English. Luís noticed that the fat director was glaring at him and when he looked to his side for a translation he realized that Marta and Ramón had left him alone. He stiffened until the guard put his hand on his shoulder and slowly drew out the word "move" and pushed Luís further down the rope.

"It's because you were in the picture," Marta explained to him.

Luís still felt like everyone was looking at him. "The boy should be playing on the beach. Maybe he'll want to get wet in the ocean."

Marta frowned. "I want to see this a few more times. He's hungry. Buy him a hot dog."

"There's still two sandwiches," he reminded her.

"He wants a *hot dog.*"

Luís wanted to argue, but once Ramón had heard his mommy mention hot dogs, he started whining again. Luís knew it was hopeless. He took his son to the nearby stand.

"One hot dog," Luís told the fry cook.

"The long or the short?" the man said in a hoarse foreign accent. "The sauerkraut, the chili, the cheese?"

Luís stared at him mystified. "I want one hot dog," he said in English.

The man stared back at Luís. "You wannit the long dog or the regular? You wannit the chili, or the sauerkraut, or the cheese? You wannit the plain or the mustard and relish?"

Luís looked down at Ramón in defeat. The fry cook, irritated, started to go over the options again, but before he finished, Ramón, in clear English, told him he would have a regular hot dog with ketchup only.

Luís returned to Marta with the news.

"He watches television, and a lot of his friends talk to him in English," she said, unimpressed. "And when I babysit for Mr. and Mrs. Oakes, the children speak English to him. The Oakes speak Spanish to you, but not to their children."

●

Luís wished he could talk to either Ramón or Marta on the way back home, but a sore throat and fever kept his son whimpering the whole way and made Marta mad at him. So he drove fourteen straight hours, secretly not unhappy that they were getting back from expensive California two days earlier than they'd planned.

Late the next night, Ramón was tossing and turning on the bed between his mommy and daddy, who had been trying everything to get him to stop his crying.

"He used to go to sleep when you sang to him," Luís reminded Marta.

"Well you see it hasn't been working this time," she said, tired. "Maybe you should tell him one of your stories. Tell him how much money we saved not going to Disneyland."

Luís, as always, ignored her sarcasm. But he liked the idea. He liked to tell what Marta called his stories, and he believed Ramón liked them too, because many times he did go to sleep hearing about the men Luís worked with or the animals they raised or the plants they grew. And, according to Luís, this was good for him since the stories would help him in the future, especially since he went to sleep with them. He considered talking about the wild burros he saw in the Mojave Desert, or those saguaros near Picacho Peak, or the piscadores in the chile fields near the Rio Grande. Any of these could have worked.

"Remember when we were at the ocean, where the waves ran up your legs? And the helicopters, and those fishing boats?"

Ramón stopped whimpering.

"Remember those birds that flew around those boats, and how they all flew onto the beach when you and I started feeding them bread?"

Ramón seemed to listen, was quiet. Already Luís felt a little like gloating to Marta, who'd rolled her head over to watch. "Those birds make their life there, mijo, and with their wings . . ."

But suddenly Ramón lost interest. He turned to his mommy and cried about the sore throat and how hot he was. Luís was truly disappointed.

Luís and Mart stared up at the darkness toward their small

bedroom ceiling. There were crickets outside, and they could hear a hard breeze rustle the trees and bushes around their house and a tumbleweed scraping against the back door screen. A cat yowled louder than the boy and that was comforting to them both.

Marta hummed a few unmelodic notes. "How did that go?" she asked Luís softly. "A and double U . . ."

Luís didn't know the words, but he tried to remember the music to the jingle. They'd heard it a dozen times or more, but things like this didn't stay with him.

"A and double U root beer . . ." she whispered, hoping that maybe Ramón had finally fallen asleep because he wasn't crying.

Marta kept trying. Luís would tell her when she didn't have it, which was every time.

Then Ramón, with his eyes barely open, sang the first words just loud enough for them all to hear.

Luís couldn't believe it. Marta laughed. She sang: "A and double U tastes so fine, sends a thrill up my spine! Taste that frosty mug sensation—uuu!" And she laughed again, hummed the rest of it, laughing still more, and Ramón fell asleep as she sang it over and over to taunt Luís, who this night was happy to lose the battle.

VIC DAMONE'S MUSIC

Our house just fits between two buildings that keep us in shade almost all day long. There used to be another house with a big yard and a new fence on the side of us, but it was torn down and replaced by a popcorn factory, which means we smell popcorn all the time. When they first started things up over there, the owner would give my mother and me huge bags of it, and I liked that then. These days I don't feel one way or the other about the smell, but please don't offer me any. On the other side of us an older chainlink fence separates our chunky grass from the laundry that's been there since I was born and before that, and its red brick walls seem to me to take up most of Cordoba Street. This is the place I know the best. Even as a little kid, if I didn't go in to visit my mother during working hours, I'd climb over the fence when the plant was closed and find a way inside. There was never anything I wanted, even when I had the nerve to think about it, so all I did was wander around the cement floors, touching those secret machines that either washed, dried, squeezed, ironed, folded, or bundled the sheets and towels, pants, shirts, tablecloths, or napkins. You can't imagine how big the place is. Each workroom must be at least two of my house, and there are seven different areas that size, and still there are all these other places where a few more people could work. It was a whole world to disappear into. I did have to be careful though, because it seemed like there was always someone there.

Sometimes that's what I did: I'd see who was around while I was hiding from them, I'd find spots I wouldn't be discovered.

My mother has worked at the folding table in the corner for as long as I can remember. It was only recently that I realized that this was a place of recognition, that it was reserved for the best-looking women in the plant. While most of the others work near hot steam, these women hand-fold dry, clean towels and linen the company owns, or the finer things a restaurant or club has done there, or maybe some personal belongings those at the top have done for themselves. They get to do this near an open window, without any machine too close to them, and they can move around and talk and laugh, all those privileges the other women don't have. The way I understand it now, my mother's appearance had a lot more to do with my getting to work here three years ago, at thirteen, than I'd like to admit.

During school, I work three or four hours a day and eight on Saturday. They never let me work more than eight because of the law, but during summer vacation I work all six days full-time. We need the money, even though it's only my mother and me. My aunt used to live with us and help when she could, though she practically stopped knowing us once she got married. That was about the same time I started in the sorting room, where all the dirty laundry is unloaded off the trucks in heavy sacks, which are untied and dumped onto the cement floor. Men gather around the pile and sort, throwing one kind of thing into a wooden cart and another in another cart, the colored things into another, like that. My first hour was almost my last. I was standing near this heap of greasy restaurant rags that were still hot, and all around them was wiggling rice, something I'd never seen before. *Gusanos,* a short man next to me smiled. Maggots, a tall black man nearby said. He offered to work where I was and he went through them with gloves on, and I let him.

The short guy who spoke Spanish was Victorio, and he was from Panama. We've worked together since that first day. He liked it when I was there because he didn't speak English well and they put him with the black crew in the sort room. That was because he worked hard and never said anything that would have given anybody the idea, at least in English, that he didn't want to be there, even though at lunch and breaks he'd go over with the Spanish-speaking guys, who were most of the other employees. Another reason he stayed with them as long as he did was that the black guys liked him. Victorio was very short around them, but he was always telling them how big his dick was, which made everybody break up. Also Victorio could sing with the confidence of someone naked in the shower, and everyone who could hear him enjoyed that, whether it was in Spanish or English. He knew a lot of old songs in Spanish, though the black guys preferred his Righteous Brothers imitations, and he tried to please them. He himself said his favorite singer was Vic Damone, not only because of the name, but because he was a lady's man.

Victorio and I work together with Raúl in the shake room now. He's happier because there are women all around us, and everyone speaks Spanish except the foreman. Victorio does miss the weekly sort through the Playboy Club laundry, which all the guys like because of the souvenirs, those plastic cocktail stirrers with the Playboy symbol at the top of them, and because once somebody found a bunny outfit, though it had to be returned, and another time a twenty-dollar bill, which got kept. I suppose the work over here is harder, worth the nickel more an hour, because it takes more muscles and endurance than going through the hospitals' bloody greens or their sheets or pillowcases, which is what our old crew still does. Here the sheets are damp and knotted up in the wooden carts. We have to pull them out and stack them so that the women who work the mangle in front of us can each take a corner of one and feed it through to be pressed and dried and folded on the other side. And no matter what we do or don't, no matter what the weather is outside, in this room we're sweating. The women don't seem to care for that much, but none of us minds it. In fact Raúl thinks it's good for him because he plays soccer and works out with weights, and Victorio because he thinks the women get sexually excited on account of it, and I don't care because I don't plan to stay here.

Maybe you already know how it is when you hear someone like Victorio constantly singing the same songs. In the shake room he couldn't sing as loud because of the windows above us where the owner and his secretaries worked and watched us, but he could sing loud enough for me and Raúl to hear. He'd bought this album, *Vic Damone Live at Basin Street East,* wherever that was (none of us knew). It had his favorite song on it, "Adios," but it also had a few new ones that Victorio liked—for instance, "When Your Lover Has Gone," which he memorized right away, and one called "You and the Night and the Music." This was one he struggled with, that he listened to every day to figure out a new word or two. He'd learned the opening very quickly:

> You and the night and the music
> thrill me with flaming desire
> setting my being completely
> on fire

After that Victorio was having his troubles, though we all knew it started out with those lines again and that sooner or later hearts would be guitars, because that was another line he'd learned.

Pulling wet sheets out of a cart may not sound hard, but really it is. After a few hours of doing it, especially in that heat, all the usual tough-guy or great lover talk doesn't leave the mouth. Victorio, though, would sing or hum during these times, and it was that tune he was stuck on. I never felt one way or the other about Vic Damone's music before Victorio, but my opinion was forming by the day. I'd tell him that if he had to sing, to sing a few Spanish songs. He told me he was trying to learn the others because sometimes he got to sing at some nightclub, and at the nightclub the American songs were what were making him famous. I couldn't blame him for that, and I didn't want to be the one to discourage him. Anybody with any sense should try to get out of this work. There were way too many people stuck here for no other reason than that they wouldn't quit. Inez, as an example, has worked the left side of the mangle I work in front of for as long as I can remember. She stands there and takes her corner of a sheet and feeds it to the hot rollers. She and her partner Rosita, who has worked her side more than a few years, talk a little in the morning and a little in the afternoon and that's how they pay their bills. The same attitude is true of my mother. Her main excuse is that we live next door and it's easy for her.

It isn't that easy for her because my mother was once the owner's lover. I think I probably knew this for a long time, but it's only recently that I gave it words. Not out in the open. I wouldn't talk about it to anyone, and if I did, who knows what I'd have to do or say. And naturally nobody brought it up with me. Not that they weren't aware of it. They told me with their eyes and indirect questions. Last year, when I first put it together in my mind, I made a point of flirting with this woman at the job the guys said was a prostitute. I'd wink and look her up and down and ask about prices and times. I wanted everyone to see, including my mother. Mostly the woman waved me off and told me to shut up and go back to work, though she did smile. Nothing happened between us, and my mother never said a word to me about it either. She only acted a little sadder than she usually was.

The owner is married to a woman his age. Yet he always seems to have a young one to hang around with. In the few years that I've worked here, it's been one of the other women that works at the folding table where my mother works. Her name is Juliana, and she's from Costa Rica. I don't know how many different ones there have been over the years, or how he manages to interest them and then give them up, just that he does. Most of the men who work here admire him for it openly, even say they'd do the same if they could, and that the women do better for it, get new clothes, jewelry, a better job on the floor. I can't say about that. To me he's an ugly old man who'd be spit on if he didn't drive a Lincoln Continental.

The way I was reading it, Juliana was being replaced by Mercedes, who fed napkins into the mangle in the corner, closest to the wall of dryers, which is about the hottest spot a woman can work. Mercedes is eighteen and just from Vera Cruz. She doesn't have papers, which is common for many of the people who work in the plant. I doubt if I'd have noticed her if I hadn't seen the owner talking to her one morning before the whistle. The only ones I even thought of paying attention to were the obvious ones, and they weren't even near my age, though Mercedes wasn't either. She was more like a woman. Also her eyes were crossed. I don't go around thinking I'm the greatest-looking guy in the world, but I suppose my tastes are normal enough to not want a girlfriend who's going to be stared at for bad reasons.

Once I overlooked Mercedes's defect, I saw the rest of her, and I saw what the owner probably did, that she was pretty and had a good body. So each day I spent more time looking at her. I've been on dates with girls from school, and I probably could have a steady girlfriend from there if I wanted to, but I've already mentioned that I have plans, and they don't include getting all mixed up with a female. I know too much about what can happen at the worst, and at the best it's like Raúl, who's only twenty-one and is married and has a kid and still works in this place.

This is what I did: Victorio was singing that song to himself and I was pulling sheets so fast and hard that sweat soaked through my pants. It seemed everyone around was hypnotized by their routine. The women behind the mangles were folding, near them a guy was tying counted piles, blue paper top and bottom. Another man opened the round-windowed doors of the dryers and tipped the spinning drums so that the whirling sheets dropped into the wooden carts. Women stood in a line in front of their mangles, leaning, tired, lazy, or bored, this way or that, those huge rollers in front of them turning and steaming. Mercedes was with them, her black hair more shiny than the older women near her. I walked over there to steer a cart to our work area and, without really asking myself about the right or wrong of it, I went up behind her and ran two of my fingers across the hard seam of her pants between her legs. She hopped and took an angry swing at me, and the other women at the trough of the machine jumped on each side of me, chattering like I'd touched them. I ran with that cart back to Victorio and Raúl and didn't say anything. My heart pumped and I felt as stupid as that Vic Damone song.

Clumsy and crude, it worked, even though I didn't plan that it would—I just did it. The next day the women were smiling and Mercedes was watching me whenever I glanced over. After I explained it to him, Victorio got excited, singing as though he'd fallen in love. To be honest, I was confused. I wasn't sure what to do next, what I wanted from Mercedes. But, like it was some obligation, at break I went over and ate with her in the lunchroom, where all those women held back their stares and voices as best as they could. Though I really did like her, I didn't want to like Mercedes so publicly, didn't want all these people judging my taste or intentions. At the same time, I wanted all to see. Both these feelings intensified when I let myself think about my mother's opinion.

That afternoon I finally couldn't stand Victorio's broken verses any more and I offered to listen to the song and get the words for him. He brought me the album the next day. When I told him that I was going to invite Mercedes over to my house for lunch so we both could listen to it, he acted like I'd announced a wedding.

Mercedes agreed to come over to the house with me as though we'd been doing that regularly, which wasn't the only thing that was different about being with her. Another was how I felt right away. Not young or old, but from up here, from this side, and therefore more natural and more like a man. I don't mean like *bad,* like *chingón,* just like a man with a woman. My usual worries, in other words, weren't playing on me since she didn't live with parents, didn't think about my style or crowd or cash. In fact she made me feel proud of our house next door, proud just as I knew my mother was that at the very least it was ours, wherever it was. She brought whole new fears and confidence out of me. Passing the time clock, I couldn't miss the owner tilting and swiveling toward us in his chair, and once through the door, moving on the sidewalk beneath the open lunchroom windows, I was more conscious of those women squealing and gaping than of my feet walking. Mercedes, on the other hand, seemed to be in complete control.

I hadn't played our record player in the living room for so long that dust covered it and the book that had been sitting on it, a hardbound picture book of President Kennedy's one thousand days. The dust didn't affect Mercedes in the slightest, and I wished my mother could see that. I knew she wouldn't say anything about my bringing Mercedes over, but that she'd be very upset about her being in the house without it being cleaned up first. I imagined that she'd be very upset about that, that she'd use extra words to tell me how wrong it was to bring someone over to a dirty house, and that she'd go on about it. And I already imagined my standing near her, listening, telling her that the house isn't so dirty, that she shouldn't worry so much. And finally she'd say that the owner wasn't going to like it that we came over here during lunch because we're supposed to go right back to work, that it was a break from work. And I'd have to say that the owner doesn't pay us during lunch break, and that some of the guys go over to the stand down the street to buy food, not everyone stays in the building, so what's the difference? That besides, he never cared when I came over here by myself, or when you did, he knows we can hear the five-more-minutes whistles fine from any room in our house. And then she'd stop arguing with me about it.

Mercedes and I listened to the first song, Victorio's, on the album twice, then let the rest of it play through. I made sandwiches in the kitchen and she shared her lunch with me. We small-talked, drank sodas, thumbed through the sad pictures of the book about the president. I started the album over again to hear Victorio's song one more time. I sat on the couch next to her, and I kissed her before we heard the two whistles telling us to go back.

That afternoon, Victorio, his dark face lit up, asked me as though it were one question whether I'd understood the words to the song and whether anything happened between Mercedes and me. I didn't say yes or no that day or any of the following ones that she and I took our lunch at my house. I worked on it for him though, until finally I had the words and almost Mercedes.

> You and the night and the music
> fill me with flaming desire
> setting my being completely
> on fire
>
> You and the night and the music
> thrill me but will we be one
> after the night and the music
> are done?
>
> Until the pale light of dawning and day lights
> our hearts will be throbbing guitars
> mornings may come without warning
> and take away the stars
>
> If we must live for the moment
> love till the moment is through
> after the night and the music die
> will I have you

I had a problem with that last line. I didn't know if it was supposed to have a question mark. At first it seemed obvious that it did, but after I'd heard it so many times I couldn't be sure. Even though she didn't know English, I asked Mercedes if she could tell, but she couldn't either. I kept listening, and the more I did the less certain I was. And then I had another problem. I couldn't get the song out of my head. It played over and over and over without the record player. And as it did I kept seeing Mercedes. Now she and the song were connected just as Victorio had joined them, and my thoughts twisted between. Dislike or like of one became dislike or like of the other. Doubt about one was doubt about the other.

Victorio was happy when I gave him the words, but I asked him to please not sing it, that if he had to, to sing anything else. He couldn't understand how I wouldn't want to hear Vic Damone, even after I told him it had nothing to do with that. One day he came to me exclaiming that my sweetheart Mercedes loved his version of the song he'd just sung for her, and he offered it as proof of how wonderful Vic Damone's music was and that I should be grateful. I begged him to not sing any of it around me. He acted hurt, like I was rejecting Mercedes's love. She was so beautiful, the song was so beautiful, he told me so sincerely. I tried to say he didn't understand, and yet he was somehow right.

Everybody waited for me to make a move, I knew it. The owner, my mother, Victorio, Raúl, Inez, Rosita, all the women at the mangles and at the tables. Mercedes waited. I just wasn't sure. How could I know what to do? I wanted and I didn't want. It was that simple and that hard. It was exactly like working in the shake room, where that hot steam pours out of everything and we sweat, wondering why we should let it run off our legs and arms for hardly enough money, and then again why not, why not when we've already got a job and know how to do it, aware or not of what other possibilities are out there.

This is what I did: I invited Mercedes to my house for dinner. I asked my mother to make something special, and I went out and bought all the ingredients. I helped her clean the house, I helped her set the table, I told her to relax because it was only a dinner. It was my favorite meal, and the whole house smelled of sauces for hours. I brought Mercedes over and I swore my mother was happy for the first time in years, in so long a time. We ate flan with the TV on.

It was still light when I offered to take Mercedes home. She didn't live very far so I told my mother we were going to walk. When we got out the front door I told Mercedes to follow me. I helped her climb the fence so she wouldn't tear the dress pants I'd never seen her wear before, I led her through the side entrance of the laundry I'd used this same way so many times, and we walked the concrete floors we both knew well during the day, but which at night seemed cool with the machinery down, and wider with no one working around them. It was in a useless corner of the building, a spot good enough to store towels but not much else, close enough to a mangle that towels passing through it could get bundled and stacked there. The pile was seven feet high toward the front, and we climbed a stairway of them, then rolled down to where the pile sloped beneath a window and leveled out like a mattress. Under us were towels that I believed had been there for ten years or more, ones I'd climbed on when I knew nothing of sex. I took a bundle from the high, recently stacked part and broke the string that kept them together and spread the clean towels around. I showed Mercedes how we could see around an edge of the pile and almost be certain no one could see us unless they knew to look here, which nobody ever had, and how through the window we could see my house and the street. A perfect place, I told her.

We lay on the towels and we kissed and touched. Finally we had our clothes off. We made love. With her eyes closed, Mercedes was the most beautiful woman I could ever imagine. I looked around the tall edge of the bundled towels and could tell the light was on in the owner's office by the way it reflected on the work floor below. In the other direction I could see the lights on at home, where my mother was alone either in the living room, still watching TV, or in the kitchen, washing dishes. I could smell the chemicals and soap in the towels under us, and the popcorn outside, and the perfume Mercedes wore. Then I thought of that song. That stupid song that had nothing to do with what I thought about or what I liked or even, if anything made sense, with this event in my life. Unwillingly, I went through the verses hearing Vic Damone's voice and intonations, and I could hear the hollow rhythm of the bass and the forced harmony of the brass instruments, and I followed a snare drum, a piano, and Vic Damone's voice rising, rising, lengthening a note, another, and then it was over, and it really was for a few seconds, longer than that, and I felt as good as I thought was ever possible, until the music began again.

GETTING A JOB IN DELL CITY

I got here about five weeks ago by bus with $50, wanting a job. They always say you can find work in the city, and El Paso is a big city, so I believed that in due course I'd be able to get a car and rent an apartment. In the meantime I was staying downtown at the McCoy Hotel for $4 a night, or $24 a week, which is how I paid after the first night because that was as cheap as I could find. I didn't mind the place that much, though I could imagine some would. There were lots of different types coming or going at all times of the day or night, but I appreciated being so close to Juárez, because for a dollar I could eat a big meal and drink a beer downstairs in the old mercado near the church.

I started moving around at about seven every morning, going down the stairs instead of the noisy elevator, toward the fresh classified ads and hot coffee, passing those Mennonites who were always in the lobby, talking some language I didn't know and dressed like they'd come off a covered wagon, the men from dusty boots to dusty cowboy hats, the women from skirts trailing their heels to bonnets tied to their chins. Outside I'd always seem to catch sight of that old man slowly peddling his bicycle, dragging cardboard and rags. The city workers would be there poking away at the street, and there'd be the prostitute working an early shift near the door of the bar that opened between eight and nine. I felt like I knew her since she lived on my floor, right next door to the woman with the baby that cried and the two older kids who liked to play in the corridor.

I tried to take the same seat at the counter in the coffee shop because I wanted some routine, especially on the days I was looking for work, which was most of the time. Up to this point I'd made only enough to pay the hotel clerk, afford some food for my stomach, and buy a few stamps for the letters I'd write to my girlfriend back home. Nobody'd paid me above the minimum yet, and sometimes they'd offered me less than that. There was nothing I could do about it because turning around and going back, by bus or foot, meant no work and no money at all. So I dug the postholes and knocked down walls, pulled nails from piles of old lumber and cleaned jobsites, and kept on hunting. At the restaurant I took the breakfast special and read the paper with a cup of coffee the uniformed waitress made sure I could only sip. I started the classifieds at employment opportunities and went to apartments for rent and to automobiles for sale, and hadn't seen a job or bargain there since the first day.

After I ate I walked up to the unemployment office on Santa Fe Street, through the guys standing around outside the glass doors in levis and workboots and colored baseball caps, men who looked used to working in the sun and drinking beer afterwards, who looked very unemployed. Inside it was stark and ugly green and too many people leaned up against the wall or sat in those lines of hard chairs, waiting for their names to be called to one of those gray desks. Fortunately for me, I'd skip this room and go up the short steps into the only other room. There, modern machines with dim lights listed jobs, and I approached one with the hope that its blue screen might brighten my day with something good.

This particular day a job was listed for a tile setter, one with some carpentry and remodeling skills for someone willing to work out of town, transportation and lodging available. The pay was $4.50 an hour to start. I wanted it, and I took it.

The man who picked me up outside the hotel after I called

seemed nice enough to me. I was immediately in love with his new GMC truck and envied the rattlesnake-skin boots he told me he'd bought the day before. His name was Joseph Hernandez, though he had almost blond hair and spoke with a drawl that was sometimes hard for me to understand. He owned the ranch in Dell City, where we were going. The job he had was to make one of his ranch houses livable for his son who just turned twenty-one and wanted a place of his own. That meant tile in the bathroom and kitchen and in a den area around a fireplace, a couple of doors to be hung, forming and pouring a sidewalk and steps, things like that. I told Mr. Hernandez I could do all of these things and he seemed very pleased. He told me if this first week worked out, if he liked what he saw, he'd bring me back next week at $5 an hour, and that there might be even more work after that.

It sounded like my break to me, and I started thinking about the letter I'd write my girlfriend, who hadn't had the same confidence about my leaving and finding us a good job as I did. I thought about the words I'd use to describe the drive out here through this country and about how she'd like it and about how easy the work was for me, even though I hadn't started it yet. I put words together for a speech I'd make to Mr. Hernandez about staying on at his ranch, how I'd do anything, how if there was something I didn't know I'd learn fast and work hard, that I'd take any pay he thought would be fair if he would keep me on somehow. I believed in the best possibilities but compromised on those by thinking I could accept much less if I had to, though in the back of my mind I didn't give up my ideals since I'd sacrificed and tried so hard and wanted it so bad, virtues said to be justly rewarded.

On the way Mr. Hernandez had explained about my staying with one of his ranch hands named Trini. He'd be helping me out when I needed it, though he had to start his chores a couple of hours earlier than me. Trini, he said, was just a boy when he started on the ranch ten years ago and was still a boy in age even now, but he was also a good man who could be counted on. He told me that I shouldn't hesitate to ask him to do any work that wasn't skilled.

The radial tires howled to a stop at a small, cinderblock building Mr. Hernandez said Trini lived in. It was unpainted block on the outside with gravel and scrub brush pushing up through it, and the same block inside with a cement floor. Two partitions with untaped sheetrock separated the kitchen and washroom area on the left side of the front door and the bedroom area on the right. In the center room a console television without any knobs, a single bed, and three wooden chairs circled a large Mexican blanket that substituted for a rug. On the walls it was impossible not to notice a large, painted figure of the crucified Christ opposite an equally large, framed photograph of a young, beautiful woman.

I dropped my bag of clothes on a metal bunk bed, one of five, that Mr. Hernandez pointed out, and he drove me and my tools over to the work. This other building was of adobe and made bigger by a wooden addition. Mr. Hernandez left me to unload the bags of cement and grout, the mesh, and tiles, and when I finished doing that I went to the bathroom and started there, cleaning and readying it. It was good to work, to be making money. I opened the window above the bathtub, let the clean blue air in, and smiled at the white clouds.

●

The shower, which like the toilet was near the kitchen sink in Trini's home, made me warm and comfortable after the day I'd put in. I was relaxing and towel drying my hair when Trini came out looking wet from his shower but already dressed.

"Who's this?" I asked him, nodding up at the photograph.

"My wife," he said.

"Really?" That was hard to believe, not only because Trini wasn't the most handsome guy in the world, but because he was in this place without her. "She's very beautiful," I told him, staring into her eyes and at her lips.

He livened up with pride. "She is the most beautiful woman I have ever seen," he said, "and if you saw her, you'd say she was the most beautiful *you* have ever seen. I know it's true," he boasted, "I absolutely know it's the truth."

I had the feeling we could talk more on this subject, but I didn't think it was something to dwell on. I'd only worked with Trini a few hours, yet already my impression of him was as a quiet, all-business, even stiff kind who particularly didn't talk about personal matters very much. I've been wrong about my impressions lots of times though, and my earlier impression of him would have had nothing to do with him being married in the first place and to this female in the second. Him making that statement to me would be the third mistake.

While there were eggs and bacon, bologna, bread, all that, in Trini's refrigerator for our breakfast and lunch, Mr. Hernandez had arranged for us to have our dinner at a restaurant in town. I got ready and Trini drove us there in his old Ford pickup. Cafe La Rosa was a combination restaurant and bar with three pool tables. Fidel, who worked the front, explained to me how I could have one beer on Mr. Hernandez but that after that the tab was mine. That seemed fair to me, and I ordered the house dish, chicken tacos and mole enchiladas. I cleaned my plate and took a second beer at the bar. Trini ate his dinner in small bites between games of eight ball. He smiled more with a few beers and talked less formally. Once in a while one of the guys not holding a pool cue would punch in a set of songs on the jukebox. The night went along like this. When I asked for still another beer, I offered to pay for it and the last ones before Fidel or I forgot.

"It's all right," Fidel told me. "After you get paid. That's what the men do who work for Mr. Hernandez."

"You can trust me to stay on that long and to pay you besides?"

"Mr. Hernandez says he has good men. Or he takes care of it."

"He has a lot of men work for him?"

"Four, sometimes five at the most. And Trini. To work on the ranch. Otherwise only one or two. Not a lot. Most of the time it's only Trini."

"He never has any other guys that have stayed on for a long time?" I was still counting on that permanent work.

"I don't know."

Fidel jumped for some beers that were ordered from the pool tables. He was quick on his feet, but not in the other ways, so I wasn't sure he understood my question, whether he really didn't know or he couldn't concentrate that long.

Then something happened at the pool table. Something said, I guessed, because I didn't see anything except that Trini had smacked his pool cue into the table and was threatening the guy he was playing with. Fidel rushed over and mothered Trini to a table to cool off. The other guy shook his head disgustedly, unafraid, and began a new game with his friend, keeping his eye on Trini, who pouted at the table with the long-neck bottle in his hand.

"What was that about?" I asked Fidel, wiping his hands on his apron as though he'd just washed them.

"Always the same. He drinks and it's worse." Fidel looked at me, which he didn't do often when he talked. "He hasn't said something to you about his wife?"

"No," I answered, expecting more, but Fidel walked away. I checked the clock and wanted to go back for some sleep. Trini agreed reluctantly, and we left.

The next day was busy and I worked hard to make the surface ready for the ceramic tiles in both the bathroom and kitchen. Trini did his share and seemed to loosen up as the day grew. We were getting along, telling stories, mostly about people we worked with over the years.

"So a lot of these guys lived in your place with you, huh?" I asked him.

"Almost all of them."

"There must have been some wild nights," I laughed.

"And sometimes my wife would get tired of it," he said.

I'd forgotten about her. "You both lived together in that place?"

"Yes."

All the sudden I could see Trini curled up on that small bed near the TV set, sleeping close to the face in the photograph. It seemed hard to believe. "What was your wife's name?"

"Reyna."

I was embarrassed that I'd asked as though she were dead. "So what did happen to her?"

"One day she was gone," he confessed. "She left me a note that said she was sorry and that's all."

It seemed so sad. It was easy to tell how much he loved her and missed her, how shamed he felt. "I'm sorry for you. She's such a great-looking woman."

He pulled out his wallet in an explosion of personality. "See how she is," he said excitedly, showing me more pictures of her. Two were of them as a couple, him with his arm reaching around her and smiling proudly, standing an inch or two shorter than her. The others were of her posing sexily, though I couldn't be sure whether that was her attitude or someone's suggestion. "She has 37–24–36," he swore to me. "I guarantee she is the best you have ever seen."

Normally I would look at someone's pictures carefully and slowly out of politeness. This was different. I could have looked longer, until it was impolite. The moment after I gave Trini his wallet back, his wife Reyna had come alive in my imagination. I didn't really like this, yet it was also not my choice. Hadn't Trini wanted me to appreciate his accomplishment and loss just as he did?

That night we didn't stay for beers or pool after we ate at La
Rosa. Both of us were tired and we came back to the house to
watch TV and drink the beers in the refrigerator. Trini was
slumped into his bed with a bottle, under the picture of Reyna,
and I rocked in one of the wooden chairs across from him. The
TV was black and white with poor reception and it was hard to
pay attention to it.

"So your wife, Reyna, lived right here with you?"

"Yes."

"In *this* place?"

"Yes."

I tried to imagine her in that bed with him. Her lying there,
ready to go to sleep just like we were. I could almost imagine all
sorts of things with her in that bed if I let myself, but I didn't. "It
must not have been so good having all those guys around," I
said out loud, sure the moment after I shouldn't have.

Trini shook his head and made a strange face at me, almost
as if I'd said it with her in the room with us. The 11x14 of Reyna
did have an unnatural life to it. You could see too well the
moisture of her lips, the softness of her cheeks, the long curves
of her lashes, the whiteness of her eyes shining against the deep
brown irises. When my own eyes shifted back down I saw that
Trini was watching them. "You must miss her," I said, setting
my beer on the cement floor. Trini shook his head slightly, as
though he were thinking of something else. I got up and said
good night.

I heard him in the morning. I smelled the bacon, saw the
light from the kitchen bend around the partition near my head
and push into the cinderblock wall. My bed and the other four
in the room stayed in the darkness. Then I heard him go out the
door.

In the undivided darkness again, I thought about Reyna
being in the bed in the other room. A woman like that all alone
in the morning, men in this room all alone, thinking about a
woman like her. Did Trini always show so much pride about

her? And did she always have the look in that photograph? I could imagine getting up, seeing her in there. It would be so easy to do. Just turn the corner and look. Would she be in bed? Would she be out of bed? Would she have to hurry and be dressed before the men got up every morning, or would she not? How would she be different if there was only one man? How would she have acted if *I* stayed here, if it was like this morning and I'd been here for a month and every morning we saw each other wake up and be alone? How could she have been satisfied with *Trini,* who was a good, nice man, but ordinary, so ordinary?

That day was short. Trini hadn't come until lunchtime because he said he had a lot of other things to do. He didn't have the energy or enthusiasm of the day before. I laid the ceramic tiles, did what I thought was a good job in both the kitchen and bathroom. I'd grout the next day. Even so, my mind was on going to La Rosa that night. I wanted to talk to Fidel.

We ate and drank beer at the dinner table and I told Trini I'd buy him a couple of rounds because I felt like sitting at the bar for a while. He bought the idea and got himself into a game of eight ball.

I leaned over the counter to feel more private. "So what did happen with his wife Reyna? Seems like something must have happened."

Fidel grimaced as though he didn't care for the subject.

"Tell me. I really want to know."

Fidel wouldn't know how to tell me to mind my own business.

"He says there were other men. Sometimes he says it's every man. When he drinks too much. He says they looked at her. And she was alone with them. She left. He says she would come here. Or over to Guillermo's Cantina. He says she wouldn't go to her mother's."

"Did she? With other men? Was it true?"

"I don't know."

"*You* don't know, or nobody knows for sure?"

"I don't know."

"Did she leave him, or did she go off with some other guy?"

"I don't know."

I'd been making Fidel miserable, and I could see how relieved he was that a man and woman at one of the tables called him over for something. He did run back to the other side of the bar when I ordered two more beers for Trini and I, but I could tell he'd already forgotten that we even had a conversation.

Then it happened again, this time with Trini and two guys who were playing at another table. The bigger of the two was pushing Trini and mocking him. An older man with a straw cowboy hat stepped in front of Trini and was telling him to leave it alone. "Reyna, Reyna, Reyna," the big guy taunted, and then he made a face like he was doing something that gave him pleasure. Fidel ran over to Trini with a cold beer and walked him to a table, where Trini slumped and sulked.

"When he drinks too much," Fidel told me as he passed my stool.

"Then don't let him buy more beer."

"I gave him that beer," he said defensively. "I didn't charge."

The big guy's friend had convinced him to leave, and as he did he said, loud enough for everyone, "I can't stand hearing about her anymore."

I thought about it and decided I felt sorry for Trini, so instead of suggesting we leave, I offered to play some pool with him. He didn't like the idea at first, but I appealed to him in a familiar voice, the way we talked the day before. He got up. He was better than me, even if I hadn't sat out several days' worth of games. Even the game I sank all my little ones, the solids, first, I lost because I couldn't bank in the eight ball. But the playing did seem to cheer Trini up, and I felt better too.

"We probably should go if we're going to work tomorrow," he said.

"Let's play a few more, drink one more beer." I motioned over to Fidel. "It's better to get our mind off her."

I don't know why I said that, or if I was innocent. It wasn't the right thing, and Trini didn't think so either. He paused, then he slapped the pool cue into the table and backed off with it still in his hand. Then he swang at me, hitting Fidel across the head by accident. The beer bottles he was carrying splintered, and a half-second later Fidel spilled like a sack of grain cut open at the bottom. Trini held onto the pool cue.

With a blue, swollen knot on the side of his forehead, Fidel was still passed-out when the sheriff's deputies arrived. Mr. Hernandez, who pulled up after they did, agreed to take Trini to the jail instead of waiting with him at La Rosa so they could care for Fidel on the way to the hospital. I drove Trini's truck back to the ranch, as I was told to do.

I didn't think I should go inside Trini's house when I first got there, so I tried to sleep on the bench seat of his pickup. Then I went in. It wasn't my fault and I was mad for going on like it might be. I turned a light on. I stared right at his woman, right into her eyes and at her lips. Then I put the picture back on the wall. I walked around looking at things with defiance. Then I heard footsteps outside. Maybe it was the beer, but I got it into my head that it was Trini with Reyna and that made me more angry. I visualized what I would first do to him, then with her. It was Mr. Hernandez who walked in. He asked me if I was okay. I told him I was having a hard time getting some sleep. He said he expected me to get some work done the next day, without Trini's help, and he left. That got me into my bunk and I slept a few hours before dawn broke.

I grouted that day, a very pretty dark brown. I was proud of my work and confident Mr. Hernandez liked it, though he didn't say so. What we talked about when he came by was whether I wanted to go back to El Paso for the weekend or stay on the ranch. I wasn't sure this wasn't some test question. I went ahead and said I wanted to go back. He told me to be ready.

I envied Mr. Hernandez driving his shiny GMC and wearing that new Stetson. I wished I could talk to him about all his success in life, but I knew it wasn't my place. He mentioned Trini. How Trini had accused me. Mr. Hernandez apologized, explaining to me that Trini had some problems with this girl he married, Reyna, that he'd been awful crazy since she ran off. He said he thought it might be hard to find someone to replace him on the ranch, though it looked like he might be forced to. I suppose that was my chance, except I hadn't done much preparing for my speech. Mr. Hernandez paid me cash and told me to be in front of the hotel, where he let me off, at 6 a.m. Monday, and that he'd pay me $5 an hour next week. I told him I'd be there.

The Mennonites were in the lobby as usual, and the kids were playing in the corridor near my room, and I guessed my prostitute neighbor was in her room trying to get some sleep. I pulled out my tablet to write my girlfriend about the drive out to Dell City, only she seemed less real to me now than the photograph of sexy Reyna. I was grateful to be in the same room. I counted my money. I opened a window. I shined my boots, took out my nice shirt, and went to a bar with live music. I met a guy there and the two of us met two ladies. We all went to Juárez, and I felt like a man that'd come to town.

ILLUSTRATIONS BY LUIS JIMENEZ

TITLE PAGE ILLUSTRATION
A veces viene a trot, a veces a galope
1991 Etching 12"x16"

PART TITLE ONE
Siempre Triunfa
1991 Lithograph 28"x22"

PART TITLE TWO
La Lucha
1991 Etching 5"x7"

PART TITLE THREE
Baile con la Talaca
1983 Lithograph 38.5"x27"